YOU CAN'T STAY

S. T. ASHMAN

Ashman Books

Contents

Dedication and a Message

*To my Abenaki consultants and sensitivity readers—thank you. Your guidance,
your stories, and your truth were invaluable.
I hope your culture and history shine far and wide, reminding the world that you
are still here—and will never be forgotten.*

Thank You!

Dear Reader,

Thank you for reading "You Can't Stay." If you enjoy the book, please consider leaving a review on your preferred retailer's website (like Amazon, Goodreads, Barnes & Noble, etc.).

I am a mom and an indie author, and every review, share, and kind word makes a huge difference and means the world to me.

Newsletter for bonus chapters:
https://www.ashmanbooks.com
Instagram:
https://www.instagram.com/booksbyashman/
TikTok:
https://www.tiktok.com/@ashmanbooks

Join Ashman's Hideout for Thriller, Mystery & Horror Book Lovers to Meet the Author & Win Signed Copies:
https://www.facebook.com/groups/295886162846929

Contact: hello@ashmanbooks.com

Thank you for your support.
S. T. Ashman

Foreword

An Important Message from the Author

You Can't Stay is a horror-fantasy novel, but its roots are grounded in real history.

I have had the privilege of working with Native communities as a psychotherapist and have witnessed the deep, lasting scars of colonization. Before publishing this book, I consulted with members of the Abenaki community and hired Abenaki sensitivity readers to help ensure the story was handled with care and respect. The majority of those I spoke with wanted this book to be published. They saw it as a chance to bring awareness to their people and to a history that most of the world has forgotten.

This story doesn't speak ***for*** the Abenaki—it just brings their name and history into the hands of fiction readers who might want to learn more.

The land my neighborhood sits on today once belonged to the Abenaki. And yet, almost no one even knows their name.

I hope readers don't skip the "Notes" section at the end. Please don't skip the history of the Abenaki people. Or the Vikings—descended from the same Germanic ancestors as my own.

Thank you for reading. You are amazing!
—S.T. Ashman

Prologue

The warm summer evening clung to Route 1 just outside Boston. It was thick with the tang of traffic fumes and the sharp, greasy scent of tacos wafting from the Mexican joint down the street. Under the flickering neon glow of a shuttered gas station, three women in tight dresses huddled together near a car that rocked back and forth in a slow, relentless rhythm. From inside, the moans of a woman were muffled by the fogged windows. Exaggerated lust dripped from each breathy cry.

"Yeah, show me, Daddy!" came the voice from inside. It was followed by a palm slapping against the glass. The woman wiped the window clear with a quick swipe.

"You like this big cock?" the man inside groaned.

"Yeah, it's so big. Oh my God!" The woman shot her friends a look, rolling her eyes hard before holding up her fingers just barely apart: *tiny as hell.*

The group fought to keep it in, shoulders shaking, but laughter slipped out in bursts, sharp and breathless against the humid night.

Jasmine bit back another laugh and grabbed her fake designer purse. Her electric-blue nails tapped against it as she shook her head, trying to keep the conversation going. "And then this sick fuck brought his fucking dog to the hotel room and offered an extra hundred if I'd screw it in front of him."

A pair of headlights swept the lot, illuminating the group's high heels and the weary shadows under their eyes.

"Fucking nasty," Annabel muttered, twisting her black hair into a tight bun. "That's why I stick with pussy when I'm off work."

"Did you actually do it?" Reese asked, her brow arched with curiosity. "Did you fuck the dog?"

"Hell no," Jasmine said. "I grabbed the poor little thing and ran like Forrest Gump. Old bastard fell five feet chasing after me."

The group's laughter echoed through the night, but the moment faded when a black SUV rolled up and came to a halt in front of them. The three women adjusted their dresses and checked their makeup in the dim light as the car's tinted window rolled down. A young man in a black suit stared at them.

Buff. Clean-shaven, dark sunglasses, baseball cap low over his face. Kinda handsome.

Not the client.

"Hello, ladies," he said, his voice silky smooth.

"Hello, handsome," Reese crooned, licking her lips with exaggerated flair. Annabel pushed her tits together with her hands.

Jasmine, always the bold one, spun around and shook her ass toward the open window. "You want some of this, baby? Fifty for the cunny, a hundred for the ass."

The man's lips curled into a cold smile. "You." He pointed directly at Jasmine. "Get in."

"Aww," the others pouted, playing along as Jasmine hurried around the hood.

"Text me when you're done!" Annabel shouted. It was their rule. They looked out for each other, a silent pact among fallen women who felt no one else cared about their heartbreaking lives.

Jasmine winked and slipped into the passenger seat. "Will do."

The door slammed shut, and the SUV purred away into the thickening night, leaving behind the greasy scent of tacos, the distant hum of traffic, and the lingering echoes of fake moans.

Esther

It was raining. The whole damn summer had been nothing but rain. The lukewarm pumpkin spice coffee in my hand had gone cold. I swirled it absentmindedly, staring blankly as droplets splattered against the windshield.

I sat in my car, parked outside Four Paws Vet Clinic, wearing my faded blue vet-tech uniform—the only one I owned. Literally. Dropping out of vet school last year left me drowning in student loans, with nothing but debt and no diploma to show for it. Money was tight. Hell, everything had been a struggle since last year.

The interior of the car smelled faintly of coffee and the humid scent of the rain creeping in through the cracked window. I heard the roar of an engine from a car parked nearby, but I barely noticed. I was too busy feeling stuck in this loop, just like the water on the windshield.

My phone buzzed. Shit. The front desk.

I pressed my lips together, braced myself, and answered.

Emily's voice—soft and apologetic—came through the speaker. "Dr. Fonders said if you don't come in right now, don't bother coming back at all." She hated being the one to deliver his message, but we both knew she had no choice.

"What time is it?" I asked, glancing at the dashboard clock.

"Four past eight," she said, her tone careful. "Your shift started at eight. You've been sitting out there for over thirty minutes."

Thirty minutes?

I stared at the clock again, realizing I hadn't reset it from daylight saving time. "God, I'm so sorry," I muttered.

And I meant it.

These time lapses were happening more often—moments when I'd zone out and lose track of everything. It was part of why I'd started failing my exams. Why I'd dropped out in the first place.

I hung up and did a quick check in the rear mirror. I looked exhausted, my blue eyes tired, as always, from the sleepless nights. My brown hair was in a lazy bun.

"Looking like shit," I muttered, shoving the door open and stepping into the cold drizzle. Rain kissed my skin as I jogged toward the clinic. Inside, the air was thick with the scents of wet dogs, antiseptic, and a faint, lingering smell of cat litter. The waiting room was packed, pets and their owners staring at me with tense faces.

"I'm so sorry," I mumbled as I approached the desk where Emily sat typing. Dr. Fonders stood next to her, stiff as ever, lips pressed into a thin line. His thinning brown hair was neatly combed, not a strand out of place. His cold, gray eyes pinned me down with a look of impatience. "I had an important phone call," I lied, holding up my phone as if it were some form of pathetic evidence.

He barely glanced at it, his gaze hard and dismissive. "Next time, don't bother coming in," he snapped before turning and stalking off.

"I'm really sorry," I muttered again, reaching for the stack of manila folders—the morning's patients—on the desk. Two other techs were on duty, but I knew I was skating on thin ice. Even with everything going on in my life, I couldn't be late again.

I opened the first folder. A cat named Pancake. Eight-year-old orange tabby, scratching at her ear, with a foul odor noted in her file. Likely an ear infection.

"Pancake?" I called into the noisy waiting room.

An elderly woman stood, struggling slightly as she lifted a crate.

I smiled warmly as I approached her. "I'm Esther," I said, bending down to peek into the carrier. "Hey there, Pancake," I cooed, my voice soft as I tried to soothe the scared cat.

Pancake's wide pupils swallowed the light, making her look like a cartoon with huge, pleading eyes.

"Don't worry, sweetie. We'll take good care of you." I straightened up and nodded at the woman. "Please follow me," I said, leading the way down the hall as the sound of barks faded behind us.

Ryder

"Thirty-one, thirty-two, thirty-three . . ." I counted in my head.

The man beneath me jerked, his bloodshot eyes bulging, veins spidering across the whites. Desperate panic fixed on me as I tightened my grip around his neck. He tried to beg, but only a strangled sound escaped. The bones of his spine pressed into my fingers. A rear naked choke would have been faster, more humane. But I wanted to see the light go out of his eyes.

"P—puh . . . ghh—esss . . ." Mr. Colter choked out as he clawed at my grip, scraping and kicking. The stench of urine filled the air. God, he pissed himself. I sat firmly on top of him, knees pinning his arms down. Eleven years in Special Forces—I fucking knew how to kill a man. Especially Mr. Colter. All five-foot-five of pure coward.

"Fifty-eight, fifty-nine, sixty . . ."

"P . . . peeeees," he gagged, then finally passed out. Most people didn't realize how long it took to choke someone to death—freaking two to five minutes. And I'd been so damn close.

The first scream echoed behind me—a woman's. I tightened my grip. They'd try to stop me soon.

"One hundred seventy-one, one hundred seventy-two . . ."

The panicked voices of a crowd grew louder. Hands grabbed at me, trying to pull me off. First one person, then two. A strained breath slipped from my mouth as I pressed down harder, pushing back against the arms that were trying to drag me away.

Kirsten's voice sliced through the noise. "Ryder! Ryder, stop!"

"Two hundred twenty-five, two hundred twenty-six, two hundred twenty-seven."

I stared into Mr. Colter's eyes. Wide open. Rolled back. Empty and unfocused. Maybe I should feel guilt. Maybe I should feel shame.

But all I felt was hate.

Large hands around my chest yanked hard, strong enough to drag me back. They tore me off Colter's body, but my fingers still clung to his neck, so I just dragged him with me. I swore I'd hold on until the job was done. Until he was dead. Or until I was.

"Three hundred one, three hundred two . . ."

"Stop!" screamed the man who had pulled me off. He hammered his fists against my hands to break my grip. But Mr. Colter's weak pulse had stopped pounding against my grip thirty seconds earlier. Now, it was gone. His vacant stare settled into that dull, empty look. The stare of death. I'd seen it many times before during missions. But never this close. Never like this.

Finally, I let him go.

I collapsed backward along with the people who'd tried to pull me off. My hands trembled, aching and drained from minutes of unrelenting force.

Mr. Colter just lay there, lifeless on the ground.

"Call an ambulance!" someone shouted. People cried, screamed. It was pure chaos.

"Don't bother," I muttered as I allowed whoever was pulling at me to tackle me to the floor. "He's already in hell."

▭

MY EYES SNAPPED open to the grating clank of the prison doors sliding open. The sound bounced off the cold concrete walls, pulling me from a dream that clung to me like smoke. It had been a dream but also a memory. I could still see my son's small frame hunched over on the rug in the TV room. He was playing timidly with his little soldiers, his fingers tense as if he were afraid he might break them. He'd been silent, not even a whisper of pretend explosions or shouts. Just silence, as though breathing too loud was a sin.

The memory twisted my gut.

I sat up on the hard, unforgiving metal bed. Its thin mattress did nothing to ease the ache in my back. Above me, the tiny window let in barely enough light for me to tell that it was morning. It was the only view of the outside world I had. On sunny days, I could see bits of blue sky. If I squinted and let my mind wander, I could almost picture the treetops swaying beneath it, like they had on our last family hike. My wife and son had bolted ahead toward the parking lot, shouting, "Lunch!" in wild, rebellious cries as if I'd dragged them through a survival course instead of a one-mile loop. I smiled at the memory, but it faded quickly, replaced by the cold reality around me.

The metallic smell of disinfectant hit my nose as I brushed my teeth in the communal sink. Everything in prison smelled sterile, like they were trying to scrub joy out of it.

I made my way to the chow hall. The air was colder than it had any right to be. Gray tables, gray trays, gray faces. Zombies. Miserable.

I skipped the breakfast line, instead cutting in front of the same buff guy I cut in front of every morning. Ben Gaetz. Convicted burglar. Piece of shit raped an eight-months-pregnant woman during a burglary. She lost her baby because of that worthless man.

He barely acknowledged me, his gaze sliding away like I didn't exist. I turned around, fixing him with a hard stare.

"Morning, rapist," I said, my voice loud enough for the men around us to hear.

He didn't say a word, just stood there, his jaw tightening, his hands clenched at his sides.

I stepped closer into his space until only stale air divided us. "I said, good morning, rapist," I repeated, slower this time, letting each word hit like a jab.

Tension spread through the line. Conversations dropped. Eyes turned toward us.

Ben's shoulders stiffened, but he didn't meet my eyes. Instead, he turned on his heel and walked away, heading for the back of the line.

Laughter followed him, sharp and mocking.

I watched him go, my stomach twisting with the same disappointment I felt every time. I prayed one day he'd try. Just once.

So far, no luck.

A glance over my shoulder told me no one else was looking for trouble. A few grumbles, a couple of hard stares, but nothing else. Good. Here, respect was survival. And respect wasn't given. It was taken, carved out through fear and violence.

I ate alone, as I always did. No gangs, no alliances. Not with the Nazis. Not with the Blacks or the Latinos. I was just the loner. The ex-military weapon nobody wanted to fuck with. That reputation kept me alive.

After breakfast came therapy. A joke, really, but it was the only part of the week I didn't hate. Dr. McCarthy's office had a window —a real one, with a view of the outside world. It was the closest I got to seeing trees, and I wasn't about to pass that up.

———

"NIGHTMARES AGAIN?" Dr. McCarthy asked, his voice thin but steady. He was a wiry little guy, all sharp angles and nervous energy. He had "bullied in middle school" written all over him, but he cared about others. That much, I could tell. And that made this charade bearable.

"Not really," I said, fixing my gaze on the tops of the trees swaying gently in the breeze. Reliving Colter's death at night wasn't a nightmare. Maybe I was a monster, but it felt right. Every single time.

For a moment, I let myself get lost in the view. "Had a beautiful dream last night. The kind that makes you feel . . . at peace."

I caught my reflection in the window—my sharp cheekbones, the hollows under my eyes, the faint curl of my lips.

My tattooed hands twitched in my lap, just enough for me to notice. I clenched them into fists, forcing them to stop, but I could still feel the phantom weight of Mr. Colter's neck in my grip. That brief, animalistic satisfaction.

A faint smile tugged at my lips, and I looked back at McCarthy. He didn't press me, just nodded, his pen scratching lightly against his notebook. I shifted in my chair. My six-foot-two frame was too big for the cheap plastic.

"Jimmy told me you declined your wife's visits again," Dr. McCarthy said.

"Jimmy needs to find another fixer-upper to make himself feel good."

"He did a tour before he took his job as prison guard. He's just watching out for his own," McCarthy countered.

"I'm not his own."

Fifteen years in the service. But now I was trash.

McCarthy cocked a brow at me.

"Not anymore, at least," I added, trying to soften it a little. "And she's my ex-wife, remember? Married that doctor last year. All six feet of vegan burgers and sunshine shining out of his ass."

God, had it really been five years in here already? Five fucking years, sucking the life out of me, turning me into some empty, walking shell. As I rubbed my face, the calluses on my hands scraped against the stubble on my jaw.

"No. I don't remember," McCarthy said with a shrug. "This is the first time you've ever told me that. You don't talk much. It makes me wonder if you're ready for this."

Shit. He was right. My words weren't exactly flowing these days.

"She's better off without me," I said quickly, tossing him a treat. There was a goddamn waiting list to get into McCarthy's office. Everyone wanted the Skittles in that glass bowl on his desk and a few stolen minutes staring at the trees. I wouldn't give that up. Never.

"What about your son?" McCarthy asked as carefully as if he were handling live explosives. "I was told he was here with your ex-wife."

My fists clenched instinctively, and my gaze dropped to the Nordic runes inked on the backs of my hands. A reminder of a life I couldn't forget even if I wanted to.

"He's better off without me too," I said, forcing the words out like they weighed a hundred pounds each. Not much could hurt me anymore, but the mere thought of him crushed me. Every. Single. Time.

"Don't you think that should be his decision to make?" McCarthy prodded, his tone calm but firm. "If he's better off without you?"

"Ouch." The word slipped out before I could stop it. "Aren't you supposed to use gentle parenting in here?" I always got an attitude when pain hit. Coping in healthy ways had never been my strong suit.

McCarthy laughed and leaned back in his chair. "I've got a two-year-old, a three-year-old, and a five-year-old at home. They're probably burning the house down as we speak. This *is* my gentle parenting."

That pulled a grin out of me. I liked McCarthy. He was the kind of guy I might've been friends with before all this. Just a regular dad trying to scrape by while making the world suck a little less.

"Time's up," McCarthy said, glancing at his phone. "I have an extra spot on the fifteenth now that Sean is—"

"I'll take it," I said.

His eyebrows lifted slightly, but he nodded. "I'll put you down."

My eyes wandered to the window, and I caught the last few seconds of the view. The trees swayed lazily in the breeze, their tops brushing against the wide-open sky.

Freedom—so close it hurt to look at.

3

Esther

The cool fall breeze brushed against my cheeks as I turned the key in the glass doors of the office. The faint scent of leaves lingered in the air, leaving a bittersweet reminder of the season slipping away.

"You shouldn't let him treat you like this," Conny said, digging through her purse for her vape. The jangling of keys and coins filled the quiet. She was barely nineteen but always talked like she'd lived through a lifetime of bad decisions and hard lessons. "I mean, the shit you're going through with your sister? That man's chest is made of ice." She exhaled a thick vanilla-scented cloud.

"Those vanilla flavors can cause popcorn lung," I said, pulling at the door handles to double-check the lock. The glass rattled faintly in its frame. "If you can't quit, at least stay away from the vanilla."

Conny blew another plume of smoke, her lips pursing in defiance. "I think he feels threatened by you."

A dry laugh slipped out before I could stop it. "Threatened by what? I'm one step away from homelessness or the psych ward."

She shook her head, her ponytail swaying. "He feels threatened by you, I'm telling you. Matt has been late for one year straight. But not a word about that, huh? Just think about it. You were the best in your class in vet school. One semester away from your doctorate.

And we all know it was you who fixed those misdiagnoses in the patient charts—saved that pregnant dog and the parrot. And the two cats with cancer. Dr. Fonders might act like he walks on water, but he'd be neck-deep without you."

I didn't reply. Instead, I turned and walked to my car, my sneakers scraping against the pavement. Conny's hurried steps trailed close behind.

"Dr. Fonders is ranked the best in the state, top fifty in the nation," Conny continued. "And you still know more than he does. You have a gift, Esther. And he knows it. That's why he acts like such an asshole. He can't handle being outshined by a woman in the one thing he thinks makes him special. A tale as old as time. A small-dicked man—"

The low hum of an approaching vehicle interrupted her rant. We froze mid-step and turned toward the sound.

A sleek electric SUV rolled into the parking lot. The canoe hitched to the back swayed slightly as the car came to a stop in the fading light.

"Shit," Conny muttered, crossing her arms. "Why can't people read the damn opening hours on Google?"

The man who stepped out was tall and broad-shouldered. His patterned burgundy and blue jacket caught the dying sunlight. Colorful ribbons sewn into the fabric fluttered in the breeze, outing him as Native. Around his neck hung a small turtle pendant whose polished surface gleamed faintly against his chest. His long, gray hair was pulled back neatly, and an air of quiet wisdom softened the sharp lines of his face.

In his hands, he carried a crate. Inside, a fox lay curled up. The creature's large eyes fixed on me with a sharp warning.

The man glanced at the fox and spoke softly in a Native tongue, his voice a soothing balm for the frightened creature.

"We're closed," Conny said. She blew a thin stream of vanilla-scented vapor into the cool evening air.

The man hesitated, his hand tightening around the crate's handle as he stepped closer. "I found him on the side of the road. There was a lot of blood."

I leaned down and looked inside the crate. He wasn't lying. Blood was smeared across the base of the crate and matted into the fox's white fur.

"I was coming back from Boston with my cat and saw him at the side of the road," he explained. "I didn't know what else to do, so I put him in her crate."

We glanced over at his SUV. A cat sat perched on the dashboard, its green eyes glaring at us like an annoyed queen surveying her subjects.

"Sorry, but this is a wildlife problem," Conny said, her words clipped. "You'll have to call the New Hampshire Fish and Game Department."

"I already did," the man replied, his brows knitting together. "They said they wouldn't be out until tomorrow morning. I don't think he'll make it that long. There are almost no white foxes left in North America. Please help us."

I looked into the fox's eyes, which were wide and glassy with pain. Its body trembled in the cramped space, its sides heaving with shallow breaths. Every instinct I had screamed at me to walk away, to leave this to the authorities. But those eyes—sharp and pleading —held me.

"I'm really sorry," Conny said, "but—"

"Come with me," I interrupted her.

"What?" Conny protested, her voice rising in disbelief. "No. You can't."

But I was already hurrying back toward the clinic.

"Dr. Fonders will fire you for this, Esther!" Conny hollered after me.

The man followed with long strides to keep up.

Inside the clinic, the hum of the fluorescent lights buzzed faintly overhead as I led him straight to the surgical room.

I grabbed the crate from his hands and placed it on the cold metal table. My hands moved on autopilot as I slipped on surgical gloves and slapped the latex against my wrists. From the cabinet, I retrieved a vial of sedative. The liquid shimmered faintly as I drew it into a syringe. I tapped it to dislodge a stubborn bubble, then pressed the plunger just enough to release a fine mist from the tip.

"How you gonna get him out of there?" the man asked.

I didn't answer. Instead, I turned back to the crate and reached for the latch.

"I wouldn't—" he started, but it was too late.

The moment the door cracked open, the fox lunged. It sank its teeth through my jacket and into my forearm, latching on tightly. A sharp, burning pain radiated from the bite, but I didn't flinch. This pain was nothing but a dull joke compared to what life had given me so far.

The fox's eyes met mine. They were wild and expectant, as if the animal was bracing for a fight or a blow. I stayed still, holding its gaze with a calm, steady expression.

"I could've told you he still had some fight in him," the man said. "Took me over an hour to get him into that crate safely."

"It's okay," I said to the fox, my voice soft despite the throbbing in my arm. "I won't hurt you. But you're bleeding a lot, and we're running out of time. I'm trying to save you." On the animal's belly, I could just make out the nubs of swollen nipples. "You have little ones, don't you? I know you fox mothers stay with your babies for many months. Some of your girls might even stay with you to help you raise the next litter. Don't you want to see them again?"

The fox's grip didn't loosen, but her breathing slowed, and her trembling abated.

I locked eyes with the fox, holding her gaze for what felt like an eternity. Finally, the pressure of her bite softened. As if she trusted me, she released her grip and retreated slightly.

"Good mama," I murmured. I gently lifted her onto the metal table and injected her with the sedative. Her body stiffened momentarily before relaxing into stillness.

I waited a few moments to ensure the sedative had taken full effect, then carefully rolled her onto her side to examine her injured back leg. The flesh was swollen and bruised. Crusted blood surrounded the edges of the wound.

"Are you the vet?" the man asked.

"No," I replied flatly. My fingers moved methodically over the wound, searching for anything that might have been lodged beneath the skin. Nothing stood out, but when I turned the leg slightly, I found an exit wound on the back. "She was shot," I said. "The bullet went straight through. She's lost a lot of blood, but she'll be fine once I stitch her up."

The man's eyes tracked my every movement as I walked to the cabinet and pulled open drawers to retrieve antiseptic and a suture kit. Setting the supplies on a metal tray, I took a deep breath, steadying myself. It had been over a year since I'd performed surgery during my veterinary residency.

I returned to the fox and carefully shaved the fur around the wound. Fine hairs drifted to the table like wisps of dust. The exposed skin was mottled and tender. I wiped it clean with antiseptic until the wound gleamed under the light.

With steady hands, I positioned a sterile drape around the area and then threaded the suture needle. The curved metal glinted as I worked, each stitch deliberate and precise. The needle weaved through the torn edges of the wound and pulled the flesh back together.

"I'm John Bear," the man said, breaking the silence. "What's your name?"

"Esther Smith," I replied, my focus still on the stitches.

From the corner of my eye, I caught him nodding, his expression unreadable.

"No," he said slowly, "I mean your real name."

I paused briefly, the words catching me off guard. Nobody ever asked me that. My mother's blue eyes had always silenced any questions about my high cheekbones and slightly darker skin.

"I don't know for sure," I said finally, my voice quiet but firm. "But I think my last name was Obomsawin when I was little."

He nodded again, his gaze heavy with something I couldn't quite place. "What are you—Sokoki?"

I shook my head. "My father was Pequawket."

John Bear's brow furrowed. "The people of the rivers of the White Mountains. Not many of you left."

I tied off the last stitch and cleaned the area again, then applied a light dressing to protect the wound.

"Where's your father now?" John Bear asked, his tone softening.

"Dead," I replied, my voice hollow.

"And your mother?"

"Dead," I said again, stripping off the surgical gloves and tossing them into the bin. Then I shrugged off my jacket so I could look at the bite wound. "You can grab a towel from the cabinet and use it to line the crate," I said, inspecting the angry red marks on my forearm. I dabbed antiseptic onto the punctures, creating a sharp, fleeting, stinging sensation. The bite marks weren't deep, but they would hurt for a while.

"Don't you need a rabies shot or something?" John Bear asked as he gently placed the sleeping fox onto the towel in the crate.

"I don't think so," I replied. "If she were rabid, she wouldn't have let go. But a booster wouldn't hurt. If she scratched or bit you, I'd recommend you get one too."

I slipped my jacket back on and began cleaning the surgery site. The clink of instruments and the faint hum of the overhead lights filled the silence.

John Bear closed the crate with slow and cautious movements. Then he turned to me. His dark eyes searched mine as though he were trying to unearth the secrets of my past, present, and future all at once.

"You know," he said, "I'm an elder of the Penobscot Nation up north in Maine. I could help you. Be with your own people again. Find out who you are. Help you go to college. You have a rare gift, Esther." He gestured to the sleeping fox. "For healing. You tamed the fox's spirit. Saved her life. Our people call people like you M'teoulin."

My head snapped up, and my eyes locked onto his. "M'teoulin?" I repeated. The word was like a ghost from my childhood. "That's what my grandmother used to call my father. What does it mean?"

John Bear's lips curled into a soft smile. Pride and reverence tinged his expression. "It means healer," he explained. "Your father must have been a healer. A M'teoulin can transform into animals, travel great distances in spirit form, or protect our people from harm. Legends tell of them battling spirits or helping their communities survive disasters. A M'teoulin carries great honor and respect."

Respect?

A bitter, hollow laugh threatened to rise but never fully escaped my throat. Instead, I swallowed hard, pushing back the familiar sting of old grief.

"My dad, mom, and grandmother burned to death," I said, trying to keep my voice flat. "It was an arson attack on our home. The police said white supremacists thought we were illegal immigrants from Venezuela. My sister and I made it out only because a water pipe burst over our room when the fire spread. After that, we were shuffled around in foster care, and the state took our land when we failed to pay the property taxes. They sold it for millions to the biggest mining company in the Northeast. Makes you wonder if it was about the land all along. My dad wouldn't sell. But who knows? Doesn't matter. They're dead."

The words brought memories rushing back like a gut punch: the piercing wail of sirens, the stench of smoke, the heat licking at my skin as firefighters carried us away from the crumbling house. Past the stretchers. Past the blackened, unrecognizable bodies of my parents and grandmother, their mouths torn wide in horror.

"Not a very respectful thing to do," I added, holding the door to the surgical room open for John Bear to leave. "Burning people alive."

His gaze lingered on me, searching, before he nodded and lifted the cage. I followed him down the hall, wondering if the gas station down the street was still hiring.

We reached the glass entrance doors, and I opened one for him. But John Bear stopped and turned to face me.

"What keeps you here?" he asked. "Why not come north where I can help you?"

I sighed, my shoulders sagging under the weight I'd carried for too long. For a moment, I considered telling him about my sister, the real reason I couldn't leave. But the urge passed as quickly as it had come, and I forced my face to harden again.

"The White Mountains," I said abruptly, the words clipped and final. "The White Mountains hold me here."

It was the truth, in some way. But it was not the answer he'd expected.

"The mountains? How?" he asked.

This man was trying. I had to give him that. Out of kindness, most likely, I reminded myself. But I wasn't used to it.

"The mountains have something very dear to me," I said.

He nodded slowly as though piecing something together in his mind. "Your tribe always had a strong bond to the mountains by your rivers. And their spirits."

If only he knew half the truth about what the White Mountains were hiding from me—the horrors they'd dragged me into. They had taken the only thing I had left in my life. The only thing I loved.

"The sutures are self-dissolving," I said. "You can drop her off at the New Hampshire Wildlife Refuge in the morning. Or release her yourself. Where you found her, so she can return to her children. Given that it's fall, they'd be several months old and wouldn't need her to survive anymore. But female foxes often stick together. It might be nice for her to find her family."

John Bear's expression turned serious, his eyes betraying a mix of pity and gratitude.

"I'm sorry for any trouble this caused you," he said. "Thank you for saving the fox. She waited for me to find her . . . to bring her to you."

"Yes, yes, don't worry about it," I said quickly, my words tumbling out as I tried to end the conversation. I wanted to get home. There was new information I had to analyze—information that had taken me over a year to find.

I started to close the door, but John Bear's boot wedged into the gap.

"The fox is known for its cleverness, strategy, and adaptability in challenging times," he said, his tone deliberate. "When you need it, her spirit will show its gratitude to you."

"That's good to hear," I replied, my voice tight with impatience. "But I really need to go."

John Bear studied me for a moment, then stepped back, allowing the door to close.

The soft click of the lock echoed in the empty clinic. I turned and walked briskly to my workstation.

Saving this fox was a promise to get fired. Why even bother showing up tomorrow to let Dr. Fonders yell at me in front of everybody? He loved that shit. It made him feel powerful to belittle others. Probably jerked off in the restroom right after destroying someone's self-esteem. If I didn't come back, at least I wouldn't give him the satisfaction. I'd keep my dignity. Or whatever dust-covered scrap was left of it.

I grabbed my mug, the one that read "Best Sister in the World" in faded block letters. It was a gift from Jasmine for my fifteenth birthday, back when she still cared enough to celebrate life. Hers or mine. The mug was one of the only things she hadn't stolen to pawn for drug money later on. It was worthless to most people. Yet, not even its weight in diamonds could make me part with it.

I stared at it for a moment, my grip tightening, then set it carefully in my bag alongside a few other personal items.

The clinic was silent. My footsteps echoed as I hurried out and locked the door behind me.

John Bear was gone. The parking lot was abandoned in the dark.

The cool night air hit me like a slap, sharp and bracing.

I needed to get home. I had to see if there was a new message from my source.

A message that might tell me where Jasmine was.

Because God be my witness, if the White Mountains had her, I would get her back.

Dead or alive.

4

Esther

I stepped into my shitty studio apartment just outside Newmarket off Route 1. The air hit me like a wet rag—stale and damp, thick with the stench of mold. The carpet, once a beige color, was a graveyard of stains from previous renters—years of beer spills, ground-in dirt, and the unmistakable reek of pet urine. Six hundred bucks a month didn't get you much these days.

Against the yellowing walls stood stacks of boxes, teetering like they might fall at the slightest bump. Papers were shoved into every corner, crowding the tiny space. My so-called living room doubled as my bedroom. A thin blanket, half-covered, lay on the couch where I slept.

The clutter spilled into the kitchen, which was a cramped alcove with peeling linoleum and a fridge that hummed louder than my thoughts.

The walls had become a goddamn obsession board. Maps, photos, phone numbers, scribbled notes, lists of names—my sister's case spread out like a twisted jigsaw puzzle.

A big whiteboard dominated one corner. "White Mountains" was circled in furious red marker. Below it, in jagged black letters, were the words "Cersei Lannister." No phone number. Just a fucking TV show username from a website. Useless.

I shuffled into the kitchen, my feet sticking to the tacky floor. The smell of mildew hung around the sink, where a stack of unwashed dishes leaned like a drunkard. It was almost unbelievable to think I'd once prided myself on my immaculate cleanliness. Every surface in my home used to gleam. Every corner was dust-free. But when your sister is missing, the search consumes every second of your life, leaving no time for anything else. The chaos around me—the piles of paper, the cluttered walls, the forgotten dishes—mirrored the storm raging inside. Anger, frustration, and despair spilled out of me, ruining everything they touched.

I flicked the switch on the electric kettle and grabbed my mug from my bag. No milk. No sugar. Just black tea—bitter, like my mood.

Back on the couch, I pulled my laptop from under a pile of crumpled receipts and opened it. The screen flickered to life, and I navigated to the forums I frequented. Amateur sleuth websites. "Never Forget" was the main one.

Sure, it was filled with keyboard detectives, but they had more grit and heart than the local cops, who'd given up the same day my sister had gone missing.

The police hadn't even pretended to care. Drugs. Prostitution. Case closed. To them, she was just another statistic—a junkie whore whose life didn't matter. Not many people gave a fuck about women like my sister. And for Jasmine, that list was down to one name: me.

But there was hope. There were still good people in the world. And after I posted Jasmine's story on the site Never Forget, it caught fire. Strangers started digging, submitting FOIA requests to police stations up and down the seacoast. A few police officers from different towns even helped. Within months, what had felt like a dead end was showing cracks of light. Patterns emerged.

Mainly one.

Every September, people went missing along the stretch from Boston to Portland, Maine. Prostitutes. Homeless. Addicts. Vulnerable people no one would miss.

And many times, there was a black SUV.

Witness reports came in from Portsmouth, North-Conway, Belmont, Portland—different states, same detail. A black SUV lingering near the scenes of the disappearances. However, when I'd taken this new information to the Newmarket PD, they'd treated me like a joke.

"Oh, a black SUV," one of the detectives had sneered, leaning back in his chair like he was auditioning for the role of douchebag in a B-list cop film. "Like one of a million on the streets? What's next, Colombo? You want us to visit every McDonald's in the state?"

His partner snickered, adding, "Grab me a Happy Meal while you're at it."

"Most likely dead in a ditch somewhere," a third one said with a shrug, his voice so casual it made my stomach turn. "Or ran off with a trucker, sucking his . . . well, they ran off."

I'd never wanted to hit someone so bad in my life. Not a slap or a shove—a full-force punch aimed to shatter the nose. And I almost did. Almost. But then what? I couldn't afford bail, let alone a lawyer. They knew that. Bastards.

What they *did* do was take my sister's dog from me—Mr. Snuggles. I'd brought him with me to the station that day. The cops said he was reported missing by some local councilman. They claimed my sister had snatched him right out of the park while the councilmember was walking him. Called her a thief, said she probably wanted to trade him for drugs.

I went home with tears burning in my eyes. Tears of rage. I didn't let them fall, though. Crying wouldn't fix a damn thing. Instead, I let it all out on the wall. My fist went straight through the drywall, leaving my knuckles raw and bleeding. The pain was sharp, blinding—good in all the ways I needed it to be.

But once that moment passed, I was back on the floor of my shitty apartment, staring into the dark.

Nothing left.

Not even the damn dog.

Just the deep, sinking thought that maybe I should quit.

Then my phone had buzzed. A notification about a message in my Never Forget inbox. A woman calling herself Cersei Lannister. Fake name, obviously. But I didn't care. She said she had information—claimed my sister might be in the White Mountains. Said other people went missing there too.

She didn't answer many questions, just said she'd reach out with the location when the time came. Told me time would be critical.

That was two weeks ago.

I opened Never Forget again tonight, desperate, my fingers shaking as I logged in to check the inbox. Maybe I missed something. A new message?

Nothing.

Losing that lead felt like losing my sister all over again. A gut punch, hard enough to knock the air out of me.

I sat on the couch, holding a bowl of untouched microwave mac and cheese. I wasn't hungry most of the time. I ate only to stay alive, to keep searching for her.

My eyes landed on the wall across the room. A map of the seacoast, covered in red pins marking every disappearance I could find. The map stretched straight onto the drywall, forming a giant evidence board of chaos. I pulled my laptop onto my lap and started Googling again. Searching the same locations where the people had disappeared. There had to be a connection—something more than the goddamn SUV.

As always, I started with my sister. Her picture hung on the wall —a snapshot of her holding Mr. Snuggles. His fluffy white fur glowed against her tired smile. I went over her case again, combing through the details for the hundredth time. Had I missed something?

She'd been working. A middle-aged man in a black SUV had pulled up. He'd been wearing sunglasses and a baseball cap. She'd gotten into the car with him. After that, she was gone.

Nothing else popped up.

So I moved to the next case. Dover, New Hampshire. Last September. An elderly homeless woman vanished just a week before my sister. Her mug shot from a police file stared back at me. Sunken cheeks. Dark, hollow eyes. A worn, grimy coat clinging to her like a second skin. She looked half-dead already, like a walking corpse. The group and I had found her police report from an incident a week before she went missing. She was arrested for stealing bread.

Bread.

Fuck the cops. Fuck the store manager. Fuck every asshole who saw a hungry homeless woman steal bread and played Rambo.

Anger curled in my chest, hot and sharp.

Fuck them all.

If no one else cared in this world, I would. I'd keep searching, keep connecting the dots, keep making noise until the cops could no longer ignore me.

I moved on, case by case, person by person. A grim procession of names and faces, each leading nowhere.

Hours blurred together until my eyes grew heavy. By 1:00 a.m., the laptop's glow was the only light in the room. My head lolled back against the couch, exhaustion pulling me under. The laptop slipped off my lap as sleep took over.

And then, like clockwork, the nightmares began.

The whoosh of roaring flames swallowed everything. Black smoke invaded my lungs, choking me, making me gag and cough until my chest burned. My ears rang with the wail of distant sirens. Water poured from a burst pipe above, soaking my skin and mixing with the oppressive heat around me.

"Jasmine!" I croaked, my voice raw. My stomach lurched as bile rose, and I doubled over, coughing violently. "Jasmine!"

I'd held her hand only moments ago, both of us screaming for our parents as the fire consumed the house. We'd tried to make it to the hallway, but I'd lost her grip in the chaos.

Had she made it out without me? Had she . . . left me behind?

"Jas—" Another fit of coughing cut me off. I curled into a ball by my bed, pulling my knees to my chest in a haze of panic and smoke.

I was so scared.

I would die.

I knew it.

But then I felt it. A small, desperate hand grabbed my arm.

"Esther!" Jasmine's voice was hoarse but strong as she yanked me to my feet. "The window!"

"You came back," I gasped, tears cutting streaks through the soot on my face.

"Of course I did!" she wheezed, pulling me toward the window. A firefighter reached through. His strong hands grabbed us and yanked us out moments before the roof collapsed in a fiery roar.

We stumbled away, coughing and trembling, past the ambulances and stretchers. My legs gave out when I saw them—blackened, unrecognizable figures. My parents. My grandmother. Their bodies were charred beyond recognition, their mouths frozen in silent screams. Their eyes . . . hollow, endless pits.

Horror.

Absolute horror.

A sudden sound jolted me awake. My breath hitched as I sat up, sweat dripping down my face. The laptop had fallen to the floor, and I was curled up in a fetal position on the couch, still wearing yesterday's clothes.

My pulse quickened when I realized what that sound was. It was a notification—the one for Never Forget messages.

Adrenaline surged as I grabbed the laptop and fumbled to open my inbox. My heart nearly stopped when I saw the message.

Cersei Lannister.

Meet me at the old Portsmouth cemetery next to the train tracks in 30.

I reread it, my mind racing. What the hell?

What's going on? I typed back with trembling fingers. No reply.

I glanced at the clock: 2:34 a.m. Panic clawed at me. What if this was a trap? A pervert? My sister's murderer?

But what would the cops do if I called them? Nothing. Or worse, they'd scare off whoever this was, and I'd lose my only lead.

Forcing my legs to move, I got up and headed to the kitchen. The junk drawer screeched as I yanked it open. My fingers found the cold metal of my handgun. It had been my first purchase after my sister went missing. I didn't know much about guns except that pulling the trigger could kill someone. And that was all I needed to know.

I checked the safety, slipped it into my coat pocket, and took a breath.

I should have more doubts. I should call the cops. Hell, I probably shouldn't go at all.

But I *had* to find my sister.

Whatever happened to me in that cemetery tonight wouldn't be worse than what countless other women had endured before. I'd survive—or I wouldn't. Either way, I was willing to endure more pain to find my family.

If I was going to die chasing this lead tonight, at least I'd already be in a graveyard. Make things easier for everyone. Just dig the hole and push me in. A little dirt on top. Done.

I grabbed my coat, shoved the laptop into my bag, and headed into the cold night.

To meet Cersei Lannister.

Or my end.

5

Esther

The town was dead. As I parked in front of the old Portsmouth graveyard, my headlights cut through a low-hanging fog that clung to the empty streets. The flickering glow of streetlights gave everything a washed-out, horror-movie vibe. My gut screamed at me to turn around. Nothing about this was normal.

But then nothing about my life felt normal anymore.

My hand gripped the cold metal of the gun in my jacket pocket as I stepped onto the historic graveyard grounds. The grass beneath my shoes felt soft and damp, slippery enough to make me tread carefully. The air carried the heavy scent of wet earth. Crooked tombstones rose in uneven rows. Some were so eroded they looked fake, like forgotten Halloween props left to rot. The small ones—the children's graves—hit the hardest. Thin, short, rounded at the tops. A few had toppled over and were partially swallowed by the creeping grass.

I turned on my phone's flashlight. The beam cut a narrow path through the darkness. My breath clouded in the cold air. No birds. No cars. Just my heartbeat, thundering against my ribcage.

Row by row, I made my way to the back of the cemetery,

28

cursing myself for falling for what could easily be a trap. If this Cersei Lannister had lured me out here for some sick game, I—

A woman's voice cut through the silence, calm and low. "Do you have a gun?"

I froze. My fingers tightened around the grip in my pocket. As I slowly turned toward the sound, my flashlight swung with me, but I didn't see anyone.

"No," I lied.

"Mm-hmm. Just don't point it at me. I'm unarmed."

The woman stepped out from behind a large tombstone. Her hair was dark brown like mine and pulled into a tight bun. She wore a jogging outfit—no coat, despite the fresh breeze—and clutched a military duffle bag in one hand.

"Cersei Lannister?" I asked cautiously, my hand still wrapped around the gun in my pocket.

She scoffed, the sound sharp and sarcastic. "Come on," she said, dropping the bag onto the ground with a dull thud. "We don't have much time." Her eyes darted left and right, scanning the cemetery like she expected someone to appear at any moment.

"All right," I said, my voice firm. "Let's get to the point. Where is my sister?"

She gave me a once-over, her gaze sharp and appraising. Finally, she nodded as if she had made a decision. "It might work," she muttered.

"What might work?" I asked, irritation breaking through. "And where is my sister?"

"I already told you," she said. "Your sister is in the White Mountains."

"Yeah, that's pretty much all you've told me," I shot back. "So maybe you could explain a little more, considering I'm meeting you in a goddamn graveyard in the middle of the night."

She knelt beside the duffle bag, her movements quick and deliberate as if she were racing against an invisible clock. "She's somewhere in the Pemigewasset Wilderness," the woman said as she pulled a stack of military-grade clothing from the duffle bag. I watched her every move.

"Pemigewasset Wilderness?" My voice shot up, thick with disbelief. "What the hell would she be doing there?"

She didn't answer right away. Instead, she pulled out an army camouflage jacket and walked toward me. Then she held it up, checking the size against my frame. Instinctively, I stepped back, my grip tightening on the gun in my pocket.

"Relax," she muttered, giving the jacket a shake before holding it up again. "They don't tell us who or why these people end up there." She walked back to the bag. "But forty-five thousand acres with no roads or communication? Can't be good."

"Who's *they*?" I asked, stepping closer.

She didn't meet my gaze as she stuffed the jacket back into the bag. "I don't know that for sure either."

A sarcastic laugh escaped me. "Listen, lady, you *do* see how this all looks, right? You meeting me here in the middle of the night, playing military dress-up or whatever the hell you're doing there. So unless you give me something more substantial, I'm going to assume you're some sick fuck with a weird-ass kink, and I'm leaving."

Her hands stilled over the duffle bag. Slowly, she straightened and turned to face me. For a moment, she just stared, as if weighing something in her mind.

A rustling sound made her glance over her shoulder. A bird was taking off into the fog. Then her gaze—hard and determined— snapped back to mine. "My name is Private First Class Emily Wager, Bravo Company, 2nd Battalion, 75th Ranger Regiment," she said, her voice sharp and proud. She reached into the bag, pulled out a white plastic ID, and handed it to me.

I took it hesitantly. Her picture stared back at me, and the name matched exactly what she'd just said. At the bottom, a gold chip gleamed, making it look disturbingly official.

"I was pulled from my regiment for a mission in the White Mountains," she explained.

"What mission?"

"I don't have details yet. The Operations Detail Briefing is in two days in Twin Mountains."

I shook my head. "I don't understand what any of this has to do with my sister."

Her jaw tightened. "I'll tell you what it has to do with your sister. That mission in the White Mountains . . . they usually recruit from across the country, but someone screwed up this time. And they picked me."

"And what's wrong with that?"

"I'm from Twin Mountains," she said. A bitter laugh escaped her lips. "That tiny little no-man's town at the foot of the Pemigewasset Wilderness. I grew up with its scary stories. We told them to each other around campfires."

She zipped the duffle bag closed and slung it over her shoulder.

"What stories?" I pressed.

Emily turned to me, her eyes locking onto mine with unsettling intensity. "Stories about the people who go into the Pemi every fall and never come back out."

This was crazy. Absolutely insane. "I see," I said, forcing a dry laugh. "Do you want me to get my tinfoil hat now, or should I wait until after you start talking about the aliens?"

She didn't flinch. Her expression remained deadly serious as she came closer, then stopped inches from me.

"We don't have time for this," she snapped, glancing at her watch. "Fifteen minutes, to be precise. So here's the deal. You let me finish talking, then maybe beat the odds and see your sister again. Or I walk away right now, and you can spend the rest of your life searching, always wondering if the woman in the graveyard that night was telling the truth."

Her words hit me like a slap in the face.

I didn't move, didn't speak. I didn't have to.

She nodded sharply, apparently taking my hesitation as a silent agreement. "Growing up, I never believed the stories," she said. "Left that little shithole as soon as I could. Joined the military. Proved to myself that I was tougher than ninety-nine percent of the rest out there, men or women, and became an Army Ranger. Then I got my first orders." She shook her head in disbelief. "Fucking Twin Mountains. What are the odds? At first, I was just pissed. I wanted to see the world, not get shoved back into small-town America. Whatever, though, right? Get the mission over with, don't mind those old spooky stories. But then I remembered something." She paused, her eyes distant and lost.

"What did you remember?" I pressed.

"When I was a kid, some friends and I got lost in the woods," she said quietly. "It was getting dark, and we stayed out too long, building a tree house. When we finally left, it was pitch black. We stumbled around all night, tripping over branches and roots, until we hit something." Her gaze dropped for a moment as if the memory itself weighed her down. "A huge wall," she said, her voice barely above a whisper. "It was too dark to tell what it was for, but it was made of metal or something solid. We turned around, scared out of our minds. By morning, we'd stumbled onto the road where they found us. My parents told me it was just a tree or something. That there was nothing in those woods but God and trees." She shook her head. "But I know what I saw." She paused and pushed her hands into the pockets of her jogging pants. "As soon as I remembered that night, I started looking deeper into the White Mountains. Then I found your website. And your wannabe Navy CSI friends."

"And?" I asked, ignoring the jab, my stomach knotting with suspense.

"And you're fucking right. People disappear around here. Every fall."

A chill snaked down my spine as her words settled in. Their weight pressed hard against my chest.

"So it's true, then?" I asked, my voice low. "All those missing people with the black SUV—they're connected?"

Emily nodded, her expression grim. "You're wrong about two things, though."

"What things?"

"Your radius is too broad. A few missing people here and there in Boston or Portland, sure, but those are distractions. Smoke-screens. Pull them out of the equation, and you'll see the real pattern."

My throat tightened. "The White Mountains."

She nodded. "A one-hundred-mile radius around the Pemi. Homeless people. Drug addicts. Prostitutes. Missing. Every. Damn. Fall."

It felt like the air had been sucked out of my lungs. My sister. She wasn't just missing—she'd been taken.

"What happens to them there?" I asked, my voice barely audible. I was terrified of the answer.

Emily shrugged "No idea. But that's the second thing you guys were wrong about. It's not some serial killer out there picking them off. Whatever's happening, it's big. Bigger than some psycho playing Dahmer in the woods."

My mind reeled, but Emily pressed on.

"The mission I got pulled for," she said. "It's running under Joint Special Operations Command. JSOC. That's above a lot of pay grades. Highly unusual for domestic operations. Kinda unheard of."

"What should we do?" I asked. "Go to the police? The FBI? How can we get my sister back?"

I realized I was still clutching her ID. Slowly, I stretched it out toward her, my hand trembling just enough for her to notice.

"The cops? Sure, if you want to wake up dead tomorrow," Emily said.

Her words scared me. The fog swirling around the graveyard didn't help.

Emily dropped the duffle bag at my feet. I was still holding her ID.

"The operations meeting is in two days. In Twin Mountains."

A heavy, suffocating silence stretched between us until my brain finally pieced it together. The ID she wasn't reclaiming. The bag at my feet.

"Wait. No." The words escaped me in disbelief.

Emily stayed silent, her gaze steady and unyielding.

"You joking?" I asked, almost choking on the absurdity of it. "You want me to pretend I'm you?"

Still nothing.

"To go on this mission? As an Army Ranger?"

"I thought you wanted to find your sister," she countered.

"I do," I shot back, crossing my arms. "But this is insane. And it's a suicide mission, isn't it? That's why you're bailing."

"It's your only chance," she said, stepping closer. "And mine."

Before I could respond, a sharp beep from her watch broke the tension. She glanced at it, and her face hardened.

"Shit," she muttered as she pulled her keys and phone from her pocket. She held them out to me. When I didn't take them, she dropped them on top of the duffle bag. "If my car and phone aren't back at the Motel 6 up the street in ten minutes, they'll notice. There's a manila folder on the bed in my room. It has everything you need to know. We're both tall with brown hair and blue eyes. With some luck, it can work. Now you've got two more minutes to decide. Drive to that motel as Emily Wager, or lose your only chance to find your sister."

And just like that, she walked past me.

"Wait!" I called after her.

She stopped and turned, her face unreadable.

"They'll see right through me," I said, panicking. "And then they'll arrest me. Or kill me. I can't do this."

Emily's expression softened slightly. "Up until I met you, I didn't think you could do it either. But there's a fighter in you. A born one. I can see it."

"That shit won't help me," I snapped. "I don't know anything about the military!"

"You don't need to. They won't question you. Half the time, their own secrecy screws them over. They'll assume you're CIA—or more likely, some top-secret scientist brought in for a classified op. There are only two things you need to know about the military."

"Strength and honor?" I asked, freaking out on the inside—and the outside, too, given the way the ID was shaking in my hand.

Emily laughed, short and sharp. "No. One, don't talk too much."

"And two?"

"Always shoot first."

Then she turned and jogged off.

"Wait!" I shouted again, but she was already across the street, vanishing into a side alley beyond the train tracks.

Fuck.

An imaginary ticking clock became a pounding soundtrack in my ears. Sweat formed on my forehead, feeling cold and hot at the same time. I could just walk away. Leave her car parked right there in front of the graveyard—if that red Jeep was even hers. I could go back to my apartment, find a new job tomorrow, and fall asleep with mac and cheese and my laptop in my lap, just as I did every night.

But then the memory came crashing back.

Smoke.

Flames.

The fire swallowing everything.

You came back, I'd coughed, terrified and certain I'd been about to die. My sister had risked her life in the fire and come back for me.

Of course, she'd said, as if there had never been the slightest doubt in her mind.

I owed her.

Before I realized what I was doing, I reached for the duffle bag, phone, and keys. I grabbed them and sprinted toward the red Jeep. My pulse raced as I clicked the button on the car fob. The Jeep beeped in response, its lights flashing in the fog.

Sliding into the driver's seat, I turned on the car and gripped the steering wheel. The Motel 6 wasn't far, but a few minutes had already ticked by. I sat there for a moment, staring at the empty road ahead as if giving myself one last out.

Before the thought could form, my foot hit the gas pedal.

The streets were empty, the world eerily quiet as I sped through the fog. If I drove this old Jeep like it was a Ferrari, I could make it on time.

"Don't talk too much, and always shoot first," I muttered. Strangely, the words comforted me. These were two things I could actually be good at. Two things on which my life—and my sister's life—might now depend.

As I raced toward the motel, a spark of hope flared. Hope that I'd finally find my sister and maybe, just maybe, find her alive.

6

Ryder

The doors to the chow hall swung open, releasing the familiar stench of overcooked beans and burnt coffee. It clung to the air like a threat. The line for food stretched halfway across the room—a slow shuffle of orange jumpsuits and murmured complaints.

I scanned the line. Ben Gaetz stood near the front, his hulking frame next in line for the slop. Then I spotted Jimmy on guard duty. He was leaning against the counter and chatting with one of the cooks.

Perfect.

I made my move, shoving my way through the line like I owned it. When I reached Ben, I shoved him hard enough to make him stumble.

"Move it, rapist," I said, my voice low.

He fucking did—just like the coward he was. That enraged me almost as much as his face. His filthy presence alone was enough to twist my guts, but the fact that he'd raped a pregnant woman during a burglary made me see red. She'd lost her baby because of this monster.

Maybe it was the dream I'd had last night about my son. Or maybe it was the way he just stood there like he didn't deserve to be here. Sassy. Annoyed. Or maybe I'd simply waited long enough for Benny Boy to suck dick. Either way, I wasn't holding back today.

"You hungry, rapist?" I growled, stepping into his space, forcing him to backpedal until the counter pinned him in place.

His mouth opened, but no sound came out. He glanced around at the other inmates. Their stares were heavy with the kind of malice that turns men into predators. Weakness stank like vomit in here.

"Answer me, you piece of shit. You hungry?" I pressed closer, my face inches from his.

Someone behind me muttered, "Baby back bitch." Snickers rippled through the crowd. Ben's eyes flickered with fear as he realized they weren't looking at me. They were looking at *him*. Prey. Soap-dropper. Dead man walking.

"Fuck you," Ben finally mumbled, his voice shaking.

"Fuck me? Oh, Benny Boy," I sneered, tilting my head. "Is that a backbone I hear rattling around in there? You sure you wanna test it out on me?"

Benny just stood there, staring at me with fear-filled eyes.

"All right." I grabbed the back of his neck and twisted his arm, spinning him around like a ragdoll. He grunted in pain as I slammed his face into the steaming porridge on the counter.

His scream tore through the chow hall. I shoved him in harder, grinding his face into the scalding slop as he thrashed like a fish on a hook. Cheers erupted like a fucking symphony.

"Ryder!" Jimmy's voice cut through the chaos.

I felt his hands grab my shoulders, yanking me back. I didn't resist. A fight with Jimmy wasn't on my to-do list. He was one of the good ones—a guy just here to pay his bills. Clean military record, a tour in Iraq. Not my enemy.

Ben crumpled to the floor, screeching as he clutched his face. The porridge clung to his skin, where angry red burns were already blistering. Blood and slime mixed into a mess that sent a rush through me—not from guilt but from the thrill of justice.

Guards rushed in and shoved inmates aside as they circled the scene. The noise faded, leaving only Ben's screams echoing in the sudden silence.

"He started it," Jimmy said to the guards as he pointed down at Ben.

Nobody argued. Nobody asked questions. The guards hated Ben for what he'd done. A man who'd raped a pregnant woman, causing her to lose her child? Even in here, that made him less than nothing. And after this, it would be only days until he got shanked.

Good.

The guards grabbed Ben by the arms and dragged him out to the doctor. His muffled groans bounced off the walls.

"The show's over!" Jimmy barked, his voice cutting through the lingering murmurs. "Eat!"

Slowly, the men returned to their places. Some shuffled back into the line, others slumped into chairs, poking at their food with disinterest. Just another day in hell.

"You. Let's go," Jimmy demanded, grabbing me by the arm. He shoved a few inmates out of his way as he made a path through the chow hall.

Isolation, most likely.

Fine by me. Benny Boy was worth it.

"Goddamn it, Ryder," Jimmy muttered as we passed the hallway leading toward the isolation block. "Fucking hell. This was really bad timing."

I slowed, glancing down the corridor lined with metal gates. "Bad timing? Since when does timing matter in this shithole?"

"This way," was all he said, pushing me forward.

We passed the security station and the laundry room. I frowned. "This isn't the way to the hole. Where the hell are we going? Am I getting transferred? For that piece-of-shit rapist?"

Jimmy stayed silent, his steps steady and determined. He turned into a hallway I'd never been down before. It was quieter here. The walls felt tighter. After a few more turns, we reached a hallway lined with men. Their presence was suffocating. Some wore black suits. Most likely, they were members of a three-letter government agency.

Others were military. No doubt about it. The haircuts, the rigid posture, the hard stares.

One guy in his forties, with a beard and sunglasses, stood out. Active Special Forces. Or former.

"Now, now . . . what is all this?" I asked as we passed the men in sharp black suits. I didn't see any badges, and the FBI loved flashing theirs around like high school hall passes. So definitely CIA or NSA.

Jimmy stopped in front of an open door and stretched his arm out, signaling me to go in. He shot me a final scolding look, his lips tight with a warning.

"Please try," he almost begged. "Just fucking try."

I cocked a confused brow at him as I stepped inside. A couple of the men from the hallway trailed behind. One of them shut the door behind us with a solid *click*. No guards. My hands and feet weren't even cuffed. This was new.

The room was bare. No one-way mirror, no visible cameras. Just a table with two chairs on each side. Across the table sat a man with slicked-back hair and a sleek black suit. He motioned for me to sit. Sunglasses indoors—classic government prick move.

I glanced around. Three suits. Two military guys in plainclothes —jeans and sweaters. And then there was the one who looked like he ran the whole operation. Cargo pants, work boots, and a plain white shirt stretched tight over biceps that looked like they belonged in a comic book. Beard. Crooked nose. Tattoos. He didn't sit. Just leaned against the wall, arms crossed, watching me like a hawk. His disapproval hung thick in the air.

I sat and slouched back into the chair, making myself comfortable. Then it was quiet.

"Isn't this the part where you start talking or something?" I said, breaking the silence. I tapped my fingers on the table, already tired of the theater.

The man in the suit smirked and slid his sunglasses off, revealing sharp eyes that pinned me like a knife. "Don't worry. This isn't about your murder case involving Mr. Colter. Or the guy you just blinded with porridge."

"Shocking twist," I deadpanned, not bothering to hide my lack of enthusiasm.

He lifted his brows, amused. "You already knew that?"

Yeah, I did. Military and government types didn't roll into a prison for petty shit like Colter or Benny. Whatever this was, it was bigger. I stayed silent, refusing to bite. Let him do the talking. The less I said, the better.

Another beat of silence passed before the suit leaned forward and opened a manila folder in front of him.

"You like it in here?" he asked casually, flipping through the pages. From the file, my military photo stared back at me. It contained a man I barely recognized. The buzz cut, the sharp uniform, the steel in his eyes. Someone else's face now.

The man flipped past court documents, reports, shit I'd rather forget.

It was all for show. I knew these assholes had read that file a dozen times before stepping into this room. Every detail, every skeleton in my closet, already dissected and cataloged.

"You're in here for the murder of Mr. Gavin Colter. Life sentence."

I stayed silent.

The guy in the suit cleared his throat and exchanged a glance with the buff Special Forces guy. Another suit stepped forward and took a seat across from me. He looked like a 3D printed copy of the first guy—cocky, sharp, government-grade arrogance.

"You were a survival instructor and tracker in the military, correct?"

"I taught basic survival skills," I replied, keeping my tone casual, almost bored. "Not exactly Rambo."

A flicker of a memory interrupted my indifference—a young Navy SEAL recruit in the woods, his eyes wide in panic as I demonstrated how to snatch a sharp branch off the ground and drive it into an enemy's eye in under two seconds.

"Mm-hmm," the suit muttered, his eyes on the folder. "And what about your tracking skills?"

"Some hiking here and there," I said, shrugging.

Another memory surged forward: my team sleeping in cliff tents thousands of feet above the ground, the jagged peaks of the Altai Mountains slicing through the frozen mist. Six weeks of being hunted by enemy forces, surviving on lingonberries and pine bark, and sleeping on charcoal-warmed earth to keep from freezing. By the end of it, nature had claimed all hundred of the men chasing us. We'd trekked to Mongolia, established comms, and finally gotten extracted. All of us.

Suit Man didn't buy my dismissal. His eyes flicked back to the file. "A lot of this is redacted," he said, "but it says here you led a special ops team through pretty rough terrain in the dead of winter."

"Just a little snow," I said. "Like I said, never really saw combat."

In some ways, that was true.

The suits exchanged glances again, subtle but loaded. The blond-haired suit cleared his throat and leaned forward slightly.

"We're in need of a tracker," he said, his voice smooth but deliberate. "Someone with solid skills."

I narrowed my eyes at him. Whatever these clowns wanted, it couldn't be good. For me. No introductions, no name tags, nothing. Just blank stares and bad vibes. There were plenty of good trackers on the other side of these concrete walls.

"Did you try the military?" I joked.

The suit ignored me. He leaned forward, elbows on the table.

"We were told you're one of the best trackers out there. The best, to be precise."

Silence. Their eyes bore into me, waiting for something.

"No idea who'd make up such bullshit," I said with a shrug, my eyes narrowed.

"Let's get to the point," the other suit jumped in, his voice smooth like that of an award-winning car salesman. "We have a mission for you. Here, in the US. Quick in and out. No enemy threats. Thought you might like to stretch your legs."

A sarcastic smile curled on my lips as I let my gaze wander to the window. For the first time since entering the room, I caught a glimpse of the trees. Their crowns swayed gently in the breeze. The sun hung just above them—midmorning.

"Mm-hmm. I see. A little mission," I said, drawing the words out like I was savoring them. "Here at home. In and out."

Both suits nodded, too eager, like hopeful kids pitching a bad idea.

"Okay," I continued. "Well, what time is it?"

"What?" Blond Suit blinked, clearly baffled.

"Time? It's morning, right? What time exactly?"

He fumbled for his phone. "Uh, nine twenty-six."

"Oh-oh," I said, my tone suddenly chipper. "Guess we're done here. My therapy starts in four minutes. And nobody fucks with my Skittles. Especially not the government. Who lies for a living. So here's the deal—you've got one minute to tell me why the CIA is recruiting a convicted felon for a domestic mission led by Special Forces." I nodded toward Beard Guy, who was leaning against the wall. "Or you can fuck right off."

Blond Suit's mouth fell open as he exchanged a stunned look with the others.

"We already told you—" he started, but I cut him off.

"Twenty-three seconds now," I said flatly. "I deducted the time I spoke too."

His face twisted with anger. "Who the fuck do you think you—"

"Ten," I interrupted, launching into a countdown, "nine, eight, seven."

"You asshole—" spat Suit Man.

"Three, two, one—" I rose from my chair.

A deep voice cut through the tension. "The last two teams we sent on this mission failed," Beard Guy said. He pushed off the wall and strode to the table, ignoring the sharp look Suit Man shot him. "Never reached the target coordinates."

"That's classified," Blond Suit hissed.

Beard Guy didn't flinch. "We need your help to lead the next team. A lot depends on it."

I arched a brow. "Are you saying that a team of special forces couldn't find a target somewhere in America? Who'd you send, the Boy Scouts?"

"Delta," Beard Guy said, his expression stone-cold.

"Delta is Joint Special Operations Command," I said. "For a domestic mission? Where the hell did you send them?"

"Any other details will be disclosed at the classified operations meeting," Suit Man cut in, his tone curt. "And if that's a problem, people can fuck off back to their cells or expect disciplinary actions." His sharp glare landed on Beard Guy.

The room fell silent.

"So what's in it for me?" I asked with a shrug. "Now that you've fucked with my Skittles."

Suit Man shot to his feet. "This is a waste of time. Let this fucker rot in here."

The other suit started to rise, but Beard Guy's calm, commanding voice made the whole room freeze. "Wait." His gaze lingered briefly on the Norse runes tattooed on my hands. The Raido (R) rune. People always thought all rune symbols were tied to white supremacy, but that was total bullshit. For thousands of years, Germanic and Viking tribes had used these symbols, which were full of meaning tied to their language, beliefs, and culture—long before modern hate groups twisted them to hide their little peckers and personal failures.

"What trees are those?" Beard Guy asked me, nodding toward the window.

"What's in it for me?" I shot back, leaning forward. "If I get your team to the coordinates, what do I get?"

Bear Guy nodded slowly. "If you get them there, you'll be granted a full pardon. A clean record. A fresh start."

I frowned. "Expunged records or actually fucking clean?"

"Clean," Beard Guy said. His eyes flicked toward the window again. "Now, what can you tell me from looking out there?"

I didn't need to look out again. My mind didn't work like that. Numbers? Not my thing. Drawing or singing? Forget it. But nature? That was in my blood. My breath. I'd lived it since I was a child, camping in the woods for weeks at a time. It wasn't knowledge. It was instinct, a primal connection. Something that had called to me from the time when our ancestors prayed to Yggdrasil, the holy tree, and respected the land that kept them alive without trying to "own" it.

I sighed and met his gaze. "Sycamore. Red maple. White oak. The white oak's roots took in too much salt runoff from the parking lot. Hence, the few leaves. It won't survive another winter."

Suit Man scoffed. "So he can name some trees. Call the news."

"While you're at it, you might want to change the time on your phone," I told Suit Man. "It's wrong."

"What?" Suit Man jerked his head back.

I nodded at the window. "The red maple's shadow on the dead branches of the white oak. Based on the arc of the sun over the last fifteen minutes, your phone is off by . . . sixteen minutes. Check your personal phone. It syncs with an atomic clock. CIA servers use older satellites for security reasons. Concrete facilities like this one can delay the signal."

"That's ridiculous," Suit Man scoffed, but his expression dropped from his face the second he pulled out his personal phone. As he stared at the screen, his face twisted in disbelief. He handed the phone to Blond Suit.

"Fucking crazy," the second guy muttered and passed the phone back. "He's right. Sixteen minutes off."

"Now," I said, leaning back with a smirk. "Let's talk about my added terms if you want me to lead your team."

"Forget it. You're already getting a full pardon," Suit Man protested.

"So does every congressional pervert caught with a sixteen-year-old," I shot back. "I have a couple more conditions. So either you start swallowing, or you find someone else."

The room tensed as the suit guys exchanged looks.

Beard Guy nodded. "What do you want?" he asked.

"I want to visit my grandmother before the mission," I said. "The other demand is similar. My son."

"You serious?" Suit Man laughed. "You wanna see your grandma?"

I leveled a deadly glare at him. The laughter stopped.

"Done," Beard Guy said. The room stayed quiet for another beat before a grin crept across my face.

Christmas had come early. I knew they were lying about this mission. A team of delta forces failing a domestic mission? In the USA? They'd been bullshitting left and right. Something about this reeked. Of shit. But I didn't care. If I could get my two demands in, I'd die willingly. Fair trade.

"Now," I said, standing, "shall we get the hell out of here? I haven't had a good burger with fries in years."

7

Ryder

I sat next to the towering tree that had grown from my grandmother's grave. Its roots had twisted into the soft, overgrown grass of the old farm we used to own near Salem, Massachusetts. The fields stretched out in a quiet sprawl, filling the air with the faint scent of wildflowers and damp earth. My parents had died early, and my grandmother was the person who had raised me into the man I once was. Not the man I'd become. But then again, my grandma always understood. She'd be proud of me, even the nobody I had become.

The farm wasn't mine anymore. I'd handed everything over to my ex-wife—cats and all—with the condition that it would go to my son when he was old enough. For now, she rented it out.

I glanced toward the little white house and red barn in the distance, noting the sleek black government SUV parked in the driveway. The renters had been hesitant to let us onto the property. Who wouldn't be?

I struck a match and lit a small juniper branch, as was the custom in Norse beliefs for protection and guidance. The flame crawled over its brittle surface. Smoke curled into the air, carrying an earthy scent I remembered from better days.

"Grandma . . . may Freyja keep my spot next to yours in Sessrúmnir," I muttered. I glanced up at the massive tree whose thick and gnarled trunk rose from the site of my grandmother's burial. The juniper smoke filled my lungs. Its aroma was bittersweet and grounding, even on a visit like this.

When the flame crept too close to my fingers, I dropped the twig onto the ground and let it smolder out. Then I dug a small hole with my hand, the dirt cold and damp against my skin, and placed a twist of yarrow into it. "To honor a great woman," I said, patting the earth back into place. "I didn't think I'd get to see you again."

My hand rested on a root. The bark was rough and cool under my palm as if it carried her spirit.

"I see Yggdrasil granted your wish, letting this tree grow so damn strong." I let the moment stretch as my eyes drifted to the dark ink of my Raido (ᚱ) rune tattoo. It seemed to harmonize with the tree, the earth, and the memory of her.

Once, I'd worn the symbol as a pendant, a gift from her. Raido. The rune of journeys, movement, and life's path, symbolizing purposeful travel, progress, and harmony with the natural flow of events. I'd passed the pendant on to my son the day I was sentenced in court. The sight of his big, innocent eyes filled with tears flashed in front of me.

"Of course I visited him," I said to the tree. The memory from this morning hit me like a punch to the gut—standing across the street in Boston, watching my son play during recess. He looked so much bigger now, ten years old and full of life.

It fucking hurt to see him. Hurt so goddamn bad I thought my chest would burst right there. I wanted to run to him, scoop him up, smell his hair, and tease him about his stupid, gelled hairstyle. Kids these days. I grinned at the thought, but the grin faded. He was better off without me. Better off without his convict father fucking up his life. His mom and stepdad could give him what I never could.

The wind stirred the branches above me, soft and insistent, as if she were calling me out. To call that a *visit*.

"It counts," I told the tree. "Even if I just watch from a distance.

It's better this way." The branches stilled, and I knew she understood. That was just who she was.

I smelled the cheap drugstore aftershave before I saw them—the douchebags from the black SUV. They were walking toward me in their stiff suits and sunglasses. Impatient pricks.

I sighed. "Looks like my visit's cut short." I nodded toward the suits. "Can't fucking do without me, can they?"

Her voice echoed in my head, the way she used to laugh and scold me when I made macho jokes. And then countered: "It's easy to take a life, but giving one? Until you do that, a real man is still only half a woman."

"What do you think of this mission?" I asked. She already knew what was going on. She always did. She believed in our old ways, the ways of the gods and the mighty Yggdrasil. She burned herbs, prayed to Freyja, and listened to the earth. She was still here. In the trees, grasses, and wind.

Then the world fell still. No birds. No sound. No branches moving with the wind. Just a heavy silence that wrapped around me.

"What is it?" I whispered, pressing my hand harder against the root. The warning was clear, but my time in prison had dulled my connection to the world around me.

"Hope that's not juniper you're burning there," barked one of the suits, who then sneezed. "I'm allergic to that shit." His gaze flicked to the rune tattoos crawling over my hands and under my jacket. "What's up with all this Viking crap? Burning herbs, mumbling to trees. We gotta make a stop to get your meds? There's something called Christianity if you wanna pray and look sane."

When I turned, my reflection caught in his mirrored sunglasses. "Oh, right. Praying to the old man in the sky who supposedly saved the world by stuffing two of every animal onto a boat the size of a small cruise ship. Yeah, that's totally sane. Much better than praying to the trees that keep you breathing and you can actually touch. Now here's a thought. Stop shitting on my gods, and I won't shit on yours."

The Blond Suit bit down a laugh as his friend frowned.

I ignored him and turned back to the tree. Something was wrong. The warning was still clear.

"Earth to tree-hugger," Suit Man grumbled, his voice grating. "We need to go."

I narrowed my eyes at the tree, then turned. Whatever was about to go down, it wasn't good. She was never wrong.

A deal was a deal, though. I'd seen my son, talked to my grandmother. Two things I'd thought impossible when I'd gotten life for killing a man.

I straightened. "I'll see you in Fólkvangr, Grandma," I mumbled and started walking.

"See me where?" sneered the arrogant suit. "Over the rainbow?"

"Don't be ridiculous," I shot back. "You wouldn't even make it into the hellhound's ass."

"Convict scum," he barked.

I didn't give a shit. My grandmother's warning echoed in my head. Something was coming, and it was going to be bad.

But that didn't matter now. I'd made my peace. All that was left was to see this through and hope I died with honor so Freyja would think I was worthy of her meadows and great hall Sessrúmnir.

8

Esther

When I pulled up to the security gate, I was gripping the wheel so
hard that my knuckles had turned white. Emily Wager and I looked
similar enough. Her shorter hair now matched mine after a rushed
kitchen scissors hack job last night. And we both had blue eyes. I'd
spent the whole night watching videos on military etiquette and how
to handle the weapons they used, but nothing had settled my stomach. I'd had to pull over to stop a panic attack twice on the drive to
Twin Mountains.

It was madness, all of it.

Emily's Army uniform fit me perfectly, and her hair color was
identical to mine. But my cheekbones were sharper and higher than
hers.

Shit.

The drive here had been hell. Thirty minutes before reaching
the gate, I'd lost my cell signal. The woods had grown thicker and
more feral. I'd had to rely on printed directions from the manila
folder I found in Emily's car. No more small towns or gas stations.
Just a few rotting, abandoned buildings leaning into the Pemigewasset Wilderness. Twin Mountains had felt like the last breath of

civilization before I plunged into another world—one where time had been forgotten.

I pulled up and lowered the window as the guard walked up.

"ID," he muttered, bored.

I handed it over, keeping my gaze out the windshield. He scanned the ID slowly, then glanced at me.

"What brings you out here?"

"Classified," I said, echoing the words straight from the folder.

His eyes narrowed as he studied me. Shit. My hand started trembling against the wheel. He noticed.

"Cold as hell out here," I grumbled, trying to cover my nerves. "They treat us good here, at least?"

He smirked. "Like shit. They promised me Florida, but once I signed the dotted line, they dumped me in this armpit. Lyme disease and snow from October until May."

"Yeah," I muttered, forcing a chuckle. "They sure stop blowing smoke up your ass once you ink the paper."

His grin turned into a laugh, a brief flicker of camaraderie. Then he leaned closer. "Hey," he said.

My spine stiffened. Shit. Had he figured it out?

"Can you give these to Wilkins at the next checkpoint?" He held up a pack of cigarettes. "Accidentally grabbed them this morning at the chow hall."

Relief hit me so fast that I almost sighed out loud. I caught myself and put on a scolding look. "Personal deliveries on duty? Fine. I'll do it. We gotta stick together, right?" I grabbed the pack.

"We sure do. Thanks! Tell him he owes me for my honesty."

I gave a nod, acting like I was doing him a favor. In reality, he was doing me one.

Gravel crunched under the tires as I drove through. Towers loomed on either side. In them, armed guards scanned the woods with sharp-eyed focus.

The second checkpoint came fast. Wilkins waved me through the moment I handed him the cigarettes with the message. He didn't even glance at my badge. I could've kissed the first guy for making it so easy. My first triumph as a fraud Army Ranger on a secret mission to find my sister.

There was every chance I'd get caught—or killed. I couldn't shoot or fight in close-range combat, but none of that mattered. Without my sister, I was already dead. I had to do this. No way out but through.

The base was strange. Before me stretched empty gravel roads flanked by watchtowers manned by soldiers with AR-15s. Again, they weren't watching me or the base. They were watching the woods.

The buildings were old. Really old. Some resembled wooden mountain huts. There were no signs, no commissary, and almost no life on the roads.

When I spotted a soldier walking, I pulled over. "Excuse me," I said, my voice steady despite the chaos in my chest. "Do you know where operations briefings take place?"

The young soldier scanned the yellow Ranger tag on my uniform sleeve and snapped into a perfect salute.

"Ma'am, next to the shooting range, ma'am." His voice was robotic as he pointed toward a weathered wooden building near a large white one.

"Thank you," I said, forcing a casual nod.

"Ma'am," he replied, resuming his march.

Shit. I should've saluted back. I had to be more careful.

I parked in front of the wooden building. My stomach was twisting into knots as I grabbed my black beret and stepped out. This mission was last minute. No time to shower and get cozy in whatever lodging they had for me here. I let out a breath when I realized I was literally just on time.

The hallway inside smelled of mold and old wood. At the far end, a group of men stood outside an open door, chatting in low voices.

Damn it.

I was the only woman.

Emily Wager must've been a goddamn legend to have made it

onto a mission like this. Now, there was me. And the manila folder had been useless. Of course, it hadn't included information about Emily herself. Why the hell would it? She knew her own role. I didn't even know what part I was supposed to play in this twisted action movie.

I walked slowly, keeping my head down. My eyes caught on a tall man leaning against the wall, away from the others. He was well over six feet and extremely fit. His plain white T-shirt stretched over his chest. His camouflage pants were creased and spotless.

And his tattoos.

Through Google, I'd learned that military regs allowed one small tattoo on the hands. This guy was covered. Symbols sprawled across his arms, neck, and hands—jagged signs I couldn't make out from a distance.

His gaze followed me like that of a predator watching its prey.

I held his stare as long as I could, then tugged my beret lower and looked down.

His voice rumbled behind me as I passed him. "Hat off."

Shit. He was right. No hats indoors.

I yanked it off and glanced around. Nobody else had noticed.

But he was still watching. I could feel his eyes on my back like needles.

As I approached the doorway, the laughter of men swapping deployment stories spilled from the room and into the hall. I hesitated just outside where the group clustered near the entrance—all Rangers and SEALs. Half of them looked rugged and worn—men in their thirties and forties with thick beards and lines etched into their faces. They had the air of men who'd seen too much and were hard to impress. They wore cargo pants and snug T-shirts with no jackets like they'd just stepped off a sting operation in the Middle East and couldn't be bothered to dress up.

The other half were fresh-faced, their hair clipped high and tight, looking like they'd just graduated from special forces training. Their youth stood out against the grizzled veterans' appearance. They were eager, inexperienced, and trying too hard to fit in. They laughed at everything like idiots.

I swallowed hard and tugged at the beret under my arm.

"Excuse me," I mumbled, stepping through the group. A few men glanced at me, and their conversations halted mid-laugh. The quiet spread like ripples in a pond as the others turned to look.

Their stares were heavy, assessing. Some lingered as if trying to place me, while others returned to their conversations as if I didn't exist. But I saw it in their faces—curiosity, skepticism, a silent question. *What the hell is she doing here?*

With a hammering heart, I kept my head down and pushed through. The room was dimly lit, the lights buzzing faintly overhead. The tables were arranged in a U-shape, with folders, maps, and coffee cups scattered across the surface. At the front, a projector hummed as it cast a map of the mountain forests onto the far wall. Red lines cut through the terrain like veins.

I slipped into a chair, my back stiff as I scanned the setup. No name tags, no formalities—just a folder in front of seventeen chairs.

The room fell silent as a three-star general walked in. He was tall and lean, with a posture rigid as steel. The sharp creases in his Operational Camouflage Pattern uniform, paired with his polished boots, reflected a discipline earned over a lifetime. His gray hair was cropped close, and his stern gaze cut across the room, silencing any remaining murmurs. The silver stars on his collar caught the fluorescent light, flashing with every movement.

Behind him stood a stocky man with a thick, dark beard and a crooked nose that appeared to have been broken and never properly set—more than once. His sleeves were rolled to his forearms, revealing tattoos snaking across his muscular arms. His stride was confident but unpolished, as if he didn't give a damn about appearances.

The general stopped as the bearded man stepped forward. "Sit," the bearded man barked, his low voice filling the room.

With quick movements, the men shuffled behind the chairs. Their backs were straight, their boots planted.

"I'm Lieutenant Cooper," the bearded man said. "And this is Lieutenant General Folks."

Cooper gestured to the general, who moved to stand beside him, hands clasped behind his back.

The room seemed to shrink when Lieutenant Cooper briefly stared at me.

"Please open the folders in front of you," Cooper instructed.

The general stepped closer, his arms still locked behind his back. His jaw tightened as he prepared to speak. However, before a single word could leave his mouth, the door opened abruptly. Every gaze moved toward the sound.

It was the man from the hallway. The one with the hand tattoos, the predator-like stare, and the blatant disregard for rules. He strolled in like he owned the place, holding a crinkling bag of chips in his hand. With a carefree air, he sauntered to the empty chair next to me and dropped into it, then popped a chip into his mouth as if he hadn't just interrupted a briefing from a three-star general.

The room stared daggers at him. Cooper's jaw twitched, but no one said a word.

General Folks allowed the moment to hang. His gaze bored into the latecomer, who chewed leisurely. Then, with deliberate patience, the general turned back to the group.

"You are here today because you are the best at what you do," he said, his voice calm but weighted. "For the mission ahead, we need the best. It's simple. Yet a lot depends on it. Depends on you."

I stared at the man next to me—or, more precisely, at the tattoos on his hands. They were old symbols, Germanic or Viking. The black ink was etched into his skin like battle scars. The one on his left hand caught my attention. Its jagged lines formed what looked like a rune. Raido? The rune for safe journeys? I tried to remember fragments of an ancient religions class in college. Bits of the *Poetic Edda* flitted through my memory. It was the most important written collection of Norse mythology. But here, in this room, surrounded by soldiers who were everything I wasn't, the confidence of my half-assed knowledge slipped away.

"Jensen, explosives expert," Cooper read, his voice sharp and commanding.

"Yes, sir," Jensen replied from across the room. His deep tone matched his broad, imposing frame.

I flicked my gaze to Cooper, who stood at the front with a folder in hand. My stomach tightened. He was reading from a list of people. Us.

"Carter—communications specialist," Cooper called out.

"Yes, sir," Carter answered quickly, his voice clipped and eager. He was wiry and had thick glasses.

"Graves—weapons specialist," Cooper continued.

"Yes, sir." Graves's voice was a low rumble, steady and unbothered, just like the scarred, grizzled man who owned it.

"Vargas—heavy weapons specialist," Cooper said.

"Yes, sir," Vargas replied with a smirk, his arms crossed and his muscular frame leaning back in his chair.

"Henderson—intelligence officer."

"Yes, sir," came the calm reply from Henderson, a man with a calculating gaze. He looked like he was three steps ahead of everyone in the room.

I shifted nervously in my chair, my hands gripping the edge of the folder in front of me. The list of names did not include pictures. That was the only silver lining. If there'd been pictures, I'd have been fucked.

"Erickson—lead guide and tracker," Cooper said.

"Yes, sir," replied the man beside me, his voice low and unhurried. His predator eyes stayed locked on me longer than necessary, so I looked away.

Then it came.

"Wager," Cooper said.

My chest went cold. I felt nauseous as I prayed his next words would be "medic" or "cook."

"Sniper," Cooper added.

I swallowed hard, my pulse thundering in my ears. This couldn't be real.

Fucking sniper?

The word echoed in my head like gunfire. My hands tightened around the folder. *This is a nightmare. This is impossible.*

"Wager?" Cooper repeated, wrinkling his forehead at me.

"Yes, sir," I shouted enthusiastically. "Here, sir."

"Nguyen—medic," Cooper continued.

"Yes, sir," Nguyen replied, his tone sharp and professional.

The rest of the names were a blur as I tried to stop my heart from hammering against my ribcage. Sniper? I couldn't hit a target ten feet away from me. Fucking Emily. How could she have hidden this important information? She'd done me dirty. I was done!

"Remember those names," Cooper said, his gaze sweeping the room like that of a hawk. "This list stays here. So do the folders. No exceptions."

"Yes, sir," the group answered in unison. Except for Erickson, who stayed silent beside me.

Cooper turned the floor over to General Folks, who stepped forward with an air of authority. "If you flip to the next page, you'll see a map of the Pemigewasset Wilderness," he began.

I forced my shaking hands to turn the page and reveal a dense expanse of green—trees, trees, and more trees.

"The Pemigewasset Wilderness is one of the most remote areas in North America," General Folks said. "No cell reception. No homes. No people. Nothing but forest. Some of your equipment, including compasses, might malfunction due to the area's strong magnetic activity. That is why Erickson will lead you through the terrain like in the good old days." He glanced at Erickson. "Your mission is simple: Deliver undisclosed cargo to the coordinates marked on this map."

The room filled with the sound of rustling paper as we all shuffled through the maps. Trails, satellite images, and blank topographical maps filled the folder.

"Sir," a voice cut in. Jensen, the explosives expert. In his early forties, he sported a salt-and-pepper beard that matched his serious tone. "These are all maps, sir?"

General Folks glanced at Cooper, who gave a barely perceptible nod.

"That's correct," General Folks replied curtly.

"What about enemy intelligence?" Graves asked, his deep voice slicing through the air.

"None reported," General Folks said calmly. "As far as we know."

The room stilled, and the unspoken tension grew heavier. No enemy intelligence? No contact reports? A domestic mission in the middle of nowhere, with no anticipated threats? Yet they'd drummed together the best of the best?

Something didn't add up, even for someone like me.

Ross, the grizzled engineer with a bald head and a build like a bulldozer, broke the silence. "So our mission is to go in and deliver classified cargo to these coordinates?" His tone was submissive, but his furrowed brow betrayed his skepticism.

"Yes," General Folks confirmed.

Ross leaned back in his chair and exchanged a glance with Vargas, the heavy weapons specialist, who smirked. "Is the cargo the Holy Virgin Mary? Seems like the only reason to drum up a team like this."

The room erupted in laughter, but not everyone joined in. Erickson, the guide next to me, remained stone-faced. I couldn't bring myself to crack a smile either.

"Something like that," Cooper replied, his lips twitching as if resisting a smile.

"All jokes aside," General Folks interjected, his face hardening, "the delivery of this cargo is of utmost importance. We cannot afford any mistakes. That's why you're here—every single one of you. The best of the best. This mission is simple in concept, but a lot depends on it. And when I say a lot, I mean a fucking lot." His sharp eyes scanned the room. "Is that clear?"

"Yes, sir," the group said in unison.

"What was that? The general couldn't hear you," Cooper barked.

"YES, SIR!" the group shouted back, their voices bouncing off the walls. All hesitation had been stamped out instantly.

"Good," Cooper said. "Your operational meeting point is at 0500 hours sharp, at the arms room for weapons gearing and distribution. The mission begins at 0600 hours. The drop-off location is on the east side of the base, where you'll hike the rest of the way, marching alongside a heavily armed cargo truck. All eyes on the woods at all times."

"The mission should last no more than three to four days," General Folks said. "There are strategic stops each night to rest. It's imperative you reach those points before sundown to avoid getting lost in the dark. Erickson will guide the team, with Henderson assisting."

Henderson, a thin man in his late forties with sharp eyes that missed nothing, gave Erickson a quick nod. Erickson didn't return it.

"Any questions?" Cooper asked, his gaze sweeping the room.

"Nope. Sounds straightforward," said Blake, the stocky mechanic with fiery red hair.

"Good," Cooper said, striding back toward the projector. "Let's go over the route to the drop-off coordinates. Then you guys should get some sleep."

The projector clicked on, and an image of dense, shadowy trees filled the screen. Cooper was about to begin when Erickson cleared his throat loudly. Every eye in the room turned to him.

"Well," Erickson said, leaning back in his chair with a faint smirk. "I think I do have a question, if you don't mind."

"I do mind," Cooper said when he saw that the question was coming from Erickson. "You had your chance. We're already behind."

Unfazed, Erickson shrugged and tossed the crinkling bag of chips onto the table. "So here we are, sitting with a team of the best men and women this country has to offer—half with more tours than they can count, and the other half ready to Rambo without asking questions. And yet, we're here for a domestic mission. No enemy contact expected. No distress calls. Just a delivery. Three to four days max in the middle of a forest in New Hampshire. New . . . Hampshire."

"Yes," Cooper replied curtly.

"See," Erickson continued. "Looking at all this, I'm just wondering—what's the catch?"

The room fell into a thick silence broken only by the faint hum of the projector. Cooper's jaw clenched, and he glanced at General Folks, who gave him a slight nod.

Cooper turned back to the projector and pressed a button to

skip forward. The screen flickered, and a new image appeared—a map marked with a jagged red X near the trail's midpoint.

"We would have gotten to it eventually, but why not skip to it right now so Erickson can calm his titties," Cooper said, walking up to the screen. His silhouette was outlined against the projected forest. "This," he pointed at the red x on the map, "is where we lost contact with our last team."

It felt like the whole room braced for impact.

"Lost, sir?" asked Kingston, the demolition expert, whose gruff voice carried a hint of skepticism. The man, in his mid-forties with a brown mustache, raised an eyebrow.

"Yes," General Folks confirmed with a serious look. "No contact. No trace."

"No enemy contact?" Kingston wondered. "But the team is missing in action?"

General Folks shook his head. "Complete blackout. No comms whatsoever."

"And the cargo?" asked Foster, the young intelligence officer with a long nose.

"Also lost without a trace," Cooper said.

The room was silent for a few moments.

"All evidence suggests they got lost due to equipment failure," General Folks explained. "The magnetic waves in this area are extremely strong. Maybe they took a wrong turn or got caught in a storm. We don't know for certain. But that's why we've got two of the best trackers on this team. Henderson and Erickson. The delivery of this cargo is of utmost importance, and Erickson and Henderson will guide you even if your equipment malfunctions."

"Are the drop-off coordinates for the cargo another base?" asked Sanders, the weapons specialist. His mid-thirties features were hardened, and a scar cut clean through his left eyebrow as he leaned forward.

"That's classified until you get closer to the coordinates," General Folks said, cutting off Cooper just as he opened his mouth to answer.

"When did the blackout occur?" Erickson asked.

"One month ago," Cooper said.

"So they might still be alive?" asked Collins, the breaching expert in his late twenties. He had a cigarette tucked behind his ear, just like in the movies.

"Possible," Cooper said, his voice cold. "But this is not a rescue mission. You will not deviate from your assigned objective, no matter what. If you find the old team or their cargo, you make contact and keep moving."

Erickson cocked a brow. "Leave them behind?"

Cooper's eyes narrowed. "I repeat for the last time. You will not deviate from your assigned objective. No. Matter. What. Is that clear?"

"Yes, sir!" the group shouted back.

"Good." Cooper nodded. "We'll dispatch a separate rescue team should you find anybody out there. Your orders remain unchanged. This mission takes priority."

My thoughts churned like a storm, wild and uncontrollable. My sister. Could she be out there, hidden away on some secret base deep in the Pemigewasset Wilderness? Was she part of some twisted government experiment? Or there by choice? Questions clawed at my mind, each one darker than the last.

I scanned the room, desperate for a sign that someone else felt my thirst for answers. But no one seemed fazed—except Erickson. His eyes were narrowed, and his posture was sharp. It was as if he were dissecting every word, every detail. The others, especially the younger guys, sat straight-backed and focused, their eyes fixed on Cooper as if they were obedient dogs waiting for their master's signal.

Of course, this was their world—special operations with orders that didn't leave room for morality or doubt. Out here, you didn't think. You didn't question. You executed. And from the looks on their faces, they were damn good at it.

"All right," Cooper announced. "Let's go over everything one more time. Then you get some rest. The mission starts early, and a lot depends on its success. Don't forget that."

9

Esther

I'd slept like shit. All night, I'd been glued to my phone, watching every video and reading every article I could find about Army Ranger snipers. Clip after clip, voice after voice, hammering home one brutal fact: If this mission went south and I had to fire that rifle, I'd be dead before I could take a second shot. And so would my team.

The same thoughts kept circling through my mind—quit, confess, go to jail forever. But Cooper had said it over and over. This was just a precautionary mission. The worst thing that could happen was getting lost.

So here I was. Five a.m. Standing in the arms room, surrounded by the sharp, metallic smell of gun oil and steel.

At the counter, my palms were slick with sweat. The man on the other side—Sergeant Daniels, according to his tag—set down a sleek, heavy case without so much as a glance in my direction. His movements were robotic, like he did this a hundred times a day.

"MK13 Mod 7," he said flatly, sliding it toward me like it weighed nothing. "Sniper rifle. You're carrying it."

I nodded, swallowing hard as I reached for the case. It was

63

heavier than I'd expected. I wasn't looking forward to hauling it through the woods.

He handed me the next weapon—a "Glock 19." Compact, smooth, lethal. Then came the "M4A1 rifle and ammo," all rattled off as he shoved them across the counter. The M4 slung over my shoulder was heavy. Its weight threw me off balance as I held the sniper rifle case in my other hand.

When Daniels handed me a KA-BAR USMC Fighting Knife, I fumbled it like an idiot, barely catching it before shoving it into my pocket.

Daniels didn't say a word. He just stared at me, expressionless, silently impatient for me to get the hell out of the way.

Another soldier, Miller, was stationed at the next section. He was handing out rucksacks loaded with gear.

"Two weeks' worth of supplies," he said, rattling off the contents as I adjusted the straps. "MREs for meals. Taste like shit. Grayl GeoPress water bottle. It'll remove viruses, bacteria, and heavy metals in seconds. Med kit, thermal liners, and a lightweight tent. You'll also find maps, a compass, and fire starters in the side pocket. Ammo goes in the lower compartment. Here's comms."

I nodded and watched.

"Radio check," Miller said, holding up the compact device. "AN/PRC-152. Programmed with the team's frequencies. Primary channel is 12-5-8, alternate is 15-3-9. Emergency's on 20-0-0. Memorize those. Don't lose comms, or you're dead out there. The PTT button's here." He tapped a small control attached to the radio. "Push to talk."

I nodded again as he handed me the radio, a headset, and a helmet.

The headset clicked neatly into the helmet, which was heavier than I expected. I adjusted the straps in a corner of the room, which buzzed with activity as the rest of the team moved through the line, collecting their gear and weapons. The team adjusted straps, loaded magazines, and tested the weight of their rucksacks with the ease of experience. I threw quick glances at them, trying to mimic their movements to see where everything went. Nobody paid me any attention.

Then my eyes landed on Erickson, the guide with runes inked into his skin like a map of dark secrets.

I caught his stare from across the room. He was leaning against the wall, his arms crossed, his sharp eyes tracking my every move. My stomach twisted under the weight of his gaze. I shot him a glare.

Mind your own damn business.

He didn't flinch.

I turned back to my gear, my hands trembling as I packed the extra ammo and adjusted the knife.

Then Cooper stepped into the room, all geared up himself. For some reason, I hadn't understood the fact that he would lead us.

"All right, listen up," he barked. "You've got everything you need. This gear's your lifeline. If something fails, it's up to you to improvise. Now get ready. Your ride to the drop-off point is waiting outside. We head out early."

"Yes, sir," the room shouted.

The weight of the pack dug into my shoulders, and the rifle strap bit into my neck. My breaths were shallow, and my mind raced. This gear was supposed to keep me alive, but right now I worried it would kill me in the end. How the hell would I march with that for miles? Days?

Fuck. Fuck. Fuck.

10

Ryder

"Holy shit," Carter muttered as he hopped out of the troop transport truck. The rest of the team followed, their boots thudding against the dirt in steady, heavy beats.

I was in the far back, but the moment I stepped out, "Holy shit" was exactly the thought that hit me too.

The whole team, including Cooper, stood frozen in front of massive metal gates. Attached to an equally colossal wall, the structure looked like something straight out of Jurassic Park. The wall stretched endlessly in both directions before disappearing into the thick forest. Its height was dizzying—easily sixty feet, if not more.

"Is this where you keep the T-Rexes?" joked Nguyen, the medic.

"No T-rex is jumping this shit," shot back Ross, the engineer with shoulders as broad as his grin. He was clearly impressed by the engineering feat before us.

For a moment, we just stood there, staring. Awe mixed with unease as our eyes traveled up the huge gate. Flanking each side were colossal towers manned by soldiers pacing back and forth like guards on an ancient castle wall. The hum of murmurs and half-hearted jokes hung in the air, but the same unspoken thought weighed on all of us.

What was this place?

Something just didn't add up here.

"All right," said Cooper, snapping us back to attention. "Erickson and Henderson will walk ahead of the cargo truck with me." He pointed at the hulking vehicle parked in front of the gate. The rest of the team split into two groups, five on each side of the truck. "The snipers and the medic will bring up the rear."

My gaze locked onto the cargo truck—a secure, heavily armored beast with no windows and a tightly sealed rear door. Its camo metal gleamed faintly under the cloudy sky.

"There will be no small talk. We move in silence," Cooper continued. "Pay attention to every suspicious sound, and report it immediately. No stops until I say so. No wandering off the path, no breaking from the team—no exceptions. Not even for the holy Virgin Mary. Is that clear?"

"Yes, sir!" the team responded in unison.

"Good. One more thing." Cooper's tone dropped, colder now. "The doors to the cargo truck stay closed at all times. And by closed, I mean locked tight. Anybody disobeying that order will be disciplined on the spot."

"Disciplined how?" I asked.

Cooper's iron stare locked onto me. "By whatever means I'm entitled to under military law."

Silence.

"Is that clear?" Cooper's voice boomed again.

"Yes, sir!" the team responded.

"Good. Echo—move!"

"Yes, sir!" The team sprang into action.

I caught sight of Wager a few feet away. She was frozen in place and staring at the massive wall as if it were a ghost.

"The wall," she muttered, seeming almost unaware her lips were moving. "So it's true."

"What is?" I stepped closer, snapping her out of whatever trance she was in.

"Erickson!" Cooper's voice—sharp and impatient—called me back. He was already waiting by the armored cargo truck.

"Nothing," Wager said quickly. She took her place behind the truck with the medic and the other sniper.

Blake, the kid fresh out of training, jumped into the driver's seat of the cargo truck.

The massive steel gates groaned, creating a creaking sound that sent shivers down my spine. Alarms blared like we'd triggered a war zone. Red and yellow lights spun from the guard towers as the gates slowly opened.

I took my place at the tip of the convoy, right behind Cooper and next to Henderson, the other tracker. The gates finally ground to a halt, revealing an endless stretch of forest under the gray, oppressive morning sky. It looked like a scene straight out of doomsday.

There were no enemy shots, no screams from injured soldiers, no choppers spinning overhead—but the silence screamed louder than war.

Everything felt off, from the bizarre makeup of our team—the best of the best mixed with kids fresh out of training—to the local mission with no supposed enemy forces, the top-secret location, the mysterious cargo, and Wager.

She wasn't who she claimed to be. A sniper? Not a chance. The way she walked, the way she carried herself—it was all wrong. She'd been planted here. But by who? The CIA? Or an unknown enemy?

Cooper threw me a quick side-eye as he scanned the convoy, then pressed the PTT button clipped to his vest. "Cooper to Command. Iron Wolf is initiated. Echo moving out. Proceeding to objective. Over."

Command's voice crackled over the shared frequency. "Copy that. Maintain comms. Over."

"Roger that, Command. Out," Cooper replied and started walking.

11

Esther

It was a cloudy day, and we'd been marching for hours in heavy silence. The forest looked like any other—a patchwork of trees shedding their leaves, the vibrant colors of fall scattered across the dirt. Occasionally, a rabbit darted across the path, or a bird rustled in the branches. And yet . . . that weight lingered. The unshakable sense that something wasn't right.

Every glance at the armored convoy ahead only fueled the question: What the hell was in there?

I stumbled on a rock again, my boot catching just enough to nearly send me sprawling. My arms flailed for balance, and I managed to steady myself, though my heart hammered in protest. The weight of the gear pulled at my shoulders, grinding me down with each step.

I was huffing and puffing but trying like hell to keep it quiet. These men were built for this. They were used to hiking through miles of forest with enough equipment strapped to them to sink a small boat. But me? I barely managed to finish my mac and cheese most nights, let alone haul my ass through the woods. My experience began and ended on my couch, scrolling through rabbit holes of information about my sister's disappearance.

Nguyen shot me a look. Curiosity flickered behind his smart eyes. Of course, he noticed me struggling. He was the damn medic.

Dawson, the other sniper, glanced my way too. His gaze was colder, more calculating, those unsettlingly close-set eyes practically drilling into me. It was like he could see right through the Army Ranger act I was barely holding together.

Nguyen tapped the comms button on his chest and tilted the mic away from his mouth.

"You all right, Wager?" he asked.

I fought to catch my breath, to force the words out without sounding like I was dying. "Yeah. I'm good. Don't tell Cooper, but I . . ."

But I what? Was a fraud? Wasn't a sniper or an Army Ranger? That I was a washed-up vet student trying to track down her fallen sister? They wouldn't care about the *why*. All they'd hear was the lie.

"I . . . just had Covid," I lied, the words spilling out as easily as the air leaving my lungs. "Really bad. Still not back to normal, but they wouldn't let me out of this mission."

Dawson nodded, his jaw tightening. "Shit. My grandma died from it three years ago."

"Yeah, they kinda forced me into this too," Nguyen added. "I've been trying to transfer to something quiet for over a year now. My wife and I just had a baby."

"Congrats," I said, managing a small smile.

"Thanks," he replied.

"What do you guys think is in there?" Dawson asked, nodding toward the cargo truck rumbling ahead of us. "I mean, an armored MRAP without windows? For a domestic mission? Must be some important shit."

"A what without windows?" I echoed.

"Mine-Resistant Ambush Protected," Nguyen explained, giving me a curious sidelong glance. "Run-flat tires. That thing can roll over a minefield and keep going like it's nothing."

"Yeah, of course," I said flatly. "Fuck, I'm tired. I thought you said MWARP not MRAP and was like huh?"

"I'm so fucking curious what's in there," Dawson pressed, this time dead serious.

We all stared at the camouflaged, armored MRAP—a hulking beast of windowless reinforced steel, angular plating that looked like it could deflect a missile, a turret-mounted weapon on top, and oversized tires that could crush anything in their path. It was built for survival, not looks.

"Something they don't want us to know," I finally said.

Their eyes locked onto me with curiosity that bordered on suspicion.

"Something dark," I continued. "Something fucked up. Something—"

The truck screeched to a sudden halt, cutting me off.

Cooper's voice crackled through the comms. "Echo, we'll take piss breaks in turns."

I exhaled loudly. "Finally."

"Stay within sight of the team at all times," Cooper ordered.

"You go first," Nguyen offered.

"Thanks," I said, wasting no time shedding my backpack and rifle case. The weight dropped like a curse. The cool air against my sweat-drenched back brought instant relief.

I stepped into the woods, just far enough to be out of sight but still close enough to hear the team. Something about this place put me on edge—the kind of unease that settled deep in my gut. Something beyond the fact that teams went missing here.

Squatting behind a tree, I stared into the tangled mess of branches and shadows. Trees, just endless trees. But then . . . a flicker.

I narrowed my eyes, trying to make out the shape in the distance. It moved. Small. Quick. A fox, maybe.

There it was again.

Shit. Was it white?

A rustling broke the silence behind me. It was followed by a sharp "Buh!" that jolted me upright as I yanked up my pants. My hand shot to the Glock holstered on my belt—clumsy but quick.

Vargas—the bald, heavy-weapons specialist—stood in front of

me, grinning like a kid who had just pulled a prank. His grin vanished the moment he noticed my hand on the gun.

"Calm your titties, Wager. It was just a joke."

"Fucking pervert!" I snapped. "You knew I was peeing here. Fuck off."

Vargas flipped me off with a grin and stomped into the woods, his bald head catching faint flashes of light as he disappeared between the trees.

I crouched again, hoping to finish in peace this time. The shadow—the one that looked like a fox—was gone. So was Vargas, handling his tiny pecker somewhere.

▭

Vargas

"Fucking bitch," Vargas muttered as he turned toward a tree and unzipped his pants. The forest was quiet. The only sound was the faint rustle of leaves overhead. His stream ran down the bark, pooling at the base and splashing onto his boots. "Shit," he hissed, stepping back.

A sudden shadow shifted above him, halting him mid-move.

From high in the tree, a squirrel darted down the trunk. Its fur was an unnaturally vibrant red, almost glowing against the muted browns and greens of the forest. Vargas squinted as he focused on the squirrel's freakishly large ears, which twitched like tiny antennae. For a split second, its eyes seemed to flicker—just a glimmer, as if the light were playing tricks on him.

"Where the hell did you come from?" he chuckled, zipping up as the squirrel leaped from the tree, landing with uncanny grace.

It didn't scurry off like a normal animal would. Instead, it stared at him, then launched into a somersault before landing on a patch of moss with a dramatic flick of its bushy tail. Vargas blinked, half in awe, half in disbelief.

"No way. Do that again," he said, letting out a low whistle.

The squirrel obliged, arching into a perfect backflip before pausing. Its head cocked as if it were gauging his reaction. Vargas laughed, loud and unrestrained.

"Nobody's gonna believe this. Hey, come here," he said, stretching out his hand.

To his surprise, the squirrel approached, inching closer. Vargas's excitement grew. He wondered if he could catch this fearless creature. However, just as he reached out, the squirrel darted forward and bit him in the finger.

"Ah, you little shit!" he shouted, stumbling back. The squirrel darted into the woods, its crimson tail a streak of defiance.

"Hey!" Vargas barked, lurching forward. His boots crunched over fallen twigs and leaves as he sprinted after it. The red tail flickered in and out of view, leading him a few feet down a deer path. Left, then right—it was always just out of reach, taunting him.

Then it vanished.

Vargas stopped and turned in a slow circle. He hadn't walked far from the group, yet all of a sudden, the forest around him felt wrong. The trees seemed denser, the silence suffocating. No flicker of red fur. No twitch of those strange ears. Nothing.

"Bitch," Vargas muttered, shaking his head as he trudged back toward the group. But with every step, his unease grew. The tree he'd just peed on was gone. The landscape seemed to shift with every glance as if the forest itself had rearranged itself while he wasn't looking.

Esther

When I returned to the team, Cooper gave us ten more minutes. After a snack and a quick drink from the water bottle, we geared up and took our positions.

"Listen up," Cooper said into comms. "Erickson estimates we're about three hours from our first overnight stop. We'll get there an hour before dark, right on schedule. Good job, everybody. Echo Team, status check—over."

"Echo One, green—over," Nguyen said, glancing at Dawson and me as he spoke into his comms.

"Echo Two, green—over," Collins, the breaching expert, reported from his position on the left side of the cargo truck.

"Echo Three . . ." Jensen, the explosives expert, said. He paused. "Three . . . red. Vargas is unaccounted for—over."

"Echo Three, confirm last known location of Vargas—over," Cooper demanded.

"Last seen heading into the woods about ten minutes ago—over," Jensen responded.

"Vargas, confirm position—over," Cooper said.

The response was silence.

"Vargas, confirm position—over," Cooper repeated, louder this time.

Still nothing. A knot in my stomach tightened. Where the hell was he?

I pressed the comms button on my chest. "Wager, Echo One. I saw Vargas about ten minutes ago heading deeper into the woods—over."

"God fucking damn it," Cooper cursed under his breath. "Erickson, Wager, you're with me. The rest hold position—over."

With Cooper and Erickson close behind, I led them to the spot where I'd last seen Vargas. I gestured toward the trees ahead. "He went this way about ten minutes ago."

Erickson moved a few steps forward, scanning the ground. He crouched near a mud puddle, then pointed at a partial boot print. He looked up at Cooper and nodded.

"He can't be far," Erickson said. "If we get everyone and focus our search on this area—"

"No," Cooper interrupted.

"But—" Erickson started, only to be cut off again.

"You and Wager have ten minutes. Then you'll return to the team. I'll meet you back at the truck at 1308 hours sharp."

Erickson and I exchanged glances. His jaw tightened. Frustration was clear in his eyes.

"But what if we can't find him in ten minutes?" I asked.

"Then we continue the mission without him."

"You can't just leave him out here," I countered.

"We must, and we will," Cooper said coldly. "You've got your orders. Now move. And it's eight minutes now." He headed back to the road.

Erickson turned sharply and followed the direction of the boot print.

"Vargas!" I shouted as I hurried after him. At first, I felt stupid, like I'd just announced our position to an enemy or something. But then Erickson shouted too, his deep voice cutting through the trees.

We'd barely walked a minute when Erickson stopped in front of a tree. He knelt to study something on the ground.

"Wager," he said, his voice calm but pointed as he stared at a patch of urine near the base of the tree. "Not a very Native name, is it?"

I froze, my stomach twisting. How the hell did he know about my Native roots?

"What . . . what are you talking about?" I asked, trying to keep my voice steady.

Erickson didn't look up. Instead, he scanned the ground. His eyes locked onto another boot print leading deeper into the woods.

"You're Native, no?" he asked casually, his gaze fixed ahead.

I ignored his question and pointed toward the deer trail. "Did Vargas go that way?"

He nodded, standing.

"Vargas!" I hollered into the forest, my voice echoing.

Nothing.

I stepped forward onto the path, which wasn't anything remarkable—just more trees shedding their autumn leaves. But something about it felt off. A chill crawled down my spine.

I looked back and saw that Erickson hadn't moved.

"We should follow the prints, right?" I asked.

He just stood there, listening, his head tilted slightly as though the forest were whispering its secrets to him.

"Fine, I'll go look by myself." I started walking down the trail, but Erickson's hand shot out and gripped my arm. I opened my mouth to protest, but then the comms crackled.

"Cooper here. Time's up. Return to Echo, over."

"But Vargas is still—" I started, but Erickson cut me off.

"Understood. Over." He released my arm and began walking in the direction of the team.

"Wait! We can't just leave him out here," I called after him, but he didn't stop. His steps were steady and deliberate.

"Erickson, wait!" I shouted. He didn't look back.

I peered down the trail where Vargas had gone missing.

"Vargas!" I yelled. Still nothing. "VARGAS!" My voice cut through the woods, but only silence met me.

The cold truth hit me like a hammer. If I went down that trail, I'd probably get lost too. And what good would that do? How would that help my sister? What if she was trapped as some military science experiment, waiting for me to find her?

That was my mission. She was my only mission.

I turned and rushed after Erickson.

"So we're just gonna leave him here?" I barked as we walked back.

He kept moving, ignoring me.

Frustrated, I blocked his way. "You're not very good at the whole teammate thing, are you? I mean, leaving a brother behind?"

He stopped inches from my face. His eyes locked onto mine. "And you're not very good at following orders, are you, *Wager*?" He said the name slowly and deliberately.

My legs moved before my brain caught up. I stepped aside to let him pass. "Just watching out for one of us!" I hollered after him.

But something told me Erickson wasn't buying it. Something told me Erickson wasn't like the others. And that same something told me he was going to be a problem.

When we returned to the team, Vargas's backpack had been hung high in a tree, most likely to keep it out of reach of bears.

"Echo, move!" Cooper barked the moment he spotted us.

Erickson took his place at the front of the convoy next to Cooper while I gathered my gear and fell in at the rear. Dawson and Nguyen threw me looks—worried, questioning, maybe both.

We started moving just as static hissed over the comms.

"Command, this is Echo Lead," Cooper said into comms. "Do you copy? Over."

"Echo Lead, this is Command. Reading you loud and clear. Over."

"Vargas is unaccounted for," Cooper continued. "Last seen grid two-two-four-five-eight-three. Requesting rescue assets. Over."

Static crackled before Command broke through again. "Echo Lead, copy. Rescue team en route. Over."

"Copy. Echo Lead out," Cooper said.

Dawson frowned, his lips pressed into a thin line. "Smart move on Cooper's part, calling that in over shared comms," he muttered.

"No shit," Nguyen said. "Almost makes you feel like they give a damn."

"Almost," Dawson countered.

The silence that followed felt heavier than the gear on my back. A mission that seemed so simple—a peaceful trek through the woods—had already gone sideways. One of the finest soldiers the military had to offer was gone, just like that.

Something was off here. Really, really off.

12

Ryder

The gravel road led us to a small, open space. At the edge of a clearing stood an old wooden hut, its weathered boards warped and uneven. Our boots crunched against the gravel as the forest's looming weight pressed down on us. Cooper raised a hand, signaling the team to halt.

"We'll spend the night here," he said. "Blake, park the cargo truck right in front of the hut to our left. Two-person rotations all night. Eyes on the truck at all times."

He kept talking, but his words blurred into background noise as I walked toward a large stone at the side of the clearing. It flanked a narrow, muddy path leading to the hut. Its surface was rough and cold under my fingertips. Carved into the stone was the shape of the rune Algiz (Υ)—its sharp lines deliberate, its presence unsettling.

I crossed the mud path to a second stone. The same rune, Algiz, stared back at me. My hand traced the uneven grooves. The marking caught the faint light from the gloomy gray sky.

"What is it?" Wager asked, her voice soft but curious as she nodded at the symbol.

I glanced around. Nobody else seemed to care. The men were

already unloading gear onto the porch of the hut, their laughter breaking the stillness of the forest.

"Algiz," I said, keeping my voice low. "It's an ancient rune. It means—"

"Protection," she interrupted, her tone sharper.

Caught off guard, I tilted my head slightly. "That's right. How did you know that?"

Her brows knitted together as her gaze flickered between me and the stone. "I don't know. It feels like something one might need out here. The more important question would be why. And from what?"

My eyes narrowed on the rune as suspicion curled in my gut. Before I could answer, I felt Cooper's stare from the porch of the hut. His presence was heavy, almost accusatory, as if he knew I had questions of my own.

"To be honest," I muttered, meeting his gaze, "I'm wondering the same fucking thing. Why and what."

My answer didn't satisfy her. I could see it in the way she pressed her lips into a thin line and folded her arms across her chest. She wouldn't let it go.

Pressing my comms button, I broke the silence. "Erickson here. It's getting dark. Wager and I will take first watch. Over."

"Understood. Over," Cooper replied, his voice clipped through the static.

I walked past the hut, ignoring the welcoming clouds of smoke coming from the stone chimney, and headed straight into the woods. Wager's presence lingered behind me. I knew her watchful gaze was following my every step.

At the edge of the forest, another large stone loomed, half-covered by moss. The same rune was etched into its surface: Algiz (ᛉ).

Wager's voice tore me out of my thoughts. "That's not good, is it?" she asked right behind me. She was closer than I expected, and her eyes searched mine. "More protection stones."

"It's probably good that it's here," I said, my tone leaving room for the weight of what I wasn't saying.

Her eyes narrowed. "Probably?"

"Yeah. Either that or it's very bad." I met her gaze.

She exhaled, shaking her head as if to clear it.

"Go eat something," I said. "The sun's going down, and we're up first."

Her nod was curt, but I caught a flicker of concern in her expression before she turned and walked toward the hut. Smoke curled lazily from its chimney. The scene was too peaceful for the unease that crept through my chest.

I turned and stared into the dense woods beyond the stone. Shadows stretched long. The air felt heavier, like it carried something ancient and unspoken.

Something powerful.

Something bad.

"What the fuck is going on here?" I whispered to the trees.

13

Esther

M4 in hand, Erickson stood on the porch while I sat on the steps. Around us loomed the forest, pitch-black except for the moonlight breaking through the clouds and the faint glow spilling from the hut's small window. Inside, the men were quiet except for the occasional cough. Cooper had sent them to bed like kids. After the hellish march today, none of them had protested.

I shifted my weight, trying to ease the pressure on a blister gnawing at my heel. The raw flesh scraped against my sock, creating a sharp and constant pain. Taking off my boots wasn't an option, as I didn't want to display evidence of my lies. Instead, I bit down on the discomfort, the strain from the march, and the weight of the gear digging deeper into my body.

My eyes flicked to Erickson. Of course, he noticed. Every move, every twitch—he caught it like his mission was to watch me instead of the cargo. Before I could glare back, a long, mournful howl echoed through the forest. The sound stretched out as clouds blanketed the sky, smothering even the smallest light.

"Wolves," Erickson said.

"Gray wolves," I added. "The howl is deep and resonant, vibrating through the forest. Eastern wolves are higher-pitched, shorter, often mixed with sharp yips. More coyote-like." I paused. "Nice to know they're still out here, considering white men nearly wiped them out."

Out of the corner of my eye, I caught Erickson's grin. "Impressive. Looks like your people taught you a thing or two."

"What makes you think I'm Native?" I shot back, sharper than intended.

He looked at me with a steady gaze. "Every step you take gives you away. Every breath. My people have been detached from their land and its voice for over a thousand years. Yours haven't." He turned his attention back to the trees. "The way you look at the trees, even the way you touched that rock. There's meaning in it. Respect. Curiosity. Longing."

I almost laughed at that. Sarcastic, bitter. He was right. I loved nature. And, yes, I felt a connection to it. But the only longing I had right now was for my sister. The last family I had. The only person who still gave a damn about me. If she was still alive . . .

"Maybe you're wrong," I said, keeping my tone light. "Maybe I just like nature. Maybe your dramatic interpretation isn't the colors of the wind, and I'm not Pocahontas."

That got a genuine smile out of him. "Doubt it. The people teaching at our universities these days couldn't tell wolf howls apart if the answer were taped to their pumpkin spice lattes."

He wasn't wrong. My dad had taught me about wolves, their howls, their patterns. I remembered sitting by the campfire, listening. Then, uninvited, the memory of his charred body flashed before me—his mouth frozen mid-scream.

"Who cares," I muttered.

Erickson's gaze lingered, heavy and knowing. "Yeah," he said quietly. "Who cares."

Before I could respond, a flicker of white darted through the trees. My body snapped upright, and my pulse kicked up a notch. "What was that?"

"Shhh." Erickson's reply was barely a whisper. We stood still, listening. The forest held its breath.

"Nothing," he said finally. "Just an animal."

I nodded, though the tension lingered. "I need to pee."

"Don't go too far."

"Hell no. Just behind the truck."

I glanced over my shoulder, checking to see if he bought it, but Erickson was staring, sharp as ever. Fucking eagle eyes. Always in my business.

I slipped behind the truck and crouched by the rear. With a quick look over my shoulder, I flicked on my flashlight and aimed it at the lock on the cargo doors in the back. A keypad. Numbers. What the hell was in there? I pressed my ear to the door but heard only silence.

"All done?" Erickson's voice came from behind me, making me jump.

"W-what?" I stammered, spinning to face him.

"With your little girl's business. All done?" His expression was unreadable, but his tone carried its usual doubts.

"Oh. Yeah. All done."

"Good." He stepped closer. "My turn. Hold watch on the porch. The next team will be ready soon."

"Y-yeah," I mumbled, brushing past him and heading back to the porch, my heart hammering in my chest. Erickson's gaze burned into my back, as relentless as ever.

Whatever was in that truck, it wasn't normal cargo. And Erickson? He knew I wasn't buying it. Not for a second.

14

Jensen and Martinez

Jensen and Martinez were on the last watch before dawn. The forest held its breath in an eerie silence.

"And then it turned out the woman paying me for a fun time was married to the base commander," Jensen said with a chuckle, his deep, growling voice lowered so he wouldn't wake the sleeping team inside the hut. He had the rugged air of a man shaped by too many tours—primal in some ways but with honor and duty etched into every line of his face. "Wasn't that poor woman's fault. The old bastard was as stiff as they came—just not where it mattered," he added with a smirk.

Martinez, younger and quieter, grinned. "That's insane." His eyes stayed fixed on Jensen, waiting for more. "Any complaints?"

Jensen leaned back, a lazy smile tugging at the corners of his lips. "Not about me." He thrust his hips a little.

Martinez bit down a laugh and shook his head. "You're an animal."

"A real American mustang," Jensen said with a crooked grin. "Wild-blooded and untouchable."

His grin faded. "What... do you think of Wager? No way in hell she's a sniper. CIA, maybe? You think she's tied to our mysterious cargo and destination?"

Martinez shrugged. "Not our business. They could put Mickey Mouse on this op, and we'd still smile like idiots and follow orders."

Jensen gave a slow nod.

A heavy silence followed, broken only by the forest coming alive around them.

Leaves began to rattle, their dry whispers filling the air. Even in the pitch black, the woods seemed alive, moving with an other-worldly rhythm. The dark silhouettes of the trees swayed as the rustling grew louder, carrying a strange, almost mystical song.

Martinez yawned. "Shit, I'm tired," he muttered, massaging the back of his neck.

Jensen rubbed his eyes. Fatigue was catching up to him. "Yeah," he agreed, his voice trailing off as both men stared into the shifting shadows.

They listened, unsure how long they sat there, caught in the restless movement of the forest. Eventually, the rattling leaves softened, their whispers fading into stillness. One by one, the men's blinks grew longer. Finally, the pull of sleep won.

By the time the first faint light of dawn touched the trees, both of their heads had fallen forward, and their weapons were loose in their hands.

Jensen woke with a jolt, jerking upright and elbowing Martinez hard enough to wake him. Martinez's eyes snapped open, wide and disoriented. "What the hell," he muttered, blinking rapidly as if shaking off a dream.

"Shit." Jensen sprang to his feet. His heart pounded as a mix of adrenaline and guilt surged through him. "I've never fallen asleep on watch. Not even in Syria after three straight nights of hiking. What the fuck happened?"

But Martinez wasn't listening. He was frozen, staring into the woods. His breath quickened, and his chest heaved as his gaze locked on the trees.

"What. The. Fuck," Martinez muttered, his hand tightening around his weapon.

Then Jensen saw it too.

"This . . . is impossible," he mumbled as Martinez bolted for the hut, stumbling as his boots hit the wooden floor. He reached the door and shoved it open so hard it banged against the wall.

"Sir!" Martinez shouted. "I need you to see this!"

One by one, Echo stumbled out of the hut, following Cooper as he stepped out first. And one by one, curses of disbelief slipped from their lips as they took in the sight before them.

15

Ryder

I walked toward the mud path that had led us from the gravel road to the hut.

The only problem was, the fucking thing was gone.

Poof.

The land was overgrown with massive, towering trees, their trunks thick with age. Where the mud trail should have stretched out to meet the road, there was now just a dense wall of forest, as if it had always been there.

"What the hell?" Henderson muttered beside me.

"Where the fuck is the road?" Dawson asked.

We moved to the edge of the forest, where the road had been, but there was nothing—just a thicket of trees. The two large rocks still stood in place, marking what used to be the border of the trail. Now, they framed the cruel joke this forest was playing on us.

"This is impossible," said Ross, the engineer. He pointed at the trees. "There was a path. I swear to God, there was a fucking path before I went to bed."

The men mumbled in agreement.

"Calm down," Cooper barked. "Spread out and find the fucking road. It didn't just disappear."

The men fanned out.

Kingston's voice rang out. "Hey! There's a path over here behind the house!"

We all rushed over. Sure enough, there was a trail. It was narrower than yesterday's, but a trail nonetheless.

"Look, there's a gravel road." Kingston pointed at a spot about a hundred feet away.

The team muttered in relief, but I wasn't convinced. Not for a second. This wasn't the same path. As a lifelong tracker, I knew the trail yesterday had been east of the hut. This one was west.

"See?" Cooper said, his voice curt. "We must've just been tired."

"Nah," I said. The weight of the team's attention shifted to me. "The path we took yesterday from the gravel road to the hut lay east of the hut, winding between two rocks. This one's west." I left out the part about the protection markings—no need to stoke the fire. I'd tell Cooper privately.

"He's right," Wager said, surprising me. Her tone was steady, unwavering. "The path was between the two rocks. Just like Erickson says."

I caught her eye—a silent exchange of respect. She wasn't backing down. Instead, she was boldly challenging Cooper in a way that none of the others dared.

The men fell into a tense silence.

Cooper let out a laugh, sharp and angry. "So what are you trying to tell me, Erickson? Huh? That a whole path and road picked up and moved overnight, and the fucking forest decided to grow trees over it?"

I shrugged, meeting his glare head-on. "That's exactly what I'm telling you."

"What the fuck is going on here?" Dawson's voice cracked as he ran a hand through his hair. His eyes darted between the trees and the new path.

"Nothing is going on!" Cooper snapped. "And we're not some teenage boys and girls telling campfire ghost stories to scare our crushes into our beds. We're a special ops team. The best of the goddamn best. So calm down." Then he muttered something like "fucking shit."

Cooper spoke into his comms: "Echo Leader calling Command. Confirm coordinates for the gravel road, over."

Silence. Not even static.

"Echo Leader calling Command. Confirm coordinates for the gravel road, over," he repeated.

Nothing.

"This must be the magnetic field interference they warned us about," Cooper said. He sighed. "Doesn't matter. The road's right behind the hut."

"Sir, if I may—" I began.

"You may not," he cut in.

I pushed on anyway. "That road behind the hut isn't the one we traveled on yesterday." I turned to the others. "The river you all filled your bottles with last night—it was behind the hut. Not a fucking road."

The team exchanged uncertain looks.

Nguyen broke the silence. "He's right. The river was back there. Where the path is now."

"Then where the hell is the river?" Ross shouted, pointing at the path.

The murmurs grew louder again.

"Enough!" Cooper's shout cut through, silencing them. "Henderson."

"Yes, sir."

"As our second guide, what do you make of this?"

Henderson looked between me, Cooper, and the woods. "If I didn't know better, I'd say Erickson's right."

Cooper grunted.

"But," Henderson added cautiously, "we all know that's impossible. We must've just been tired after yesterday's march. And Vargas going missing has us all on edge."

"Where the hell is Vargas anyway?" Jensen demanded. "Did the rescue team find him?"

"Yes," Cooper said firmly, shutting it down. "Command confirmed last night. I didn't want to wake you all."

A few shoulders relaxed. Breaths came a little easier. The tight grip on weapons loosened—just slightly.

"All right," Cooper announced. "The way I see it, one-half of you are ready to write a B-movie horror script. The other half are using their brains. Either way, the road behind the hut is the one we're taking. The cargo truck can't fit through those trees anywhere else. Everyone understand that?"

"Yes, sir," the team muttered, one by one.

"May I suggest an alternative—" I offered, catching the full force of Cooper's glare.

"Suggest an alternative?" he challenged.

I pointed at the trees where the old path had been. "Let's cut them down. The gravel road still has to be there somewhere." My eyes flicked to the faint glow of the sun behind the clouds, then back to the wall of trees, solid and unyielding where the path had once been. "I can find it," I said firmly, meeting Cooper's pissed look. "Yesterday, the sun was high and to our left, so the path ran east to west. By the time we hit the clearing, the shadows stretched north. The bend by the two rocks pointed west, and the stream crossed just south of the trail. That path and road were east of the hut. I'm sure of it, and I can get us back on it."

Not that any of this wasn't insane. The rune signs were there for a reason. Everything was unraveling into a nightmare. But the path's location was a fact, unshakable in my mind. And something deep in my gut told me that whatever was happening here didn't want us back on it. Wanted to confuse us.

Cooper's silence stretched as he considered what I'd proposed. "No," he finally said. "We're not wasting a day—or more—cutting down trees."

"We could blow them up," Jensen offered. Clearly, he wasn't as eager to take the new path as Cooper seemed to be.

Cooper shot him a look that shut him up instantly. "No. We can't fall behind," Cooper said. "We take the road behind the hut. Henderson, you agree?"

Henderson hesitated, then nodded. "Yes, sir."

"Good. We move in five!"

The men sprang into action, grabbing their gear. But I stayed, along with Wager, Jensen, Nguyen, and Dawson, staring at the trees where the path had been.

"I don't like this," Jensen muttered.

"Not one fucking bit," Dawson agreed.

Then they turned, grabbed their gear, and moved to join the others.

"If this were a horror movie, the odds wouldn't be in our favor taking this new path, would they?" Wager asked.

"Let's go," I said, my tone firm. But Wager hesitated as she looked at the trees. From the corner of my eye, a white flicker caught my attention. It came from deep within the forest. I turned quickly, but whatever it was had vanished, leaving only shadows in its wake.

16

Esther

We marched for hours, the only sound the crunch of our boots on the uneven gravel road. My back screamed from the weight of my gear, and the open blisters on my feet burned with every step. However, none of that mattered anymore. The forest surrounded us, its skeletal branches clawing at the gray fall sky. Even in daylight, the place felt wrong. Nobody said it, but we all felt it. A path disappearing overnight wasn't something you just shrugged off.

Maybe Cooper was right. Maybe we were all just tired. Or maybe I was losing my mind. Either way, it didn't matter. I was here for my sister. Whatever answers I needed, I'd find them—no matter what it took.

My gaze dropped to my arm, to the same spot where my sister had grabbed me during the fire that had destroyed our family. In this forest, I could almost feel her grip again like a phantom limb, aching with the weight of what I'd lost.

"I can't shake the feeling Erickson was right," Dawson said. "We should've gone back for the old road."

"Doesn't matter now," Nguyen replied. "We're almost halfway to the drop-off coordinates. Another day or two, and we're out of here."

"If we get out of here," Dawson muttered.

"Of course we will," Nguyen countered.

"Yeah? What about the last team that went missing? Or Vargas?" Dawson shot back.

"Vargas was found," Nguyen said.

Dawson scoffed. "Sure. Just like the last team, right?"

"Well, the Alpha team didn't have Erickson," Nguyen said.

Dawson seemed to accept that.

I cocked a brow. "What do you mean?" I asked, glancing at Nguyen.

"You didn't hear all that stuff about Erickson?" Nguyen asked, raising his eyebrows.

I shook my head.

"He knows his shit, that's for sure," Dawson said. "Special ops trainer and field guide. They ship him out on missions no one else can survive. Terrain so brutal, the survival rate's a joke."

"Well, that's good," I said.

Dawson frowned.

"Isn't it?" I clarified.

"Well, some say he's been . . . off."

"Off how?" I pressed.

"Well, there's the murder thing," Dawson added, almost casually.

"Murder?" I stopped mid-step.

"Yeah. Ross told me last night. He knew someone on a mission with him. Said Erickson strangled some teacher in cold blood."

My stomach churned. Erickson wasn't exactly warm and fuzzy, but he'd struck me as the kind of guy with an unshakable moral compass. The kind who'd die for a cause without hesitation. This? This was hard to swallow.

"You sure?" I asked. "Shouldn't he be in jail or something then?"

Dawson nodded, forming his hands into a mock chokehold. "Squeezed the life out of the poor bastard. For over four minutes. Ross said his eyes popped out right before he pissed himself. Erickson did time for it, but they got him out for this mission."

"You're serious?" I asked. My mind flashed to Erickson's faint smile last night when I'd talked about the wolves. Goose bumps prickled across my skin.

Dawson nodded again, this time shaking his hands like he was reenacting it.

"You can say whatever you want about him," Nguyen cut in. "But there's no one I'd rather follow out here. Erickson's never lost a team. Never failed a mission. Not even Ice Fox."

"Ice Fox?" I asked.

Nguyen nodded. "Russia. Minus fucking forty degrees, enemy forces closing in, no supplies. He led his team out of that frozen hell, living off the frozen land, sleeping on heated rocks to survive the nights. Got them all the way to Mongolia. Without him, none of them would've made it. They ran simulations with other trackers after that. No matter how experienced, every single one died in the simulation. Froze or starved."

The weight of Erickson's legend settled over us as we kept marching.

"All haaaalt!" Cooper's voice echoed from the front of the convoy.

"Halt!" The shout rippled back through the ranks.

Nguyen, Dawson, and I exchanged uneasy glances.

"Break?" I guessed.

Dawson shook his head. "Still an hour out."

We rounded a curve in the road, the kind that felt like it was hiding something. When we rounded the bend, we froze.

The road just . . . stopped.

Trees, massive and ancient, grew out of the gravel, their roots twisting over the stones like they'd been there forever. This wasn't like the hut. This wasn't a few trees. It was a wall—a forest swallowing the road whole. The gravel still glinted faintly beneath the roots, mocking us.

For a moment, no one spoke. No one moved.

"The same fucking shit," I heard Dawson say.

"Erickson, where are we on the map?" Cooper's voice was sharp but steady, the kind of tone that demanded answers.

Erickson pointed at the map in Cooper's hand. "Right near the red X. Halfway to the coordinates. Same area the last team went dark."

"If this is the same road," Cooper said. His voice faltered for the first time.

Erickson nodded toward the curve behind us. "I don't know how this is possible. But the sun's position lines up exactly as it did yesterday on the old road. It . . . turned into the same road somewhere along the march. Around 1200 hours."

"So we're back on track?" Cooper sounded almost hopeful.

"It defies any tracking laws I've ever been taught. But sure. For now, it seems so." Erickson motioned to the wall of trees. "But then there's this." His voice stayed calm, but his hand swept toward the dense forest like it was a bad joke. "This gravel is about ten years old, tops. But those trees are well over a hundred. So unless you're telling me someone laid this road by carefully spreading gravel between fully grown trees, it sure as hell looks like the trees grew out of the road. Which makes me wonder—what road did the last team travel on? And more importantly, how are hundred-year-old trees standing where a road was paved with gravel just ten years ago?"

"This is some crazy shit." Jensen shook his head. "We're also stuck. How are we gonna move the truck through there? We can't blow our way out this time. Way too many trees."

"I think we should turn around," Erickson said.

We were all thinking it. He just had the guts to say it. Echo was the toughest of the tough, and yet we were barely holding it together, trying to look calm and composed. None of this made sense. All of this was insane.

"I agree with that," said Blake, the mechanic driving the cargo truck, as he stepped out of the cab. "There's no way I can drive through that. It's just simple logic. We should turn around."

"We will do no such thing." Cooper's response shocked us all. It defied what felt like obvious reason.

Silence settled for a moment before Martinez stepped forward, his voice steady but questioning. "What else can we do, sir?"

Erickson cut in before Cooper could respond. "Find the other truck. If this is where Alpha went dark, their cargo truck has to be close. Since we didn't see it on the way here"—he pointed at the trees swallowing the road—"it's down there somewhere. That's what you were thinking, right, Chief?"

All eyes turned to Cooper. The murmurs started. Uneasy, uncertain.

"Erickson is correct," Cooper said, his voice sharp and commanding. "We are on a mission. An important one, if I may remind you. These magnetic fields are clearly messing with our equipment—and some people's senses. But if Alpha's truck is down there, intact and on the other side of this blockage, we'll abandon our cargo truck and use theirs."

It made sense, but it didn't sit right.

Silence.

Henderson stepped forward. "I agree with Cooper. Some of Alpha might still be out there. Alive."

I caught Dawson tipping his head back. He searched the gray sky like it held the answers. Whatever was happening here, it was getting to him too.

"All right," Cooper barked. "Henderson, you'll come with me and Ross. We'll scout for Alpha's cargo truck northwest. Erickson, pick two men and go northeast. The rest of you, stay and guard the cargo. If we're not back in two hours, return to the hut before dark and hold position. Understood?"

"Yes, sir," the group mumbled.

Cooper, Henderson, and Ross moved out, their figures disappearing into the tree line.

"Wager. Let's go," Erickson said.

My chest tightened, and I almost refused. Why the hell was he so fixated on dragging me into this madness when there were plenty of G.I. Joes to pick from? But then . . . I couldn't let us turn around. This was my last chance to find my sister. We had to find that truck. If we didn't, we'd have no choice but to abort the mission.

"He said pick two men," was all I muttered as I passed Erickson and headed straight for the woods. I left most of my gear behind, keeping only my Glock at my hip and my M4 gripped tightly in my hands.

The occasional snap of a branch under my boots shattered the eerie silence of the forest. Every time it happened, Erickson shot me a dismissive look. Somehow, he managed to move without making a single sound.

The woods were spooky as hell—the overgrown plants, the thick shadows, the strange stillness.

Erickson walked ahead. Every so often, he paused to glance up at the sky, study the trees, or crouch near a bush.

"What do you think is going on here?" I asked, my voice low.

Without turning, Erickson stepped over a fallen tree. "I have no fucking clue," he said. "But those protection symbols at the hut were there for a reason. That makes it the only place you want to be when it gets dark."

As I looked up, something uneasy twisted low in my gut. Daylight still clung to the gray clouds, but it felt thin, fragile.

"What do you think happens when it gets dark?"

"No idea, but I'm not planning to find out."

"That truck . . ." I said. "What do you think's in it?"

Erickson stopped and looked over his shoulder. His gaze was sharp and unreadable. "I thought you might be able to tell me."

Shit. He'd seen me snooping.

"I have no idea. Cooper might know, though."

He narrowed his eyes at me but said nothing. Then he turned and pressed forward into the woods, leaving me with the creeping unease that he had picked me for a reason.

Erickson stopped abruptly and raised his arm, signaling me to be quiet. "The river. Can you hear it?" he asked quietly.

I strained my ears, focusing on the stillness around us. Nothing. I shook my head.

"The map shows a river running alongside the gravel road, right by our resting coordinates," he said.

I nodded. It made sense to build a hut near water. We'd filled our bottles at the river just behind the hut.

"It doesn't seem like things disappear in this forest," Erickson said. "They just move around. Somehow. To fuck with us."

"To fuck with us?" I repeated.

Erickson didn't reply. He pressed forward, then froze. His fist shot into the air.

My heart pounded as I came to a halt, praying to whatever God existed that it was nothing but the wind.

The branches to our left rustled, and a white fox bolted out. It darted across our path and disappeared into the forest.

I stared, stunned. It had flashed past in a blur, but I swore I'd caught a glimpse of a scar on its back leg. "The . . . white fox," I mumbled. My thoughts spiraled to the one I'd saved—and lost my job for. I bolted after her, desperate to check that back leg. How could it possibly be the same fox?

"Wager, stop!" Erickson barked.

I picked up my pace.

"Wager! Stop!" he yelled again, but his voice faded as I pushed forward. My mind raced. How could this be? Was that a scar on the fox's hind leg? The one I'd stitched when the Native man brought her in?

The flash of the fox's bushy tail flickered in the distance, then vanished. My heart was hammering, and I sprinted toward the spot. However, when I broke into a clearing with a gravel road, I didn't see the fox.

Instead, I saw a fucking human head.

"Wager!" Erickson's voice was sharp. "Goddamn it, Wager—" His words stopped when he stepped into the clearing beside me.

It was a war zone.

At my feet lay the severed head of a male soldier. The skin was blue, the eyes half-shut, the hair matted with grime and blood. Its tongue hung grotesquely from its mouth, and flies buzzed around its foggy eyes.

My stomach churned, but I swallowed the bile. I'd seen worse. My parents' corpses were burned into my memory. Death could shock me, but it couldn't break me anymore.

I covered my mouth and scanned the blood-soaked road. Pieces of soldiers lay scattered—an arm here, boots there. A mangled soldier lay slumped against a blood-smeared cargo truck that was disturbingly similar to ours.

"Jesus Christ . . ." I mumbled against my hand. "What the fuck happened here?"

Erickson, calm as always, knelt beside the severed head. Using a stick, he tilted it slightly to reveal a deep gash across the cheek.

"Animals got to him," he said. "Wolves." Erickson pointed at the small paw prints scattered around the scene.

And there it was again—that lingering pause at the end of his sentence.

"But?" I pressed.

He stood and walked a few steps forward, staring at the ground. I followed. My boot landed inside a massive print.

"But they seemed to have brought the big guns with 'em."

I stared down at the enormous print. It had to be four feet wide —like a wolf's paw but monstrous.

My hands trembled as I took a steadying breath. This wasn't just horrific. It was insane.

"What . . . what the hell is this?" I asked in a shaky voice.

Erickson knelt beside the print and scanned the blood-soaked ground. "I don't know anything in North America that could possibly leave a print this size," he said before rising to his feet and scanning the area. "Anything on this planet, in fact."

"Is this all of Alpha?" I asked.

"I count nine team members here," Erickson said.

"Where's the rest?"

"Probably fled in panic when they were attacked."

"You think they're dead too?"

"Without a doubt." Erickson stared at the massive paw print. "Echo, do you copy?" he said into his comms.

Static. Nothing.

"Echo, copy?" he repeated.

Still nothing.

My eyes locked on the cargo truck in the distance.

That fucking truck.

All of this—my sister, the missing people, the secret base, or whatever these coordinates led to—was connected. And that truck held the key.

I stepped around a severed leg and headed for the vehicle. I could feel Erickson watching every step I took. He didn't stop me when I bent down, grabbed a blood-smeared rock, and hammered it against the keypad lock. Each strike echoed through the trees. The lock beeped every time I hit the right spot.

The last blow caught my finger, and I cursed, dropping the rock. Then I shook my hand and raised my M4, leveling it at the lock.

"Does that work? Shooting locks open like in the movies?" I asked.

"If you step back far enough to avoid catching a stray bullet to your head, you might find out."

I stepped back. So did he. I aimed and pulled the trigger.

The M4 roared as shots tore through the air. More bullets than I intended slammed into the lock. They ricocheted off the metal in sharp sparks. I stepped closer and spotted a crack in the casing.

Grabbing the rock again, I smashed it down one last time. The lock beeped before the satisfying click of unlocking metal filled the air.

I glanced at Erickson. His expression was calculating, analytical —but still, he didn't stop me.

My heart raced as I tore the door open.

The stench of decay slammed into me like a brick wall. It was nauseating—a cocktail of horrors blending rotten eggs, piss, shit, and fish.

Gagging, I stumbled back, nearly losing my footing. Erickson's arm caught me.

I tore free, launched forward, and pulled myself into the truck.

The oppressive gray light from the cloudy fall sky cast grim shadows over lifeless faces. Bodies lay crammed in the truck bed— men, women, young, old. The stench burned my eyes, but I didn't care.

"Jasmine!" I yelled, her name ripping from me like a desperate prayer. She'd been missing for a year. What if she was here, in this nightmare?

Gagging with every breath, I tried to step in between the bodies, but the floor was slick, sticky, and impossible to navigate cleanly. When soft flesh gave way under my boots, I winced and shifted my weight to find the solid metal floor beneath.

"Jasmine!" I shouted again, ignoring the obvious truth: The people in this truck were long gone.

This was hell.

This was fucking hell.

I made it to the end of the truck, my chest heaving as I scanned the bloated, discolored faces. None of them were hers.

"She's not here," I mumbled. A strange mix of relief and lingering dread sank into my gut.

I scrambled out of the truck, pushed past Erickson and his watchful, eagle-eyed stare, and gasped for fresh air. The forest's cool breeze filled my lungs, but the stench clung to me. I leaned against a tree, sucking in breath after breath, my chest tightening with every inhale.

Then Erickson was there, standing inches away.

"Who the fuck are you?" he asked, his voice low and sharp.

I took another shaky breath, refusing to answer.

He stepped closer, his eyes boring into mine. "Who the fuck are you, Wager?"

I stayed silent.

With the speed of a striking cobra, he grabbed my wrist and spun me, then slammed me chest-first into the rough bark of the tree. His weight pressed hard into my back.

"Who the fuck are you, Wager?" he growled.

"Fuck you," I spat.

"Fuck me, huh?"

The metallic click of a gun broke the air as he released me. I turned to find him aiming his Glock at my chest. His eyes were dark, his hand steady.

The story of him killing that teacher flashed in my mind—with bare hands, eyes popping out. Would he do it again?

"I'll ask you one last time," he said, his voice cold. "There's a truck full of dead civilians behind me. I saw a girl in there who couldn't have been older than eighteen. And I know, as sure as there's a sky above us, that you're not an Army Ranger. So I'll ask you again—who are you, and how did you know there would be people in there?"

Our eyes met. His were unwavering. However, the longer I stared at him, the more confident I grew about one thing: This man might have killed, but he wasn't a killer.

"No," I said, my voice firm. "You won't shoot." I stepped right into the barrel, whose hard metal pressed against my chest. He didn't step back, but he didn't step forward either.

"I'm sure you've heard the stories," he said. "About the teacher. So maybe you shouldn't put too much faith in me. Did the CIA send you to oversee this mission's success? Some sick experiment the government's running out here, away from the public?"

Holding my ground, I stared into his eyes and caught the first crack in his armor. He wouldn't shoot. But even if he did, here—on this gravel road littered with death and horror—I didn't care about dying.

I'd lost everything that made a person crave life.

So fuck it.

"Go ahead. Shoot me," I said. "Otherwise, get that fucking thing out of my face. If it's true that we need to be back at the hut before dark, I suggest we get moving . . . now."

A flicker of something unreadable passed through Erickson's eyes. Then, without a word, he stepped back and holstered the gun with the ease that came from too much practice.

I almost smirked as a small victory swelled in my chest—but Erickson wasn't done. He turned, walked to one of the gear packs on the ground, and grabbed a flashlight and some ammo. Tossing them my way, he said, "If I don't slow down for you, you'll fall behind on the jog back to Echo. Those blisters, that limp, shitty cardio—you're barely holding it together as is."

"What?" I stammered, my stomach dropping.

"You heard me. Try to find a cave before it gets dark. Or hide in that truck. Point your gun at the entrance. Don't sleep."

Then he started jogging toward the woods.

"Wait!" I shouted. "Erickson!"

He didn't stop. His figure was already fading into the shadows.

I screamed the only thing that could make him pause. "You're right! I'm not Wager!"

Erickson halted, then turned back. I slowly walked toward him, my heart pounding.

"You have one minute to explain everything," he said. "Then I'm leaving."

I steadied myself, swallowing hard. "I'm not Wager. My name is Esther."

One brow arched. "Esther who?"

"Esther . . . Smith."

He remained silent.

"Obomsawin," I added, hating how his faint smirk confirmed that he'd already suspected a Native name.

"You CIA? Enemy forces? Spy?"

"Veterinarian," I said.

His brows shot up.

"Well, one exam away from it, at least," I clarified.

"Esther Smith Obomsawin. Almost veterinarian." His forehead creased. "That might be the craziest thing about this whole mission so far."

I crossed my arms.

He studied me as if trying to decide whether I was telling the truth. Then, with a sharp, sarcastic laugh, he shook his head.

"Holy shit. I'll be damned. So what's a vet half-breed doing out here pretending to be a sniper on the most elite special ops team in the world?"

I hesitated. Lying wouldn't help now. Besides, the *why* might actually help my case.

"My sister," I said.

"Jasmine?"

I nodded. "She went missing last year. Her trail led to this forest."

"What trail?" he pressed.

"I don't know exactly," I admitted, my voice cracking. "All I know is people go missing here every year. I think the government's sending them here, probably in trucks like that one"—I gestured at the truck full of bodies—"to whatever coordinates we're heading to. Then you never hear from them again."

Erickson's icy eyes pinned me in place.

"So you're telling me you're out here climbing over corpses to find your missing sister?"

"It sounded less insane when I said it," I muttered. "But yes."

He shook his head. "This might be one of the dumbest things I've ever seen anyone do."

"So what?" I said. "She's all I have left in a shitty world that never gave either of us a chance."

His judgment hung heavy in the air. I was sure he'd report me to Cooper or leave me here to figure my own way back.

But then his expression softened slightly. "You've pulled some dumb shit here, Obomsawin. No doubt about that." He gave me a small, respectful nod. "But you're no coward. And I can't say that about most people I meet."

It was probably the most honest, decent thing anyone had said to me in years.

"So you won't tell Cooper I'm not a Ranger?" I asked.

"You? A Ranger? Come on." He let out a dry laugh. "He already knows. Most of Echo does." He shifted, lowering his voice. "But they're all thinking the same thing I did—that whoever put this team together had a reason for bringing you in. To them, you're CIA. Or some specialist they need up there for a classified project. It's not their place to ask questions. They follow orders. That's the job. Questioning superiors isn't."

He glanced up at the sky, his face grim. "We need to get back. Fast. I don't know how, but it seems like time is passing faster."

I nodded, swallowing hard. "Do you think there are people in our cargo truck too?"

"There's only one way to find out," he said. "How fast can you move?"

"Let's find out," I shot back, forcing a smirk.

Erickson cracked a faint grin before turning and breaking into a light jog. I followed, gritting my teeth against the pain in my feet, determined to keep up the pace, even if it killed me.

17

Ryder

We pushed out of the last line of trees and reunited with Echo and the cargo truck. Cooper was waiting impatiently.

I walked straight up to him and raised my M4. "What's the code to the truck door?"

"Erickson, what the hell is——"

Before he could finish, I drove the butt of the M4 into his face. The crunch echoed as he stumbled back, clutching his mouth, blood dripping between his fingers.

"Fucking detain him!" Cooper yelled, his voice muffled and furious. Within seconds, guns were on me.

As if on instinct, Esther swung her M4 toward Cooper. Its barrel shook.

"You can't shoot us both in time," she said, her voice cold and sharp. "One of these bullets will find you."

I raised my M4 at Cooper again. Goddamn, that woman was batshit crazy for even being here, but the good old saying held true: Hell hath no fury like a woman scorned.

The group froze. Tension, thick enough to choke on, filled the air. The fact that Esther was backing me had thrown them off.

Slowly, half the barrels turned toward her, their movements hesitant, uncertain.

"There are people in that truck!" I shouted, my voice cutting through the charged silence.

"What?" Dawson's face twisted in confusion. His rifle dipped slightly.

"Civilians," I said, my voice now louder. "We found Alpha's truck. It was full of dead civilians. They died in there after Alpha was slaughtered. Wolves—and something else—got them."

"Alpha is dead?" Sanders muttered, his grip slackening as his eyes darted between me and Cooper.

Esther's voice broke through. "So is Alpha's cargo. Innocent people left to rot in that truck. Shit, piss, decay—they died like caged animals."

"That's bullshit!" Cooper spat, fire flaring in his eyes. "The cargo is top secret, yes, but it's not people. Our mission is to deliver it to the coordinates at all costs. Do you understand what's at stake here?"

"There are people in there," I said. "Are you willing to bet your life on that?"

Cooper's jaw tightened. "What if I am, bastard?"

I shook my head and let out a bitter laugh. "Nobody scared of guns anymore?" I muttered. "Fine. Then how about this? Henderson!"

"Y-yeah?" he stuttered.

"Look at the sky. What time do you think it is?"

Henderson frowned, glancing upward before checking his watch. "About . . . two-thirty?"

"Wrong. Look again."

Henderson hesitated. His eyes darted between the sun's low position, the lengthening shadows across the gravel, and his watch. "What the . . . but it's impossible. I don't understand. It's way later than it should be!"

I stepped forward, seizing the moment as Cooper's confidence cracked. "Time moves differently today. We don't have enough of it to turn around and make it back to the hut before dark. Hell, we might not even have enough to reach the one ahead of us. But if you wanna give it a shot, who do you all trust to lead you there? Henderson . . . or me?"

I let the silence stretch, feeling their unease grow.

"So here's the deal, Cooper," I continued. "If you don't give me the code to the cargo truck, I'll sit my ass on that rock over there and wait for nightfall. Then we'll all find out why those huts matter so damn much. But I'll tell you right now—if my ass ends up on that rock, it'll be the end of the mission. Just like it was for Alpha."

Cooper's lips pressed into a tight line. His gaze darted to the shadows creeping across the road.

"Tick-tock, Cooper," I said, my voice low and sharp. "If we don't move now—"

"Three-eight-four-five-six!" he countered, the words bursting out as if he were summoning a dark spell.

I raced to the truck and punched in the code. With a beep, the lock clicked. I swung the door wide open.

"No," Esther muttered beside me as she looked inside. The word was barely audible over the collective gasp of the team gathering behind us. "She's not here."

Nine pairs of tearful eyes stared back at us, blinking rapidly as light flooded the dark, cramped space. Men and women, young and old, clung to each other, trembling.

"Please, let us go," a woman sobbed, her voice raw and desperate. Who knew how many times she had pleaded for the same thing before? But the truck's walls were heavily reinforced, swallowing every sound.

"I have kids," another begged. "Please let me go."

"What the fuck?" Ross cussed under his breath. His shock mirrored my own as he stepped behind me.

"We need to turn around!" Martinez demanded.

Nguyen nodded. His hand twitched toward his weapon as if he were ready for anything.

My focus was fixed on one figure—a teenage girl.

"Please, let me go," the girl cried, her words breaking into a sniffle. "I promise I won't run away again."

Her whimpering cut through the air, sharper than any of the other pleas. She couldn't have been more than sixteen. She wore tomboyish clothes and had shoulder-length blond hair.

She was just a kid. An innocent kid.

Something in her eyes froze me in place. That look. The raw fear, the hollow hopelessness—it was the same as my son's that day. The look that was burned into my memory like a death sentence.

And then it hit me.

The ringing.

That high-pitched, relentless ringing buried deep in my skull. The sound that always came just before the flashbacks tore through me and turned me into something primal. Something deadly. The monster that had gripped Mr. Colter's throat and— through the gasping, choking breaths—squeezed the life out of him.

The high-pitched ringing in my ears grew louder. It was like an alarm from a haunting I couldn't escape. My breath caught.

I was back in the locker room.

The school gym snapped into focus. The sharp tang of sweat and bleach hung heavy in the air. The door creaked as I stepped inside. It was quiet—too quiet. Except for my son's soft, broken sobs and Mr. Colter's soothing voice murmuring that everything was "okay."

I was early to pick up my son from soccer practice. He should've been on the field, but I saw only the assistant coach and the other kids.

And then, there he was. Sitting on the bench next to Mr. Colter. My son's head was bowed, his small hands clenched into fists on his lap. Silent tears streaked down his cheeks. They were the kind of tears that came from pure, paralyzing fear. Beside him was that sick fuck—his pants half-down as he jerked himself off.

The second my son's eyes met mine, they said everything.

I'm sorry, Dad. Like this was his fault.

Bile burned my throat, and my vision tunneled. Mr. Colter's gaze snapped to mine. His eyes went wide—caught, guilty, disgusting. He fumbled, yanking his pants up with frantic, shaking hands.

"Wait outside, Champ," I said softly to my son. Good kid that he was, he listened and left.

"I swear I never touched any of them——"

That was as far as Colter got.

I lunged.

My fist hit his jaw. The crack of bone snapped through the room. He went down hard, his skull bouncing off the cold, unforgiving floor. But I wasn't done. Not even close. I pinned him down as he scrambled under me. Gasping breaths filled the air, but my grip around his neck was like steel. His panicked eyes flicked frantically around the room for help. The sharp stench of piss hit my nose as the realization dawned on Colter—those hands weren't letting go. Not for his begging. Not for his tears.

Not until he was dead.

I didn't care if this man had never touched any of the kids. I made sure he never would. I sent him straight to hell, that piece of shit.

A scream yanked me back to the present, the woods, the mission. The girl's cries crashed over me like a wave.

My gaze locked onto the girl's eyes again—the raw, paralyzing fear of a terrified child. The thought hit me like a punch. She could've ended up just like the others—a rotting corpse in the back of a truck.

Too much.

Like a machine on autopilot, I turned and marched straight to Cooper.

My fist collided with his face before I even realized I'd swung. He stumbled back, and a grunt escaped him as blood dripped from his nose. His hand shot for his gun, but I was faster. My second punch drove into his stomach, doubling him over.

Cooper recovered quicker than most men would have. His fist connected with my chin, sharp and brutal. The force knocked me back a step, but I lunged again, grabbed him by the collar, and yanked hard. I swept his leg out from under him, sending him crashing to the ground. He clung to my jacket, yanking me down with him.

We hit the ground hard, then rolled in the dirt in a blur of fists and rage. When Cooper's fist landed on my temple, stars exploded in my vision. My fist found his jaw, sending his head snapping to the side.

Esther's voice cut through the chaos. "Stop it!"

Neither of us listened.

Finally, I gained the upper hand and pinned him beneath me, my gun pressed firmly against his temple. His was against my stomach. Our chests heaved. Every muscle was coiled and ready to fire.

"Stop it!" Esther yelled again. Her hand landed on my shoulder, firm and demanding at first, then gentle. "We don't have time for this! We need to get these people to the hut before dark!"

My hands trembled. The monster inside me was clawing to pull the trigger and send Cooper where he belonged. A man who could kidnap a girl and drag her here to die had no place on this earth. But Esther was right. We couldn't waste another second.

"You're getting us all killed," she said.

Her words hit harder this time. Cooper and I froze.

"We need every man if we want to make it out of here alive," she added.

I exhaled slowly and heavily, then stepped back. Cooper wiped his bloodied chin with his sleeve and glared at me like a wounded dog.

"You stupid bastard," he spat, blood hitting the ground near my boots.

"We need to get the civilians to the hut," Esther repeated, cutting through the tension before it reignited.

I glanced at the sky.

Shit. We did, indeed.

"Dump all the gear except weapons and ammo!" I ordered.

The team snapped into action.

"Partner with a civilian. Keep them moving."

"I'm not going anywhere," growled one of the civilians, his face defiant. He looked skinny and sickly, like a man who'd just clawed his way through addiction withdrawals. "You fucking monsters locked us in here. I'm not going anywhere with you."

"Yeah," chimed in another civilian. The group's anger swelled into a chaotic chorus.

"We don't have fucking time for this!" Cooper snapped. "We need to get to the hut now. Or—" His voice faltered.

"Or what?" Esther stepped forward, her tone daring him to finish. "Or what, Cooper? What happens when it gets dark? I think it's time you tell us. Especially after you made us kidnappers."

The team started murmuring their agreement.

"What the hell happens after dark?" I pressed.

"Tell us, Cooper!" The demands grew louder.

"I don't fucking know!" Cooper finally snapped. "I don't. And I didn't know about them!" He jabbed a finger toward the huddled, crying civilians. "I'm just following orders, like all of you. But one thing I do know. We have to make it to that hut before dark. Or we'll end up like Alpha."

"Who is Alpha?" A woman's voice cut through, raw and broken. "And what happened to them?" She looked just as unkempt as the others, her face pale and drawn like someone who'd been locked in a truck for days.

"Let's not find out," Cooper shot back. "Erickson, let's go!"

I glared at him, then turned and started jogging toward the path.

"Let's go!" I shouted.

The hut was about two miles north of the Alpha truck's location. I'd lead the group around it, along the river—no need to trigger more panic.

"Move like your life depends on it," I shouted over my shoulder. "Because it does. If you think you can't run another step, remind yourself what happens if you stop."

Some fell into step immediately, fear driving their legs. The girl followed, which was a huge relief. Others hesitated, dragging their feet until they realized no one was waiting for them.

And just like that, the chase began.

Us on the run, an unknown enemy at our heels, and the sun sinking fast. A race against nightfall, with no guarantee we'd see another sunrise.

18

Esther

As twilight crept over the trees, the last weak rays of sunlight cast a faint glow across the leaves. Darkness was coming fast, and with it, every fear we'd been running from.

I flopped forward, hands braced on my knees. My lungs burned. My chest felt like hundreds of needles were stabbing out from the inside.

Most of the civilians had fallen behind, huffing and puffing but still within sight. Echo was ahead, constantly turning back, yanking another civilian to their feet every time one collapsed. They kept shouting that we couldn't stop. That we had to keep moving.

The woman who'd tearfully said she just wanted to go home to her kids clung to a tree beside me, then doubled over and vomited. Her cheeks were hollow, her hair matted with sweat.

"I can't anymore," she croaked, wiping her mouth with a trembling hand.

The man who'd earlier shouted about not following "a bunch of kidnappers" stopped beside me, his chest heaving. His face was pale and sickly.

"I'm not taking another step," wheezed an older man between

violent coughs. His sweater looked like it had seen decades of hard labor, and his boots were cracked and worn through.

Echo halted, their formation breaking as Erickson and Cooper jogged back. Even they were breathing heavier now, their brows furrowed with frustration. Cooper's jaw clenched as he sized up the group.

"Get moving," he ordered.

"No," the pale man rasped.

"Get the fuck moving!" Cooper yelled, stepping forward. "We don't have time for this!"

The pale man didn't budge, just shook his head, his legs trembling.

Erickson's gaze flicked to the teenage girl, who was lingering a few feet away. She was watching silently, her wide eyes full of the same exhausted terror as the others.

Erickson exhaled heavily and ran a hand through his sweat-slicked hair. "Listen up," he said, pointing to where Echo was waiting. "The river is right over there. The hut is closer than you think. We just need to keep going a little longer."

The older man in the wool sweater staggered a few steps and threw up violently. He wiped his mouth with the back of his hand and shook his head. "I can't. I'm done."

Cooper stared at him for a long, tense moment. Then his voice came low and sharp. "Leave the two men and the woman. Echo, move!"

"Yes, sir!" Echo shouted, already shifting back into formation.

"Wait!" I yelled, stepping in front of Cooper, blocking his path. "We can't just leave them here!"

"Yes, we can," Cooper snapped. "Anybody who wants to live, follow me. The rest of you, do whatever the fuck you want." He shoved past me, not sparing a glance.

My eyes drifted to the civilians who'd stopped. Two men and the woman with kids. She leaned against a tree, her body trembling as she dry-heaved. She looked completely spent, her pale face slick with sweat, her legs barely holding her up. None of this was their fault. The government had kidnapped them, and now they were about to be abandoned here to die.

"Erickson, lead the way," Cooper barked.

Erickson hesitated, throwing me a look that screamed, *Move, Esther. We have to.*

But then the teenage girl stepped forward. She walked up to the mother, whose shaky hands gripped the rough bark of the tree for support, and gently grabbed her arm.

"I'll stay here with you," the girl said softly.

They must've bonded during whatever hellish journey had brought them here. Afraid for their lives.

Erickson froze.

"Erickson, move!" Cooper barked. But Erickson didn't budge. His gaze remained fixed on the girl, who was holding the mother's trembling arm.

"Goddammit, Erickson, you bastard piece of shit, I said mo—"

"Bwooooooooorrrrrrr!"

The deep, bone-rattling wail of a horn tore through the forest and my chest, silencing us. It wasn't just a sound—it was a presence, a force, like the roar of something ancient waking from a long slumber.

"What the hell was that?" Dawson hollered over to us as he glanced around.

Another blast followed.

"Bwooooooooorrrrrrr!" Longer, louder, vibrating in my ribs. It was long and mournful, like the warning cry of some ancient army readying for war.

"What the fuck is that?" Cooper muttered in a mix of awe and anger.

Erickson stood completely still, his head tilted slightly, listening. His face was unreadable, his eyes scanning the shadows like they held an answer.

"It's . . . a signal," he said. Then he snapped his head toward us. "It's our fucking signal to RUUUUN!"

Cooper didn't wait. "Mooooooove! Everyone up the river!"

The team erupted into motion, dragging the civilians with them as the horn wailed again.

"Bwoooooooorrrrrrr!"

Its echo chased us, relentless and unforgiving, like it wasn't just warning us that something was coming—it was calling it closer.

The two civilian men still hesitated. Panic was freezing them in place. I grabbed the girl by her arm and forced her into a sprint. She resisted at first, her thin frame shaking, but the first low growls echoing through the forest sent her running without argument.

Gunshots cracked ahead, sharp and sudden, blending with the growling that now seemed to come from everywhere. Shadows moved between the trees—quick flashes of fur that made my heart race.

A scream—loud and primal—tore through the chaos. I turned to see a massive wolf lunge at the pale man from behind and slam him into the dirt. A pack of wolves followed, covering every inch of the man, shredding flesh as his screams cut through the air.

I stopped and raised my M4, trying to aim. My hands shook as I locked onto one of the wolves, but then I froze. These weren't just wolves. They were massive—easily the largest wolves I had ever seen. Their fur was thick and matted, and their eyes glowed in the darkness.

The girl's scream pulled my attention away from the horrifying scene. I whirled around just in time to see a wolf in midair, leaping straight for her. But Erickson was right beside me, and his M4 rattled off a burst of gunfire. The wolf crumpled at her feet, dead before it hit the ground. Another one charged, then another. Erickson took them down with a precision that seemed inhuman— each shot a hit, each kill instant. Wolf bodies piled up around us as the forest exploded with more growls, gunfire, and screams.

"Run!" Erickson shouted during a rare break in the endless wave of wolves.

We fucking did.

Our feet pounded the earth like thunder. Branches whipped my face, though the sting barely registered. Constant growls and gunfire surrounded us. Growing louder. Closer.

The river came into view, its rushing water darkened by the fading light. The forest seemed to close in, shadows stretching and twisting. A few Echo members were already ahead, running along the riverbank, pausing only to fire as wolves lunged from the tree line.

The girl veered suddenly and splashed through the shallow water, running into the woods on the other side. The wrong direction!

"Wait!" I screamed, my voice cracking.

She didn't stop.

I had no choice. My legs burned as I ran after her, catching up just as she tripped and slammed to the ground. I grabbed her trembling fingers and pulled her back up.

From the river charged a wolf. Its huge frame crashed through the water like a nightmare. I raised my M4 and fired on instinct. Most of the shots went wide, but enough hit to send the creature yelping. Its massive body crumpled to the ground just feet from us.

"Run!" I shouted, my voice breaking. The wolves weren't stopping, and neither could we.

Twilight cast its final glow, faint and fleeting, reflecting off the trees and rippling along the water's surface as I pulled the girl up the river. Darkness had nearly consumed the woods, whose shadows were thickening like a living thing, pressing in on us. Gunfire lit up the gloom like bursts of fireworks—brief, violent, and disturbingly beautiful.

We ran like maniacs, our feet pounding against river stones. Ahead, the silhouette of a pitched roof emerged. I tugged the girl toward it. Could we make it?

From the direction of the hut, a shape—thin and frantic— darted toward us. It was Blake, the skinny mechanic who had been driving the cargo truck. He sprinted straight at us, panic etched into his face. His wide eyes locked on mine.

"The hut is the other way!" I shouted, but he didn't stop. He bolted straight past us, his head whipping over his shoulder again and again as if he expected death to grab him from behind.

Then the gunfire and screams faded. A suffocating silence

followed. Even the growls stopped, leaving only the sound of our racing breaths.

We slowed as one of the civilians stumbled toward us. Her cries were jagged and desperate. "Help!" she wailed, her voice splitting the silence. "HELP!"

She had barely closed the gap when a shadow erupted from the tree line. It was accompanied by a thunderous growl that reverberated in my chest. A massive wolf, at least twenty feet tall, surged forward. Its teeth, impossibly large and glinting in the faint light, snapped around the woman mid-scream, silencing her in a sickening crunch.

Frozen. My limbs locked in place. The creature loomed like a nightmare, its dark fur blending into the shadows of the forest. Glowing yellow eyes pierced the darkness and locked onto us. Suddenly, ancient rune symbols flared to life across its massive body. They pulsed with an eerie red glow. The symbols flickered for only a moment before winking out like dying embers. The beast's eyes closed, and darkness swallowed it whole—gone as if it had never existed.

My heart was pounding so hard I thought my chest would explode.

Then a warm breath swept past me, ruffling my hair. It pulled back with a forceful inhale before sweeping by me again.

The girl's hand tightened around mine. Despite a grip so fierce it sent a jolt of pain up my arm, I didn't let go. Neither of us dared to breathe. Right in front of us, two bright yellow eyes snapped open—wolf eyes, but the pupils were slit like a snake's. My breath caught in my throat, and I could practically feel the scream building in the girl's chest. I put my hand to her mouth, clamping down hard to stifle any noise. Hypocritical. Because when the wolf's mouth slowly opened, revealing blood-smeared teeth the size of swords, its jaws so close I could feel the warmth radiating from inside, I realized I was on the verge of screaming too.

Or at least saying my last words. They clawed at my throat, desperate to escape. Something like *Don't be scared, we're going to a better place.* Or maybe a final whisper: *Mom, Dad, Jasmine, Grand-ma . . . I'm coming home.*

But whatever noise built in my chest, it stayed there, strangled and trapped.

"Shhh." Erickson's voice came low and firm. His hand pressed hard on my mouth. I could feel his muscles tense against my back, holding me in place. I held the girl in front of me the same way, trembling as we braced for the inevitable.

The giant wolf loomed above us, its massive head lowering as it let out a deep, bone-shaking growl. Its breath was rancid, hot, almost suffocating. It began to sniff us. I tightened my grip on the girl's small, trembling hand.

The beast's eyes burned into us, and my mind whispered that this was it. Death was here. I'd finally see my sister again, wherever she was. Erickson's hand loosened slightly, as if he had accepted the same fate.

The beast jerked its head, and I braced for the strike. However, as its jaws widened, I realized it wasn't looking our way anymore. Its gaze had snapped toward the sound of a scream tearing through the darkness. The sharp crack of gunfire followed. The wolf reared back, and its growl morphed into an enraged roar before it lunged toward the source of the noise.

Why didn't it kill us?

The other wolves weren't as hesitant. They charged straight for us.

Erickson didn't wait. "Run!" he barked.

And we did.

We bolted faster than I thought humanly possible. My legs burned, and my lungs were on fire, but I didn't stop. The girl tripped over a root and hit the ground, dragging me down with her. Rocks rammed into my knees, but I ignored the pain and yanked her up. We ran, our bodies fueled by desperation and fear.

Branches whipped against my face, slicing my skin. Darkness engulfed us, broken only by the faint flicker of flashlights ahead. The wolves' growls surrounded us again—left, right, behind.

Gunshots cracked. Erickson's M4 was clearing our path with deadly precision.

Then I saw it. The clearing. The hut. A beacon of hope slicing through the nightmare.

The growls closed in, monstrous and deafening. A scream ripped from my throat as I lunged into the clearing, the girl at my side. Grass cushioned our fall as Echo team members sprinted toward us. Their flashlights glared in our eyes.

Strong arms grabbed me and pulled me backward, away from the tree line.

"Get them to the hut!" Cooper barked, his voice slicing through the chaos.

My stomach dropped when I realized Erickson wasn't with us.

"Erickson!" I screamed as I stumbled to my feet. Instinct took over, and I stormed toward the tree line. What was I doing? Charging back into that darkness to save him? Me?

But before I could step inside the shadowed forest, Erickson burst out of it like a flying bullet. He rolled to the ground, then spun into a sitting position. His rifle snapped up, its muzzle flashing in the dark.

"Shoot!" he roared, unleashing a hail of bullets into the black shadows of the woods.

The first line of wolves broke free, snarling and lunging toward him, only to collapse mid-leap to the ground as Erickson's shots found their mark.

In seconds, Echo was right next to Erickson. The roar of our M4s turned the clearing into a chaotic symphony of sparks and fire, lighting the night like the Fourth of July. Wolves fell in piles at the forest's edge, their yelps and growls blending with the relentless sound of gunfire.

Then, as suddenly as it started, it stopped.

"Hold fire!" Cooper shouted.

The silence that followed was suffocating. Dread hung in the air. Distant pops of handgun fire echoed from somewhere deep in the woods. A single, blood-curdling scream accompanied them. Then nothing.

I was trembling, my hands shaking against the cold steel of my weapon.

Another growl came, low and menacing, vibrating through the clearing as if the beast was mere feet from the tree line, restrained only by some unseen barrier.

Then came the beast's roar.

It wasn't a wolf howl. It was a raw, guttural scream—a sound from hell. It ripped through the air so loud I thought my ears would bleed. A few of the civilians let out panicked cries. Even Cooper's usual steely demeanor faltered for a second.

Then the roar faded, leaving us in an oppressive stillness. We stood frozen for what felt like an eternity, listening as we pointed our weapons into the darkness. A wolf howled in the distance, and then another, but the beast was gone.

"Erickson," Cooper called, his voice steady but quieter now. "Clear?"

"I think it's safe to move," Erickson replied, scanning the tree line.

"Let's get to the hut and tend to the wounded," Cooper ordered, rising from his crouched position.

The team moved slowly, their steps heavy with exhaustion. Only six civilians remained—the girl, a woman, and four men. Their sobs were quiet now, muted by shock. Echo had also suffered a few losses —though it was hard to tell in the dark who hadn't made it.

Erickson stayed behind, his eyes fixed on the black stretch of woods. I walked up to him, my throat dry. My words came out shakier than I intended. "What the fuck was that?"

He didn't answer the question. "Let's go inside and make a fire," he said. "You're soaked."

For the first time, I noticed how drenched I was. The icy grip of the river, which I'd forgotten in the rush of adrenaline, now bit into my skin. My uniform clung heavily to my body.

"Yes," I said.

Erickson started walking toward the hut, but I reached out and grabbed his wrist. My grip was firm, and I didn't let go until he turned to face me.

"Thank you," I said, my voice breaking under the weight of emotion.

His gaze was unreadable, but his words were steady.

"Let's go."

He turned and led the way inside.

19

Ryder

The wooden hut was nothing more than a weathered shack. A small stone fireplace was the only source of warmth. Its flickering firelight danced across the old wooden walls. Dusty shelves held forgotten supplies—cans of beans and a first aid kit.

Nguyen hunched over the civilian woman, tending to a wolf bite on her shoulder. I saw a bandage wrapped tightly around the mangled leg of a wiry man with sunken cheeks. Two Echo members, blood-soaked and pale, sat nearby, nursing their injuries until Nguyen was done with the civilians.

Cooper walked into the center of the room. "We lost Blake, Ross, Kingston, Foster, and Sanders. And half the cargo."

"I'm not your fucking cargo," the woman snapped. Mud was streaked across her face, and her tangled hair told the story of a frantic chase.

Cooper didn't even glance her way. "We lost a lot of people today," he continued. "But the mission is still intact. Tomorrow, we get these civilians to the third hut. The drop-off coordinates are half a day north of that hut."

"Fuck you," spat a man in a wool sweater. His voice was raw and trembling. His close-cropped hair stuck to his sweat-slicked forehead as he set a dented can of beans down with a *CLANG*. "Let's call the cops. Some guy in a black SUV said he'd give me a ride to my parole hearing. Next thing I know, I'm waking up in a fucking cell and then getting shoved into a truck to . . . to whatever this hell is. What the fuck is going on?"

Chaos erupted. Civilians shouted over one another, their voices a storm of anger and fear. The wooden walls seemed to amplify their demands, causing every "Why?" and "What the hell?" to bounce back at us.

"Shut up!" Cooper's roar silenced the room instantly.

He let the quiet hang heavy before speaking again.

"If you want answers, I'm not the guy," he said. "I don't know why you're here, and I sure as hell didn't put you in that truck. And a lot of my men were killed out there too. Slowed down to protect you. Their kids are now without fathers. Their wives left to raise them alone."

The weight of his words settled uneasily over the group. The fire crackled in the stillness.

"I was ordered to deliver you safely to coordinates north of here," Cooper continued. "And considering there's a giant fucking wolf trying to eat us just south of here, sticking to that plan seems like the only option that doesn't end with us all dead."

"I just want to go home," the girl sobbed. "Why can't we just go home?"

"Yeah, we want to turn around," spat the woman with mud smeared across her face.

"It makes sense," Esther said, "considering the mission seems compromised."

"I decide when the mission is compromised," Cooper said.

Nguyen, tending to Martinez's bite wound, spoke without looking up. "Respectfully, sir, half the mission is dead. We might as well turn around."

"And the other half will be dead if you go back through that beast's hunting grounds," Cooper shot back, his finger jabbing toward the dark window. "That thing out there—I've never seen a wolf like that in my life. I'm not about to march through its turf again tomorrow with the little ammo we've got left."

"The beast will follow us wherever we go," I said, my voice steady despite the unease tightening my chest. "North, south—it won't matter."

The room fell into a tense silence. Civilians exchanged wary glances, their faces exhausted under the dim firelight. One man, lanky with a short nose, fidgeted nervously with his hands. The girl held her knees tightly to her chest as if bracing for the worst.

"What the fuck is that thing?" Jensen asked, his gaze locking on me. "And why the hell isn't it scratching at the hut right now?"

Every eye in the room locked onto me. I could tell them about the carved stones outside—the ancient protection rune that seemed to ward off the creature. I could mention its uncanny resemblance to Garmr, the hellhound of Norse legend. But their wide, fearful eyes didn't need more fuel for ghost stories. They needed calm. They needed a thread of hope.

"I can't say for sure," I said at last, choosing my words carefully. "I've never seen anything like it. But these woods are old. Uninhabited. Anything could survive out here, away from human interference."

"You mean it's prehistoric or something?" asked Carter, the young comms specialist with sharp features.

I didn't answer, just let the question hang, unanswered but heavy. It was better than admitting the darker possibilities circling in my mind.

"Won't it come and eat us in our sleep?" whispered the girl. Fresh tears filled her swollen eyes.

"I don't think so. It seems . . . to avoid the huts for some reason," I said.

Esther and Cooper exchanged glances, quick but loaded. No one brought up the runes carved into the rocks outside, the ancient symbols protecting the hut like a barrier.

"We need to head north," Cooper said, his tone final. "The third hut is closer, and there's a point of contact up there."

"A point of contact?" I repeated, narrowing my eyes. That was new information.

"Yeah," he said. "We'll stock up on ammo, establish communication with Command."

Cooper wasn't giving up on delivering these people to the coordinates. Whatever was waiting there, he intended to finish the job.

But going back to the first hut was suicide. The civilians could barely make it this far, and the forest itself seemed to be fighting us—roads disappearing, time slipping by faster than it should.

"He's right," I admitted. "The north hut is only half as far as the first hut. Without more ammo, we're dead when the wolves come again."

Esther shot me a glance of approval. She was too smart not to see the truth. I knew she wouldn't stop until she found her sister—no matter what waited at those cursed coordinates.

"Is there a base or something at the drop-off?" Nguyen asked, glancing up as he wrapped a bandage around the bitten arm of a pale, trembling man.

"I don't know," Cooper said, "That was classified information. They didn't tell me. I follow orders. And our orders are clear. Drop off the cargo, return to base. You got that, Echo?"

"Yes, sir," the soldiers replied, their voices hollow.

Cooper's eyes found mine and Esther's. "Tomorrow, Erickson will lead the way north. Anyone who wants to turn around can do so. But if you do, you're on your own."

The crackle of the fire filled the silence. The flames cast an eerie orange glow over the somber faces. Echo sat in grim thought. Civilians wept quietly.

Esther sat beside the girl, who said her name was Ava. She held the girl's hand, murmuring something too soft for me to catch. Whatever it was, it seemed to help. They talked for a while. At one point, Esther even got a tired smile from her. Then Ava lay down and closed her eyes. Esther pulled a jacket over her, tucking it around her like a quiet promise.

Esther stood, walked to the window, and stared out into the

clearing. At first, she seemed lost in thought, but then her posture shifted. A flicker of surprise crossed her face.

"What is it?" I asked, rising to join her.

In the grassy field stood a white fox, its fur almost glowing against the dark backdrop of the woods. It was the same fox she'd chased earlier, the one that had led us to the dead Alpha team and their truck.

"The white fox," I muttered.

That was rare enough around here. But one following a Native woman like a dog was something to note.

"How long has it been following you?" I asked, keeping my voice low so the others wouldn't hear.

"It's not following . . ." she started, but then she stopped and met my gaze as if surrendering to the absurdity of the truth. "Since we left."

The fox stood motionless, its gaze fixed on us like it carried a message. Then, without a sound, it turned and slipped back into the darkness.

"Why?" I asked. "Why is a white fox following you?"

For a moment, she looked ready to dismiss it all as a coincidence. But then, with a resigned sigh, she looked straight at me.

"You first," she said. "What the hell is going on here?"

I smiled despite the craziness of it all. This woman wasn't one to back down. And of course, she didn't buy the whole prehistoric-wolf explanation.

"I'm not sure," I said. "But this forest . . . it's like it's still connected to the old ways. The old gods."

"Old gods?" she repeated, her voice a little too loud.

Cooper's cold stare locked onto us from across the room.

I pulled her closer and lowered my voice to a whisper. "Christianity's young. Humans believed in spirits and gods for thousands of years—living in harmony with the rivers, land, and forests."

"So you're saying this forest is full of ancient creatures?"

It sounded insane even to me—someone who believed in the power of Yggdrasil, the holy tree. But everything about this place was insane.

"If that's true, there's a bigger problem," I said.

"A bigger problem than that monster wolf out there?" Her tone dripped with disbelief.

I nodded, watching as the faint light in her eyes dimmed. This was why I hadn't told anyone else. Somehow, though, I knew she could handle it—even if it made no sense. She was a failed veterinarian who'd never held a gun before today, but crazy or not, she was the only one here whom I felt like I could trust.

"What the hell could be worse than that thing?" she pressed.

"The runes and symbols we saw out there by the first hut," I said. "They're Norse. Germanic or Viking."

Her brow furrowed. "But?"

"But this isn't Europe. These woods aren't Norse. If this forest is still tied to the old ways, it should be full of *your* people's spirits and gods. Not mine."

Her gaze shifted toward the window, to the spot where the white fox had been just moments ago.

"So tell me," I said, my voice barely above a whisper. "Is that fox following you for a good reason . . . or because you accidentally ran over its pups?"

"You two," Cooper barked from across the room. "Eat something, then try to sleep. You're on the last watch tonight."

Esther nodded, but as soon as Cooper turned away, she leaned in close. Her voice dropped to a quick, secretive murmur. "Good news. I think the fox is following me because I saved its life."

20

Esther

The night passed uneventfully. We woke at the hut by the river just as we'd found it. However, the walk that morning was tense. A suffocating quiet wrapped around us. Our boots crunched against the stones as we walked up the rocky riverbed in silence. I was positioned in the back with Dawson and Nguyen. The rest of Echo flanked the civilians. Erickson led with Cooper. We kept our rifles raised, aiming at every snap of a twig or rustle in the trees.

I wanted to talk to the girl—earlier, she'd told me her name was Ava—but every attempt to connect had been met with the hollow gaze of a traumatized soul. And Erickson had made it clear: Silence was survival.

Suddenly, Erickson froze. His hand shot up in a signal to halt.

We stopped, gathering close without a sound.

He pulled the map from his pocket and traced a finger along the river from the second hut.

"We're here," he said, tapping a spot about two miles from the third hut. "Doesn't look like we've got much farther to go."

"Then why the hell are we stopping?" Cooper asked.

Erickson glanced at me, then walked to a large tree by the riverbank and placed his hand on its rough bark. He listened to the faint rattle of its leaves.

"I think it's happening again," he said. "The forest is shifting us off track."

Cooper scoffed. "What the hell does that even mean?"

Erickson crouched, running his hand along the bark where moss clung thick and damp. "Moss grows thicker on the north side. It avoids the sun." He glanced at the sky, squinting as the sun briefly broke through the clouds. "Look at our shadows. They point east." Erickson motioned to the stretching shadows. "The map says the hut is north along the river. But the shadows aren't matching the map anymore. We're getting pulled off course. North's shifted—away from the river."

"How can you be sure?" Cooper asked.

"Wager," Erickson called, motioning me forward. "What's your take?"

I opened my mouth to answer, but Cooper cut me off. "Who the fuck cares about Wager's take? She's not a tracker. Henderson!"

Henderson jogged over, his M4 clicking with the movement.

"You still breathing, Henderson?" Cooper barked.

"Very much so, sir," Henderson replied.

"Then why the fuck are we wasting time asking Wager for advice when we've got one of the best trackers in the military right here?"

Erickson's expression didn't waver. "Wager seems to have a connection to this land," he said. "And I stand by it. The forest might fuck with us, but the sun is still up there doing its own thing. The hut is north, and north is not along the river anymore."

"This is insane."

"Fucking amen it is, but as crazy as it sounds, the forest itself is leading us astray again. If we want to find the hut, we need to head north—this way." Erickson pointed at a narrow trail away from the river. "Wager, what do you think?"

Cooper sighed. He looked up the river, then shifted his gaze to the narrow path Erickson was pointing at. "We're staying on the river," he finally ordered. "Henderson, you're with me. Erickson, you take the rear with Wager."

Erickson's jaw tightened, but he didn't argue. Instead, he narrowed his eyes and watched as Cooper and Henderson signaled the group to move along the river.

"What now?" I asked Erickson.

"We follow this idiot," he said grimly. "Strength in numbers. It's the only way we'll survive another wolf attack."

I nodded, falling in step beside him.

Each step felt heavier, like a silent warning. It was as if the forest had decided our fate and was guiding us toward another disaster.

21

Esther

We marched for another thirty minutes. The river curved gently ahead. Its steady murmur broke the silence, creating an almost soothing atmosphere. Around a bend, the river split to form a large, tranquil pool tucked against the bank. The current slowed here. The water was dark and glassy.

We stopped.

I crouched at the edge of the river and filled my water bottle. The built-in filter took a while, but it would make the water safe to drink. Then I scooped some water in my hands and splashed it on my neck. The icy sting was a small relief against my overheated skin.

When I stood, wiping my neck, I froze. Everyone else had gone utterly still. Their eyes were locked on the swimming hole.

"What's wrong?" I asked.

Erickson didn't answer. His gaze remained fixed on the trees by the pool.

With slow, deliberate movements, Dawson began walking toward the pool. The effect was almost robotic. The others followed. One by one, they drifted in the same direction.

Even when they reached the pool, they didn't stop. Dawson was the first to step straight into the water.

"What the hell is he doing?" My voice cracked as I grabbed Erickson's arm, but he didn't flinch. He just kept staring at the pool where Dawson was already up to his chest. So was Nguyen. Henderson. Cooper. Several civilians. In eerie unison, all of them walked into the water.

"Stop!" I yelled, the command catching in my throat. But none of them turned. None of them hesitated.

Erickson pushed past me, his body heavy, unstoppable.

I staggered but managed to grab his arm. "Erickson, stop!"

His gaze was glazed, empty, as though he were dreaming with his eyes wide open.

At the pool's edge, Ava waded in. The water climbed to her knees. Dawson, Henderson, and several others were already gone, their heads having slipped under the dark surface like stones pulled by an unseen hand.

"Ava!" My voice tore through the woods. She didn't stop. None of them did. I scrambled toward her and tried to pull her back, but she pushed me off.

Then she appeared.

A woman.

She emerged from behind a tree, her skin pale as snow and her hair a vivid cascade of red, burning like fire. She was naked, and her flawless body radiated a stunning beauty. Her mouth moved, wide and singing—but no sound came. Her glowing green eyes locked on mine as she stepped closer, slowly, every motion a work of art. Her lips kept moving, the silent melody unnerving, hypnotic.

"Who are you?" I demanded. "What are you doing to them?" I splashed into the water after Ava. The icy grip of the pool bit into my legs, but I barely noticed. My hands found her arms, and I yanked, pulling with everything I had. She twisted, fighting against me, her movements mechanical and unrelenting.

"Ava, stop!" I begged, my voice cracking, but she didn't even glance at me. With a sudden shove, she broke free, sending me stumbling backward. The water surged around her knees as she took another step, then another until she sank beneath the surface.

"No!" I screamed, lunging toward the spot where she'd disappeared. The rippling water had already smoothed over, swallowing her completely.

I clawed at the empty space, my breath hitching as air bubbles rose lazily to the surface—silent proof that she was gone.

Behind me, the others marched forward, one by one, following the same haunting path. Echo. The civilians. They moved like puppets, lifeless and detached, marching into the water until nothing remained of them but a scattering of bubbles.

I stumbled out of the water and fell hard against Erickson.

"Wake up!" I yelled, grabbing his shoulders and shaking him.

His blank eyes stared past me, unseeing. I slapped him, hard, again and again. His head snapped left, then right, but there was no reaction. No fight.

"Stop!" I screamed, spinning toward the woman by the water's edge. She stood motionless, her wide mouth curling into a wicked smile. Her glowing green eyes pinned on me as her lips moved, again forming the shape of a song I couldn't hear. It felt like she was performing just for me, savoring my desperation as I fought to keep Erickson from the pull of the water.

He was too strong. Erickson slipped free and waded into the pool. I collapsed onto the ground, helpless, as he disappeared beneath the surface like the others.

"Do something!" I yelled at myself.

Instinct took over.

My M4 lay farther down the bank where I'd dropped it while trying to stop Erickson. So I grabbed my Glock and bolted toward the woman. With a heaving chest, I skidded to an abrupt stop in front of her. My gun snapped up, trembling in my grip. Its barrel was aimed straight at her flawless face.

"Stop singing!" I yelled, my voice raw with rage and fear but also awe at her beauty.

Her eyes flared, bright and unnatural, as her lips kept moving in their silent rhythm. Defiant.

I fired a warning shot into the air.

"Stop singing!" I screamed, but she didn't flinch. She didn't even blink.

That was when I noticed it—the cow's tail swishing lazily behind her. And the grotesque, webbed duck feet. The sight—an absurd contrast to her beauty—sent a chill racing up my spine.

Time seemed to slow. The world tilted, spinning as I leveled the gun at her face once more. My breath hitched.

"Please," I begged, my voice barely a whisper.

The last of the team and civilians were gone, swallowed by the pool. Silence pressed in, broken only by the wind rattling the trees. And still, she stood there, her lips moving to a melody I couldn't hear, her glowing eyes locked on mine.

My grip tightened on the trigger. My chest heaved with the weight of what I was about to do.

And then I did the unthinkable.

I pulled the trigger.

The shot echoed, ripping through the air and scattering birds from the tree canopies. The bullet struck her dead center in the face. Blood splattered across me, warm and metallic, clinging to my skin. The woman collapsed to the ground. Dead.

Instantly, Echo surfaced in the swimming hole, followed by the civilians. They clawed their way out of the water, hacking and coughing, collapsing onto all fours as water poured from their mouths. Their gagging and retching filled the air. Raw. Desperate.

I doubled over and vomited. Once. Twice. My stomach twisted, emptying until nothing was left of last night's beans—only dry heaves that left me shaking.

I thought I was past this kind of weakness. After life had burned my parents alive and forced me to walk past their charred corpses. After it had dragged me through years of watching my sister waste away in addiction before taking her too. After all that, I thought I'd seen the worst.

But killing someone? Close range? Somehow, I hadn't factored that in.

"Did you fucking hear that?" Nguyen rasped between gags. "That song?"

"It was a woman," Henderson choked out, water dripping from his lips. "Her voice . . . the most beautiful thing I've ever heard."

A hand gripped my shoulder, startling me. I turned to find Erickson, soaked, his breaths fast.

"You okay?" he asked.

My gaze dropped to the lifeless body on the ground. The beautiful, naked woman lay in a growing pool of her own blood. Her mouth hung open, frozen mid-song, as if her melody had carried on into the afterlife.

"You didn't hear her singing?" Erickson pressed.

I shook my head as I wiped my mouth with the back of my hand.

He nodded slightly.

"What the fuck is that?" Cooper asked as he joined the others gathering around the corpse.

"I . . . I don't know," I said, my voice barely audible.

"Whatever the hell it is," Jensen said, stepping closer, "you saved us, Wager."

"Yeah," the others murmured.

"Good shot, Wager," Cooper said. "Do you know what it is?" His question was directed at Erickson.

Erickson's expression darkened. "I think it's a . . . huldra."

"A fucking what?" Cooper asked.

"In Norse mythology, it's a forest spirit," Erickson said. "They appear as beautiful women with long hair but always have some feature that gives them away. Like the cow's tail or the feet." He gestured toward the woman's grotesque, duck-like feet, stark against the perfection of her form. "Huldras lure people into the forest— sometimes to protect them but more often to trap or kill them."

We all stared in disbelief at the creature.

As his words sank in, the reality of what we'd just faced pressed down like a boulder. My eyes lingered on the blood-soaked figure, her twisted beauty, her frozen lips. Whatever she was, it wasn't human. And it wasn't done haunting us.

"Why was it trying to k—" Cooper started, but the thunderous blare of a horn cut him off.

"Bwoooooooooorrrrrrr!"

The bone-rattling wail tore through the forest, slamming into us with a harsh, gut-wrenching reminder of last night's horror. Erickson looked at the sky. It was getting dark again. The light was vanishing even faster than it had the day before.

"No!" cried out one of the civilians. The man in the wool sweater crumpled to his knees, clutching his head as if trying to shut it all out. The others followed, sobbing, their desperate pleas merging into incoherent mumbles.

"Fucking shit. Echo!" Cooper barked. "Shoot at whatever the fuck you see that isn't us!" He spun toward Erickson. "Which way?"

Erickson scanned the trees, his gaze darting back and forth.

"Bwoooooooooorrrrrrr!"

The horn blared again. Louder. Closer. It seemed to be right on top of us.

The civilians screamed, their voices slicing through the chaos.

"Shut the fuck up!" Cooper roared at them. "Erickson, lead the goddamn way! Now!"

Erickson froze as his eyes locked on something in the shadows. My gaze followed and landed on the white fox in the distance. It lingered for only a moment before darting through the trees and vanishing into the forest.

"This way!" Erickson shouted, breaking into a jog.

Echo's soldiers yanked the civilians to their feet and screamed at them to start running. I grabbed Ava's trembling hand and dragged her into a desperate sprint after Erickson, who kept glancing back to ensure we were still there.

"Bwoooooooooorrrrrrr!"

The horn mocked us, its call relentless, causing the ground to vibrate beneath our feet. Branches clawed at me as I tore through the forest. My lungs burned from the punishing pace.

Then came the first growls, low and guttural. Flanking us.

I whipped my head to the side and spotted a wolf. Its massive body was streaking toward us. Before I could react, Cooper fired. As the crack of his M4 split the air, the wolf dropped. However, more howls erupted, mingling with the gunshots and screams.

It was chaos. Hell on earth. I had no doubt we'd all die tonight.

Ava clung to me as we ran, our hands like one.

We burst into a clearing, then came to a dead stop. A massive rock wall—sharp and impassable—loomed ahead.

It seemed to be a death trap until I saw Henderson and Dawson clawing their way up the rock. Hope flickered, but it was fleeting. A wolf lunged at Henderson and dragged him off the wall by his leg. He hit the ground hard, and within seconds, more wolves descended, tearing into him with ruthless efficiency. Henderson's screams pierced the night as the soldiers fired shot after shot, trying to hold back the onslaught. Wolves launched from the forest, their feral eyes locked on us as we scrambled to climb the rock—the only barrier between survival and a savage end.

However, the wolves weren't just attacking. They were hunting with terrifying precision, grouping to target us one by one.

"Kill them!" Cooper barked.

I shoved Ava behind me and fired at the wolves that were leaping out of the woods and into the clearing.

Then my rifle clicked empty.

Quickly, I grabbed my pistol and unloaded it into the next wolf that charged. But the magazine drained too fast. The last round echoed like a closing bell.

The gunfire grew more sporadic.

Erickson was the first to draw his knife. He gripped it tightly as he prepared for the inevitable. Cooper followed. One by one, as their ammo ran dry, the rest of Echo did the same.

The first wolf lunged at Erickson. He caught the massive head of the beast, whose jaws snapped inches from his face. With a guttural roar, Erickson drove his knife into the creature's throat. Crimson spurted over his hands as he wrestled it to the ground.

Another wolf pounced on Cooper. Its teeth sank into his arm as it dragged him down. Cooper stabbed it over and over, each thrust desperate and savage. He was so close I could see the blood spray. Without thinking, I jumped in and plunged my blade into the wolf's side. The resistance was brutal—nothing like slicing butter. It was muscle, bone, and fur, and it took all my strength to shove the knife deeper. It didn't help that these wolves weren't normal. Their eyes held something unnatural—something monstrous.

We couldn't keep this up. There was no way.

The civilians knew it. Echo knew it. Erickson knew it. Cooper knew it.

And I knew it.

This was the end.

However, just as despair settled in my stomach, another horn echoed through the clearing. This one was high-pitched and piercing.

The wolves froze. Their ears twitched as they turned toward the sound.

The horn blared again, sharper this time, and the wolves broke. Most scattered, darting back into the trees, but several beasts remained. One of them leaped, hurtling straight for me.

Before it could strike, a spinning axe slammed into its side with a force so brutal it sent the wolf flying into a tree.

Then a figure burst from the woods—not a man but a giant of a human. He stood at least six foot seven, a mountain of muscle wrapped in a wolf-fur coat. His braided blond hair—streaked with blood—fell past his shoulders. A silver-threaded beard framed a face marked with black and blue war paint. Piercing blue eyes locked onto the remaining wolves.

The man's leather tunic was reinforced with iron. Muddy boots pounded against the ground as he charged in, twin swords clenched tight. Ancient runes shimmered faintly along the bloodied steel.

He looked like a Viking dragged straight from myth.

The wolves split. Some bolted into the forest, like they knew and feared him, while others lunged, their snarls mixing with the warrior's own savage roar. The man moved with terrifying precision, slicing through them as if the fight had been sped up. With each swing of his blade, he severed heads and limbs with ease. Blood sprayed the clearing as howls, yelps, and the warrior's guttural battle cries filled the twilight air.

The last wolf turned to flee, but the man was faster. With a single, brutal strike, he severed the head of the snow-white wolf, which rolled to my feet. Its yellow eyes stared lifelessly at me. Its tongue lolled grotesquely from its mouth.

The clearing fell silent.

The man stood with his back to us. The fur of his cloak swayed with his heavy breaths. His hair spilled over a round Viking shield strapped to his back. A large rune was carved into its surface, and it glinted faintly in the dim light.

Suddenly, all weapons were pointed at him. Most of us were out of ammo, but some had found the time to reach into their pockets and reload—a luxury they hadn't had earlier.

Bodies littered the clearing. Two civilians lay dead, their flesh torn wide open. Two members of Echo—Henderson and Nguyen —were crumpled not far from them, surrounded by dead wolves. Nguyen's death hit me like a punch to the gut. He'd just wanted to survive this and get back to his wife and baby. Then get out. Live his life as a husband and dad.

The silence was deafening. Guns were pointed at the man, and knives were held in shaking hands. Erickson stood motionless. He was the only one not aiming a weapon. His body was smeared in blood from the wolf he'd killed on top of him. Beside Erickson stood Cooper, who pointed his pistol for a few seconds before quickly reloading from a magazine in his pocket and aiming again.

Finally, the man turned to us. He appeared to be in his fifties, massive like a bear, with muscles that seemed to have been carved from stone. Everything about him screamed, *Don't fuck with me.* His gaze passed over each of us, though it lingered a moment longer on Erickson and then me.

He moved suddenly, and we tensed, but he wasn't coming toward us. Instead, he headed for the tree where his axe was buried, still lodged in a dead wolf's body.

The man glanced up at the sky. It was almost dark.

Then it came—the horrifying scream of the beast, echoing through the woods. It sounded like something from a nightmare, a dragon's roar tearing through the trees. The man narrowed his eyes at the forest.

"Garmr is roaming the woods tonight," he growled in a strong accent that could best be described as northern European. "We need to move."

He scanned us briefly again as though deciding whether we were worth the effort. "Follow in my footsteps," he said, his voice vibrating.

Without waiting for an answer, he strode toward the line of trees.

We all looked at Cooper.

"Let's go," he said, breaking into a jog after the man.

"Wait, what?" Jenkins protested, but I grabbed Ava's hand and followed Cooper. Behind us, a few more civilians voiced their objections, but Cooper barked out orders, and soon everyone was scrambling to keep up. The Viking didn't slow or wait.

Once we hit a trail, it became easier to follow him. The night thickened around us, and the cold bit into my skin. We were running again, forced into a brutal, unforgiving pace. The howls of wolves intensified. They were accompanied by the same gut-wrenching scream from the beast. The sound tore through my skin as if it were alive.

Suddenly, a human scream cut through the night. I turned to find one of the civilians impaled by a swinging trap of wooden spikes that had dropped from a tree. Blood dripped down the wooden stakes as the man's wide eyes froze in horror. His face was contorted in agony. He'd left the trail, apparently trying to take a shortcut around a rock. Now he was dead.

We all stopped.

The Viking's voice carried back to us, cold and unfazed. "You don't listen well, do you?"

Shaken, we picked up the pace again, running after him as darkness fully enveloped the forest. The trail twisted and turned. It was lined with strange, ancient totems—stick figures, animal skulls, rocks etched with runes. It was like some twisted Viking version of The Blair Witch Project. My chest burned as I struggled to keep up.

After another grueling sprint, we burst into a clearing by a spring. At the center stood a large wooden hut, its weathered logs darkened by rain and time. Smoke curled steadily from a stone chimney, and a warm, flickering light spilled from the open door. It cast jagged shapes across the ground.

A rough fence enclosed a scraggly garden of root vegetables and herbs. The smell of rosemary and thyme floated through the air. Inside the fence, a few goats and chickens huddled near a small barn whose roof was patched with straw and moss.

The Viking stopped at the hut, where his hulking frame cast a shadow over the doorway. His expression was carved from stone, and his sharp eyes swept over us as if he were weighing whether we were worth the trouble.

"Garmr won't come here," he said. "Stay out there with the animals if you like. Or step inside. Your choice."

We exchanged uneasy glances. Cooper's face was hard to read. Erickson's was set like stone. Ava's hand trembled in mine. Her skin was ice cold. The wolves' howls seemed closer now, more desperate.

"Let's go," Erickson said.

"We'll stay in the barn until morning," Cooper ordered.

"Be my guest," Erickson replied. "Come on, Wager."

"Erickson, that was an order!" Cooper barked, but Erickson led the way into the hut. Ava and I stayed close. The two surviving civilians—the man in the wool sweater and the middle-aged woman with mud on her forehead—followed us.

"I honestly don't give a fuck anymore who kills me," the woman muttered as she walked inside. "At least I'll die warm."

Cooper hesitated but eventually followed, cursing under his breath.

22

Esther

The hut smelled of wood smoke and earth. It looked like something straight out of an ancient Viking camp. Everything about this was insane. A fire crackled in the stone fireplace. Its flickering light danced across the timber walls, which were reinforced with stone and clay. Thick beams stretched across the ceiling. Bundles of dried herbs, braided ropes, and preserved meats hung from the rafters. The walls were lined with wooden shelves that held a mix of tools, carved figures, and polished bones. Axes, spears, and shields also hung on the walls. Near the fireplace sat a broad table whose surface was cluttered with clay and wooden bowls, cups, drinking horns, and a large, weathered map sketched onto animal hide. A heavy bed —layered with thick furs and surrounded by runes carved into the frame—was tucked into one corner. Next to it, an iron-bound chest hinted at secrets and treasures. There was probably another room, but the small wooden door was shut tight.

When the door closed behind us, one thought burned in my mind: *What the hell does all of this have to do with my sister?*

We stood in silence, staring at the beast of a man who now sat at the table, tearing a piece of meat off a roasted rabbit. The table contained more food: dried meats and bread.

"Eat and drink," the man said, gulping down a thick, yellowish liquid in a wooden cup. It ran down his beard. Honey wine?

The civilian in the wool sweater, Dawson, and Jenkins moved to grab chairs around the table, but the Viking hammered his fist onto it. The wood shook, rattling the dishes and startling me to my core.

"Your leader and the tired women will sit," he clarified, his voice low and sharp. "My goddess watches over this house. I won't have swine dishonor her."

Cooper, Erickson, and I exchanged glances. Then Cooper and I carefully pulled back two wooden chairs and sat. Ava and the woman with the mud-smeared face pulled back chairs as well.

"No wonder your women no longer stand by your side, bearing shield and sword," the man muttered.

For a moment, we stared at the food.

"Eat," the man said again. "All of you."

The standing men hesitated before slowly stepping forward and grabbing food from the table—careful, cautious, but starving. I slowly reached for a piece of bread and pulled off a chunk. Cooper grabbed some of the meat, and Ava and the mud-smeared woman took pieces of bread. The bread was rough, unsalted, with a faint taste of herbs—rosemary, maybe.

"Thank you," I mumbled. The rest of the group murmured the same. The man gave a small nod but didn't look up.

"Who are you?" Cooper asked, biting into the meat.

"I am Sigvarðr Þorsteinsson of Eystribyggð, son of Þorsteinn the Iron-Headed. They call me Fjallgarðr, the Mountain Guardian. My strength stands as unyielding as the peaks of Greenland."

Silence reigned for a while. I caught a brief glance from Erickson.

"I'm Lieutenant Ian Cooper, US Navy SEAL," Cooper said, shifting in his chair as the Viking eyed him with a wrinkled fore-head. "Commanding officer of Echo . . . these brave men and women," he added quickly, though the words sounded hollow next to Sigvarðr's grand introduction.

Sigvarðr nodded when nothing else followed.

"You said you're from Eystribyggð," Erickson repeated. "You mean the settlement of Erik the Red?"

Sigvarðr's head shot up, and his sharp gaze locked onto Erickson. His eyes roamed over Erickson's tattoos—runes etched into his hands and neck—with a glint of recognition.

"That name has not reached my ears in many winters," Sigvarðr said. His voice was distant as he stared at the table as if lost in memories.

"You knew him?" Erickson asked.

"Knew?" Sigvarðr mumbled, his voice gravelly. "That red beard burned on the shore as we sailed to our doom. It will stay with me until the goddess calls me home."

"Erickson," Cooper said. "Can you translate?"

"Erik the Red was a famous Viking explorer," Erickson explained. "He founded the first Viking settlement in Greenland."

"You knew Erik the Red, tracker?" Sigvarðr asked, his eyes narrowing as he looked at Erickson. "You bear the Raido on your hands. Just like him."

Erickson shook his head. "No. I didn't know him. Erik the Red . . . he lived almost a thousand years before me."

The room grew silent. Then, with no warning, Sigvarðr stood. Echo's guns were up in an instant, their reflexes automatic.

Sigvarðr growled, his hand tightening into a fist. "No honor, já?"

"Echo, lower your weapons," Cooper ordered.

The team hesitated for a split second before complying.

"Listen to your leader," Sigvarðr said, his tone cold as he turned to the fire. He tossed a few more logs onto it and stirred the embers with a metal rod. The flames crackled and roared to life. "If I am not mistaken, your weapons that spit tiny iron arrows are spent, já? Unless you wield axe and sword better than I, think twice before raising them at me again. In my home. After I fed you." He turned, his icy blue eyes locking onto Cooper with a stare that could have frozen blood. "Have you no honor at all?"

"I apologize," Cooper said. "It's been a rough few days. We lost a lot of men."

Sigvarðr gave a curt nod, then walked to a wooden shelf. He

grabbed a stack of mugs and returned to the table. Calm and relaxed, he set the mugs in front of me and the mud-smeared woman with a suggestive grin, then placed one in front of Cooper with a deadly glare. Finally, he filled each with a golden liquid from a large clay vase.

"Erickson," Cooper muttered over his shoulder. "Please talk to our 'contact' and bond over whatever Viking shit you two share. See if you can get anything useful to help us make it to the north hut."

"That's our contact?" I whispered.

Sigvarðr walked over to Erickson and handed him a mug with a small nod. "Here, tracker," he said, his tone heavy with respect.

"Thank you." Erickson took the mug. "The wolf out there. It's Garmr, isn't it?"

Sigvarðr settled into his seat at the wooden table. His gaze shifted from me to the mud-smeared woman, then finally rested on Erickson. "As I'm Sigvarðr Þorsteinsson of Eystribyggð, son of Þorsteinn the Iron-Headed, so it is. Its hunt begins as soon as the sun falls."

"Its hunt?" I asked.

Sigvarðr looked at me, his stare long and unflinching. Then, slowly, a thin grin spread across his face.

"Já. Garmr hunts your men," he said, nodding toward Echo. "Me as well," he added, taking a deliberate sip from his cup. "Even . . . her."

Something about the way he said *her* made my skin crawl.

"Her?" Erickson asked, leaning forward.

Sigvarðr hesitated. His eyes dropped to his cup as though the answers lay at the bottom. After a moment, he spoke.

"The seer."

"The fucking what?" Dawson scoffed, a nervous laugh escaping before he could stop it.

Sigvarðr's glare shot across the room, silencing Dawson instantly.

"What seer?" Erickson pressed.

Sigvarðr leaned forward. His piercing eyes cut through the dim light. "Her name is Yrsa the Cruel, but once, she was more than that. A shield maiden, fierce as any man. Erik the Red himself burned for her. She fought like a man. Fucked like one too. No fear in raid or war. If any earned a place in Sessrúmnir, Freyja's great hall, it was her." He paused. The flicker of the fire caught on his weathered face. "I am Sigvarðr, son of Þorsteinn the Iron-Headed, and I tell you this—every word I said is true."

"What did you mean when you said Garmr is hunting her too?" Erickson asked. "This Yrsa the Cruel . . . is she here in this forest? Alive?"

Sigvarðr leaned back in his chair, his eyes burdened by the weight of centuries. "Já. We brought her here to Vinland to banish her. Many winters ago."

"The Vikings called North America Vinland," Erickson explained.

"But Viking voyages happened hundreds of years ago," I said.

We all exchanged confused glances.

"You're telling us that you sailed to this land to banish a seer?" Erickson asked.

"None of this makes sense," Cooper said. "You expect us to believe this? That all of this"—he gestured to the dark woods beyond the cabin—"is because some Viking warlord exiled a fucking witch hundreds of years ago to America, and she's somehow still alive?"

"She is no witch," Sigvarðr said, his voice firm. "She is Yrsa the Cruel. A seiðkona once, weaving powerful magic—the craft of prophecy and fate, of speaking with the dead and bending the elements to her will. But in time, she became something darker. A trollkona."

"A what?" I asked.

"A seiðkona is a sorceress in Norse mythology," Erickson explained. "Someone who uses magic to predict the future, cast spells, or manipulate people. A trollkona is . . . the really messed up and brutal version of it."

"Is that why you banished her here?" Cooper asked. "Because she became too cruel for your people?"

Sigvarðr's expression darkened. "Erik the Red is not named for his beard. He is named for the blood he spilled—the same fury that saw him cast out by his own before the gods sent him to Eystribyggð. At first, Erik welcomed Yrsa. Thought her gifts as a Seiðkona were a blessing, a strength for our people. But the winds shifted. It began when we raided the borderlands. Yrsa was lost in the chaos, gone many weeks. When she returned . . . she was not Yrsa the Seiðkona anymore. She spoke of voices from the underworld, said the dead and Hel herself whispered secrets to her." Sigvarðr paused to drink deep from his honey wine. "But Erik saw only her power. She was stronger, sharper, fiercer than any man. He was bewitched by her. Even when she began spilling the blood of our own for her dark gods, he hesitated. He did not stop her."

"What happened next?" Cooper asked, leaning closer.

Sigvarðr's jaw tightened. "Yrsa the Cruel called for the blood of Erik's own bastard—a gift to Odin. Said it would make her the first woman to walk the halls of Valhalla. Even Erik could not look away then. But it was too late. She had grown too strong. No sword could kill her. No man could strike her down. No Seiðkona could break her will."

"How did you stop her?" I asked.

Sigvarðr drained his cup before speaking. "The wisest of our Seiðmenn made a plan. We would trick Yrsa the Cruel. Told her she would rule a new land, one meant for our people. A land far across the sea. Erik chose me to lead. Promised Yrsa she would build a great kingdom of her own. She believed us, and so we brought her here, to Vinland. But it did not take long before she saw the truth. That she was cast out. That this was no kingdom—only exile. And when she knew, she killed us all."

"How did you survive?" Cooper asked.

"I saved her life once. The goddess Freyja wove our fates together. Yrsa owes me a life-debt, a bond sealed by the greatest Seiðmenn of Eystribyggð. As long as I draw breath, she cannot wander far from me. And as long as she lives, neither can I from her."

"Why don't you kill her?" Erickson asked.

"If I could, I would. But she is too powerful. Stronger than any

Seiðkona or warrior before her. She bends wind and sea and calls sickness upon men. Soon, she will find a way to kill me. And when I fall, she will be free."

Erickson narrowed his eyes. "The people my leaders send here, what happens to them?"

Sigvarðr nodded. "When we first came, and she slaughtered her own, the people of this land brought her offerings. Gave thanks, thinking she would keep us at bay. We were at odds with the people of this land. We fought them fiercely."

"But the Natives of this land welcomed her?" I asked. "They thought she was on their side?"

He nodded. "They did not know she came to take their land, to rule over them. She lived in this forest, at peace not far from them. They gave her deer, bears—what they could. Then the white sailors came in their great ships, offering more than beasts and herbs."

"Humans," Cooper concluded.

"Já. The people of this land would not bind themselves to such darkness. But the white sailors—like Erik the Red—were fools. Thought they could wield her power. Bring plagues, floods, curses to feed their greed with her help. But the tree of life does not forget, nor do I, Sigvarðr, son of the Iron-Headed. Stories always walk the same path. And so this one did. It was not long before Yrsa the Cruel turned on the white sailors as well. Now they grasp and claw, trying to keep her silent with offerings for as long as fate allows."

"With human sacrifices?" I protested, my voice breaking. My head spun. These people. Ava . . . my sister.

Sigvarðr seemed unfazed as he filled his cup. "A handful of lives before each winter to sate her hunger and keep the storms at bay. Else, she wakes in wrath, and thousands may perish. Seems a wise trade to me."

It started to click. Runaways. Junkies. The homeless. The government sent people nobody would miss. Nobody but me. As sacrifices to an ancient power they thought they could control—but lost their grip on. And now they tried to keep her quiet with human blood.

My throat tightened as nausea clawed its way up. My sister was most likely dead. All of this for nothing. Her life taken by the people at the top. A story as old as time. Of course, they didn't send their own—just us peasants.

Her laugh echoed in my mind. It was bright and sharp like sunlight catching on broken glass.

Gone.

Erickson's hand gripped my shoulder just as I felt a scream build inside my chest. His fingers tightened, almost painfully, as if to say: *Wait. Not yet. Something about this still doesn't add up.*

"But our last deliveries failed," Erickson said.

"If the people are for her," Cooper added, "why is she killing them? Us? Our teams?"

Sigvarðr's expression hardened. "Já. I have not seen your kind in over two winters. You are the first to make it this far. Whatever happened with the last offering, it must have angered the forest and its gods. As I said, the hellhound hunts her too. Garmr does not answer to her. Whatever upset the balance of these woods two winters past . . . it was not done by her choice."

My fists clenched, nails digging into my sweaty palms. "Two years ago," I whispered. That was when my sister disappeared.

Sigvarðr's heavy gaze settled on me. "Whatever upset the spirits of this land doesn't matter. She will still blame you for breaking your pact. And she will punish your people for it soon."

"But it's not our fault some crazy wolf demon is killing us and the cargo," Cooper said. "We're holding up our end of the bargain. Why punish us for something we can't control?"

Sigvarðr shrugged, his face indifferent.

Cargo? I wanted to punch Cooper in the face. He had zero regard for the people being slaughtered—sacrificed in god-knows-what horrible ways. Ava, sitting right here at the table, was one of the *cargo*. I saw her expression, the way she gripped the edge of the table until her knuckles turned white. She stared downward in silent terror.

The room was suffocating, the air so thick with dread it felt impossible to breathe.

Ava let out a shaky breath. Her voice trembled. "I'm not going to the north hut."

Across from her, the mud-smeared woman grabbed Ava's hand. "No, you won't. We'll turn around tomorrow at first light. I don't give a shit about these assholes with guns. We're not going another step north."

Cooper's jaw tightened. "Yes, you will. We're moving north tomorrow morning. To complete the mission."

"No, we won't," I snapped. "Take your lapdogs and go to hell for all I care. We're turning around tomorrow. There's got to be a way out of here, and I'll find it—or die trying. But I'm not escorting anyone to get slaughtered by some psycho witch."

"She's right," Dawson said. "There is no mission left. We won't make it to the coordinates one way or the other. It's best to turn around. Try to make it back."

"Yeah," Jensen agreed.

Kingston, Ross, Martinez—one by one, the men agreed.

"Get a fucking hold of yourself!" Cooper shouted.

Sigvarðr sat back in his chair, curious. Entertained.

"What fucking part of 'threat to our country' did you not understand?" Cooper's voice boomed. "Do you think we're here because some goddamn witch won't leave a dollar under the pillow like the fucking Tooth Fairy if we don't deliver the cargo?"

He pointed at Sigvarðr. "If anything this man has said is true, we're talking about a full-scale national emergency. The kind that kills thousands if not tens of thousands of people." He shook his head. "Tornadoes. Blizzards. Plagues. If anyone here wants to be responsible for their own family's death, be my guest. Just say the fucking word. And God be my witness, I'll personally pack that coward a fucking lunchbox with a treat inside for their trip back tomorrow."

Silence. Thick, suffocating silence.

"I said speak up now, you fucking traitor, or shut the fuck up all the way north!" Cooper yelled, slamming his fist on the table.

"I . . ." the man in the wool sweater stuttered after a long pause.

Terror flickered across his face. "I'll head back tomorrow." His hand rose hesitantly as if he were a kid in school. "A-anybody else?"

Nothing. Not even Ava moved.

Brave little girl. As a runaway, she'd probably already survived another kind of hell before getting into this one.

"I'll go north with you," Erickson was the first to declare.

Our eyes met. Of course he'd be the hero. The man who saved the world. Maybe he had a wife or kid out there—someone to fight for.

"Me too," I said.

What the hell did I have to lose? At least I'd finally find out what happened to my sister. Maybe she'd died quickly—a clean cut to the throat on some stone altar, her body buried deep in the dirt.

"I didn't suffer through Dawson's farts all night just to die like a bitch now," Jansen muttered.

Dawson shot him a glare. "It was the beans, asshole."

They must have known each other from previous missions—the way they joked, even with death breathing down our necks.

Carter let out a shaky breath. "I have two kids out there. I'm in."

Jansen shrugged, gripping his rifle. "Might as well see how this shitshow ends. Dying by a shield maiden's hand—kinda kinky. And I like kinky."

Collins cracked his knuckles and shook his head. "Hell, I didn't survive my divorce to run from another witch. Let's finish this."

"This is insane," muttered the woman with mud on her face. Then she sighed. "But I'll go too. My mom is out there. She takes care of my sick brother. She doesn't need more shit to deal with."

I turned to Ava, who sat there silently sobbing, tears rolling down her face.

"Can she stay here?" I asked Sigvarðr.

He leaned forward, his massive hands pressing against the table. "She is safe here," Sigvarðr said. "Had a few daughters of my own back then." A flicker of sadness crossed his face, and then it was gone. He turned to the woman with mud smeared across her face and grinned. "You can stay too if you like. You have nothing to fear from me. My goddess watches over this home. Nothing will happen against your will." He bowed slightly. "But I must ask, what do they call such a striking woman?"

The woman's cheeks flushed beneath the dirt, and a corner of her lip curved in the beginnings of a smile. "Erin."

Sigvarðr repeated it, rolling the name over his tongue like a prayer. "Erin." He nodded. "A fine name."

Cooper frowned. "She's coming with us."

Sigvarðr's smile vanished. He rose to his full height, easily a head taller than Cooper, who himself was over six feet.

"Erin shall do as she pleases," he growled.

Erin's grin widened.

"Of course she will do as she pleases," Erickson cut in, throwing Cooper a sharp look.

Cooper's jaw clenched as he appeared to bite back a string of curses, but he stayed silent.

Sigvarðr gave a nod and settled back into his seat. "With or without the woman, it matters not," he said. "You're too weak to kill Yrsa and too few to be her sacrifice." He nodded at the man in the wool sweater, who fumbled with his sleeve, avoiding everyone's gaze. "Even with the coward, Yrsa the Cruel demands the blood of nine for her sacrifices. A sacred number to our gods."

"But we are nine," Dawson said. "Even without the woman and the girl."

I counted too: Erickson, Jansen, Martinez, Carter, Dawson, Cooper, Collins, the man in the wool sweater, and me.

Nine.

Sigvarðr's gaze flicked toward me. "She counts not."

Every pair of eyes in the room turned to him, then me.

Grinning, Sigvarðr reached across the table to fill Erin's cup. She met his grin with an even brighter smile.

"What do you mean?" Cooper asked.

Sigvarðr nodded toward me. "She's from this land. Is she not?"

A cold bolt shot through my spine. He knew. He fucking knew I was half-Pequawket.

"Wager." Cooper's voice was sharp. "What does he mean you're from this land? Last time I checked your file, you were just as much white trash as I am."

I struggled to find a response.

"Wager," he repeated, more firmly this time. "Explain."

"I'm not Wager." The words slipped out before I could stop them.

Cooper exhaled. "No shit."

My head jerked back. "You . . . knew?"

Cooper scoffed. "The moment you huffed and puffed your ass up that trail on day one. But the fucking CIA was all over this mission. You're one of them, aren't you?"

I shook my head. "I'm . . . a civilian. A vet student. My sister was kidnapped for your cargo shipments two years ago."

I left out the part about how the real Wager had approached me, how she'd gotten me in. What did it matter now? Most likely, we would all die anyway.

A sarcastic snort escaped Cooper. "Let me get this straight. You're a lying Native vet student who hijacked a top-secret mission, impersonated an Army Ranger sniper, shot a bunch of wolves, and killed some huldra bitch trying to murder us . . . all to find your missing sister?"

I nodded. "Ex-vet student," I corrected.

Ava and Erin exchanged glances with me, their eyes soft. Understanding. Like I was one of them now.

Disbelief flickered across Cooper's face before he turned to Sigvarðr as if none of this mattered anymore—as if everything was just another problem to solve, and he would get it fucking done.

"So why the hell does a lying Native civilian looking for her sister not count as a sacrifice?"

"Because her people have been living on this land for thousands of years, at one with its trees and its spirits," Erickson cut in. "And we haven't. This isn't our land. At least, not according to this forest."

Cooper's gaze met mine.

"And I assume Yrsa the Cruel didn't live in peace with the Native tribes. She didn't suddenly turn into Yrsa the Saint of the

Pequawket, did she?" Erickson added. "She had no choice but to leave them be or risk angering the land she was bound to by rituals—a bond that ran deeper than blood."

Sigvarðr's grin widened. "I see now why you bear the Raido upon your hands, tracker." He nodded in approval. "I do not know for certain, but I think Yrsa's bond with the land here is weak. Harder to control than in Noregr, our homeland, where our gods have lived and ruled since the very first winter. It seems the people of this land may be resistant to her magic, blessed by the forest itself."

Erickson appeared to process this.

Then came the shift. His posture straightened. His eyes sharpened.

"The swimming hole," he said.

A knot tightened in my stomach as the memory flashed—blood splattering across my face, the gunshot echoing into the sky.

"The huldra," Erickson said. "Esther, you were the only one she couldn't lure into her trap."

Sigvarðr studied me. "Your sister, was she by blood?"

I nodded.

Cooper's voice remained steady. "If that's the case, then two years ago, the witch might've accidentally sacrificed a Native among the cargo. And that could've pissed this place off, yeah?" He leaned forward. "But the real question now is—how do we use that? Turn her mistake into our advantage."

The room blurred. A cold ringing filled my ears.

My sister was dead.

I pushed up from my chair too quickly. The ground swayed.

The wooden door swung open under my weight, and I stumbled into the night. Its cool air splashed me like water. For the first time in weeks, the sky was clear. The stars shone down like they had been waiting for this very moment—my misery—to reveal themselves.

I stumbled past the garden, where the goats' white fur almost glowed under the moonlight. My boots sank into the damp earth. Each step pulled me closer to the forest.

What did it all fucking matter now?

Let the world burn to the ground.

It had given my family nothing but storms and silence. Now, I was ready to leave this shithole behind.

Erickson's voice sailed through the night behind me. "Esther!"

I didn't stop. His words were blurred, distant.

"Esther, stop."

A rough grip yanked me back, and my body twisted as he spun me around.

"Let me go," I growled.

He didn't.

I shoved against him, my breath sharp. "Let me go!"

I was inches from his face, yelling, my fists clenched, ready to swing if I had to.

His grip tightened, and his eyes locked onto mine like he was really thinking about it—about granting my wish and letting me walk into the woods to get myself killed by wolves. For a second, I saw it in his eyes. That hesitation. That tiny doubt as to whether he had the right to stop me.

But then he exhaled sharply. "No."

"What?" I couldn't make my voice louder than a whisper.

"I said no."

"How dare—"

"There's still fight in you."

A bitter laugh tore out of me. "I'm not the strong woman you think I am."

"Oh, yeah?" His voice hardened. "A little late to make that claim after you ran straight into the pits of literal hell for someone most people wouldn't see as a human anymore."

My jaw clenched. "They aren't fucking human for treating people like my sister like this. Human trash."

"You're right. And those same people wouldn't have done what you did out here to find anybody—not even baby Jesus himself."

His hands finally dropped, but he didn't move.

"But go ahead," he said, his arms crossed. "If I'm wrong, then go. Walk into that forest. Let the wolves rip you apart or whatever the fuck else is out there. But I don't think you will."

Something cold stirred in my chest. "And why not?"

"Because, Esther, not only would you be throwing away our only chance to kill this witch and save lives, but you'd never find out what really happened to your sister."

I barely choked out a laugh. It burned. "I already know what happened to her."

Erickson just stood there, waiting.

"The fucked-up government sent her here to die," I spat. "A junkie whore in their eyes. Nothing more than disposable cargo."

"We don't know if she's dead."

My head jerked back. "What?"

"Sigvarðr knew you were Native the second he saw you. I did too. You think Yrsa the Cruel would be stupid enough to slaughter a Native after centuries of keeping peace with them?"

His words churned my insides. I wanted to believe them. God, I wanted to. But hope was a freaking trap. At least knowing she was dead meant closure.

"At the very least," Erickson said, "make that bitch fucking pay."

My fingers twitched.

"Die standing like your people always have. No matter how much they endured, they never crawled like animals."

I exhaled, shaking my head. "Maybe my people are fucking tired now."

His stare burned through me. "Nah. Not you."

I was. I was so goddamn tired.

Then a haunting voice from the past filled my head like a storm.

"You came back," I'd gasped, my words swallowed by thick smoke as the fire devoured our home, our family.

"Of course I did!" Jasmine had wheezed, barely holding onto breath.

I scrubbed a hand down my face. "Why the hell are you doing this?" I asked Erickson. "Why are you kind to me?"

Erickson's lips curled into a half-smirk. "Kind." He said the word as if it were the most ridiculous thing anybody had ever said to him. "I'm not kind. You remind me of someone. The only other person I've ever known who would have done what you did to save a person they cared about."

I narrowed my eyes. "Some badass Chuck Norris Navy SEAL?"

His grin barely held. "Nah. My grandmother."

A dry chuckle scraped its way up my throat. "Your grandmother?"

"What? She was a hell of a woman."

"She must have been, putting up with you."

His smile widened, then vanished. "I have a son out there." His voice dipped lower. "If this witch really decides to send a plague . . ."

He didn't need to finish. I knew exactly what he meant.

I swallowed. "So what now?"

Erickson sighed, rubbing the tension from his jaw. "We'll listen to Cooper's fragile male ego in that Viking hut, get some fucking rest, and tomorrow, we come up with a plan."

I gave him a sharp nod.

He turned to leave but paused when I didn't follow.

"That man you killed," I said. "The teacher." I shouldn't have been bringing this up, but I needed to know before I threw my life into this man's hands. "It was for your son, wasn't it?"

Erickson's stare burned into mine. Something unreadable flickered behind it. Then he nodded. A long beat of silence followed.

"We'll sleep in the barn," he said. "We have no choice but to stay. But that doesn't mean we trust our host."

Then he turned and walked back.

I stared up at the stars. Their glow was almost mocking.

For the first time, hope felt heavier than grief.

What if I made it to the witch, and my sister was dead after all?

What if all of this was for nothing?

But then what choice did I have?

Erickson was right.

I would get revenge.

I wouldn't crawl into the dark like a coward.

I'd stand tall. Fight back. And if I had to, I'd die on my fucking feet.

Flames clawed up the walls, devouring everything, turning my home to ash. The fire's heat rolled over me in suffocating waves as smoke choked the sky—thick, unrelenting, searing its way into my lungs.

I couldn't breathe. I couldn't move.

But this time, I realized I wasn't inside my childhood home.

I was standing in front of it, watching it burn.

A sound rose from the fire—not a scream, not the tortured groan of collapsing wood, but something else. Low at first, barely audible beneath the roar of the fire. Then the melody rose, deep, steady, unshaken by the destruction surrounding it. This was different. My nightmares of the past had never included this voice.

And I knew that voice.

My father's.

His melody flowed like a river, steady and strong, weaving through the chaos.

A loud thunderclap vibrated through my body as a white fox stepped out of the flames. It moved slowly, deliberately, its fur untouched by the fire licking at its legs. Golden eyes locked onto mine. Watching. Unwavering.

Something cold grazed my cheek, and my hand shot up. It was rain. A single drop. Then another.

Then the sky ripped open, and a mighty storm crashed down. The rain hammered my skin, soaked my hair, and slammed against the earth like war drums. The wind tore through the trees, bending them to their breaking point. The chanting grew louder. So did the storm. Like a retreating army, the fire shrank beneath the down-pour. The scene before me transformed into a merciless battle of the elements—water against fire, my world caught between destruction and salvation.

Just as the flames seemed to retreat, a gust of wind slammed into me. It knocked me back violently—and I woke up.

23

Ryder

I'd been up most of the night, drifting in and out of a light, restless sleep—never fully under, always on alert.

Esther lay beside me, twitching in the straw, curled up near a few resting goats. The barn smelled of damp wood, hay, and animals—the kind of scene ripped straight from a medieval film. Except this wasn't a movie, and we weren't supposed to be here.

Echo and the civilians had insisted on sleeping inside. Even Ava had refused to change her mind, no matter how hard Esther tried to convince her.

I heard a sudden sharp inhale, and Esther shot up. Her chest rose and fell as panic flashed across her face. It was a look I knew all too well.

"That's why I usually don't sleep," I muttered.

She pressed a hand to her forehead, still catching her breath. "I usually don't either." Glancing around as if she were piecing reality back together, she let out a shaky sigh. "I was hoping this was all just a nightmare. How long have I been out?"

"A few hours."

Footsteps. Dawson approached, carrying a chunk of bread and a small clay mug. He handed them to me.

I sniffed the mug. Goat's milk. I passed both to Esther, who ate and drank eagerly.

"Cooper wants you inside for a mission debrief," Dawson said.

I didn't answer.

He nodded like he expected that. "Right. See you soon," he said before heading back into the hut.

Esther wiped her mouth with the back of her hand. "Anything happen while I was out?"

"A bunch of piss breaks by Echo." I stretched, rolling the tension from my shoulders. "Sigvarðr walked the clearing with a burning juniper branch. Other than that, the forest was quiet."

She slowed her chewing. "Too quiet?"

I nodded.

Her fingers tightened around the piece of bread. "What do you think about all this?"

"I think we need to kill Yrsa the Cruel. No matter the cost."

"So you believe the man in the hut?"

I met her gaze. "I do."

She held my gaze for a moment, then nodded.

We finished the food in silence before heading inside.

The heavy scent of burning juniper hit us the second we stepped into the hut. From the corner, Jensen sneezed loudly and rubbed his bloodshot eyes. "I'm allergic to this shit," he muttered, cursing under his breath.

"Stop bitching," Cooper growled.

I scanned the room. Sigvarðr and the civilian woman, Erin, were missing. The rest of Echo and the civilians were scattered around, looking strangely at ease—no weapons in their hands. However, the weight of the situation sat heavy on every face. No one needed to say it. The truth was tattooed across their foreheads.

Esther took a seat beside Ava, who sat cross-legged against the wooden wall. An owl was perched on her forearm.

"You okay?" Esther asked softly.

Ava nodded, her eyes full of quiet fascination. "Sigvarðr has three owls," she murmured, stroking the soft feathers with delicate fingers.

The bird's chest rose and fell with a steady rhythm as Esther brushed its feathers.

"He gave me this too," Ava said, pulling a thin leather cord from beneath her shirt. From it dangled a wooden amulet with a single rune carved deeply into its surface. *Eiwaz (ᛇ).* The symbol of resilience, endurance, and strength to endure suffering. "He said the gods are watching me. That they see my strength. I like him." Her voice was barely audible. "I think . . . I'll stay here if that's okay. Until you come back."

"Of course," Esther said.

A heavy wooden door creaked open. Sigvarðr stepped out from behind it, adjusting his pants. A moment later, Erin followed, avoiding everyone's gaze.

"You've got to be fucking kidding me," Jensen muttered.

Every pair of eyes locked onto them as the Viking and Erin exchanged grins.

"Unbelievable," Cooper bit out, his expression tight.

Esther moved beside me, lowering her voice. "Six feet seven inches of pure Viking muscle with good manners? That"—she nodded at them—"might be the only thing that makes sense out here."

Cooper shot her a sharp look. "All right, listen up," he said, pulling the room's attention to him. "Now that we're all here." His gaze flicked to Sigvarðr, who took a seat at the table and nonchalantly assembled a plate of food. He set it in front of Erin and watched as she took a bite of bread and then a piece of what looked like goat cheese.

Cooper exhaled, pressing his hands onto his hips. "Well. As you know, we're heading to the northern hut today—our third stop—which is not far from our final coordinates. Coordinates that apparently lead us to some kind of Norse witch."

Silence.

"We'll spend the night at the hut," he continued, "then move on at first light. We can't risk getting caught in the woods at nightfall."

"I shall lead you to the northern hut," Sigvarðr muttered between bites. "After that, your path is your own. I cannot draw close to Yrsa. It is too dangerous. She will do all in her power to break free of me . . . and the bond that binds us and traps her here with me."

Cooper met his gaze and gave him a firm nod. "We appreciate that."

Sigvarðr returned the curt nod, then took another bite of bread.

"So what exactly are we doing when we find this witch?" Dawson asked.

"Yeah, are we just walking in and offering ourselves up?" scoffed the man in the wool sweater. He was close to a breakdown, no doubt. "For some crazy demon ceremony or something? Cannibalism maybe? Sex orgies with the devil?"

The look Cooper shot him was so sharp that the man shut up instantly. "We won't just let her kill us," he said. "But we're also not storming her turf with guns blazing. According to Sigvarðr, that would be suicide."

"Já," Sigvarðr agreed. "She can sense your presence from fifty paces away. Your weapons won't work. You'll be dead before you even lay eyes on her."

"So what's the plan then?" Martinez asked.

"We play along," Cooper said. "We tell her the cargo was lost. That we'll take its place."

Dawson frowned. "And that will do what exactly?"

"Buy us time," Cooper said. "Enough to get close. I assume she'll have some kind of ritual before she makes those human sacrifices. That's when we strike. All at once. Distract her." He let the words settle before finishing. "So Esther can kill her."

His gaze slid toward her. Every eye in the room followed.

"M-me?" Esther's voice wavered.

"Yes," Cooper said. "We've already seen that Norse magic doesn't affect you—like back at the swim hole with the huldra. This seer lived in peace with the Native people of this land, which is rare for Vikings. They typically conquer and raid. I think Erickson and Sigvarðr are right. She stayed peaceful because she had no choice but to leave the people of this land alone. So, if anyone has a chance at killing the witch, it's you."

Dawson voiced what everyone was thinking. "But how? She's not even a real soldier."

Every eye turned back to Esther.

"How well can you shoot?" Cooper pressed.

Her lips parted, then closed, and she shook her head.

"Fucking hell," Martinez muttered.

"What about close combat?" Collins asked.

Esther's gaze shifted downward. She shook her head again.

Low murmurs spread among Echo.

Sigvarðr's chair scraped against the wooden floor. The harsh sound sliced through the tense air as the giant rose.

A few massive strides brought him to Esther's side. She backed up, step by step, until the wall met her spine, cutting off any escape. He loomed over her—three heads taller, a wall of muscle, his shadow swallowing her whole.

His voice rumbled low. "To kill Yrsa, you must carve out her heart. Or cut off her head." He reached above Esther to grab a sword from the wall. The weapon hung beside an axe and a shield. Its steel gleamed in the light from the fire. Sigvarðr pressed the massive blade into her hands.

She wrapped her fingers around the hilt, her grip tightening—but the weight dragged her down. Her shoulder dipped, and she almost fell over under the sheer force of the weapon.

Sigvarðr stepped aside, clearing her path. "Swing it."

Silence.

"Swing it, woman," he repeated.

Esther sucked in a sharp breath and hauled the sword up, her muscles straining under its weight. The blade wobbled, unsteady in her grip, before crashing down with a heavy *clang*. Its tip bit deep into the wooden floor. Her breath was fast and ragged as her fingers slipped against the hilt to yank it free. The wood groaned, resisting, until the blade finally tore loose with a violent jolt—ripping her balance with it. Esther staggered, her feet scrambling for control, but the weight dragged her down. With a sharp gasp, she hit the ground hard.

"Shit," Dawson muttered.

"We're all dead," Collins added.

Sigvarðr studied her, unimpressed. Then his gaze shifted to Cooper. "How long have your women forgotten war? It was our way to gift them a sword and shield on their wedding day so they could die in battle at our side.

Esther lifted her chin, eyes blazing. "Some of our men decided we should fight wrinkles in their pants instead of our enemies. Soothe their fragile egos by oppressing us rather than die by their side."

Sigvarðr held her stare and gave her a slow, understanding nod. "Then they've chosen the fate that awaits them." He took the sword back from her, hefting it with ease. "This won't do, woman."

Defeat filled the room, marking every face like the silence after a lost battle.

Then Esther straightened.

Slow. Deliberate. Chin high. Her eyes locked onto the mighty Viking as if she were David facing Goliath.

"We might have been robbed of our swords, shields, and voices for a long time," Esther said, stepping in close, "but that only taught us to fight with this." She tapped a finger against her temple before slipping a hand into her side pocket and drawing her military knife in one fluid motion. Firelight caught the blade as she held the tip just below Sigvarðr's jaw.

Esther's voice was low and steady. "The carotid artery." Her gaze stayed locked on his as she shifted the knife, its tip hovering just over the artery. "One small cut and you're out in seconds—bleeding out like a slaughtered pig." Slowly, she pointed the knife lower at the inside of his thickly muscled thigh. "The femoral artery. Biggest in the leg. A tiny stab right here, and you'll pass out. No time to fight. No time to run. No swinging sword. That bitch will be dead within seconds. If you know where to cut. Which I do."

Sigvarðr didn't move. Didn't blink. That unreadable, ice-blue stare stayed fixed on Esther, as if daring her to prove it.

A grin pulled at my lips.

This woman . . . she was something else.

Esther stepped back. Her gaze swept over the rest of us before she arched a brow. "So are we going to kill that witch and save the world or just stand around wasting time?" she asked. "Because if you're out, speak up now, and I'll pack you a nice little lunch for the long, sorry trip home. No gold star. No parade. Just you tucking tail and running."

Even Cooper grinned. Respect flickered in his expression.

Sigvarðr's deep, rumbling laugh shattered the silence. His massive hand came down on Esther's back in what could have been a gesture of brotherhood—if it hadn't nearly sent her sprawling. She coughed, stumbling forward.

"So it's decided," he said. "Eat. Drink. Then meet me outside." He turned to Cooper, and something darker flashed behind his eyes. "The woman Erin and the girl will stay."

Cooper didn't protest.

"And wash yourselves," Sigvarðr added, glancing over the rest of us.

Jensen frowned. "To cleanse our spirits or something?"

"No. You smell," Sigvarðr said flatly. "The witch will sense your odor from a hundred strides away."

Without another word, he walked out the front door.

We ate, drank, and cleaned up as best we could before gathering around the stone firepit outside. The pit sat at the heart of the clearing. It was a solid ring of blackened stones carved with deep runes. Smoke curled high into the cloudy sky. The sharp scent of burning juniper mixed with the damp chill of the forest.

Sigvarðr stood before the flames, whose light flickered across his scarred face. He kept his massive shield and iron-forged sword lifted high over the rising smoke as he spoke. His deep voice rolled through the clearing like an oath sealed in the ancient ways.

"Freyja, great goddess of war and life, may you take the worthy of us to your great hall. May Sessrúmnir open its doors, and may the battle-scarred find peace in your embrace. If we fall, let it be with axe in hand and fire in our hearts so we do not arrive empty-handed at the gates of Fólkvangr."

Lowering his weapons, he swept his gaze across Echo's ranks before waving them forward. "Come. Bless your weapons."

Hesitation rippled through the group. Jensen stepped forward first, gripping his M4 like it didn't belong in a ceremony meant for blades, shields, and iron forged by hand. He lifted it hesitantly, shifting his stance before mumbling, "Why are you telling Freyja to take us? I thought great warriors go to Valhalla."

Sigvarðr cast his eyes to the gray morning sky. "Dying with a blade in hand and feasting in Valhǫll is one of the highest honors the gods ever bestowed on a man. Odin's hall is full of warriors, drinking deep and boasting of battles long past. But they'll take up arms again when Ragnarǫk is upon us. And I've spilled enough blood to fill many tales. Freyja takes half of the bravest warriors to her great hall, Sessrúmnir. And she keeps company with strong women." A grin tugged at his scarred mouth. "I want to wake with a woman's thighs wrapped around my hard cock, not sit shoulder to shoulder with men in Valhǫll." He chuckled, low and rough, like rocks grinding in his chest. "I'd die a thousand deaths to open my eyes in Sessrúmnir—ale in one hand, a woman in the other." He shrugged, slow and careless. "As for you—go wherever the fuck you please.

Laughter rippled through the group. "No shield-maiden wants to be wrapped around Jensen's little toothpick," Dawson said.

"Oh, shut up," Jensen shot back, raising his M4 toward the fire. "Those maidens are gonna be all over this American steel."

Not all members of Echo participated in the weapon blessing ritual. Some murmured prayers to God instead. Nevertheless, most weapons passed through the smoke. Grips were tightened, and minds were sharpened for the battle ahead. Whatever gods were listening tonight, Echo would take any protection they could get.

I stepped forward and held first my M4 and then my knife over the smoke. Sigvarðr's gaze flicked to mine before I closed my eyes.

Grandma, has the mighty tree Yggdrasil not spoken to you? I haven't heard a whisper since I entered this forest. As if Yrsa has silenced you to doom us all.

No answer. Not even the wind stirring the branches.

I pushed the worry down and opened my eyes. The warmth of the flames licked at the steel. Juniper embers sent tiny sparks into the air. This wasn't just a ritual—it was an ancient form of blessing, one that warriors had observed for thousands of years.

Turning, I caught Esther watching from a few feet away. Her expression was unreadable in the firelight. I held out a hand. "Give me your knife."

She hesitated, then started to place it in my palm—but I stopped her. Instead, I wrapped my fingers around hers and guided her hand over the smoke. The knife was still in her grip.

She didn't flinch at the heat above the flames, just watched me, her stare steady. The rising smoke curled around our hands, the embers drifting like restless ghosts. Her gaze flicked back to mine.

"Do you want to say anything? A prayer of your people?" I asked.

Her lips parted, then pressed into a thin line. Not fear, not hesitation—something else. Something deeper. A sadness settled in her bones.

"I don't remember." Her voice barely broke above a whisper. "It's been bred out of me. My father's words. My people's voice."

I tightened my grip around her hand. "Impossible. It's who you are. It's still in there."

The fire crackled between us. The scent of juniper was thick in the cold air.

"It's still in there," I repeated.

Letting go of her hand, I stepped back as the fire carried the smoke into the sky. Esther had been stripped of her past, her people, her traditions. But the fire still knew her. The smoke still carried her name. So did the trees and earth of this land.

Tonight, I would burn more juniper and call to my grandmother and the holy tree, *Yggdrasil.* And maybe, just maybe, the trees in this cursed forest would finally answer.

24

Esther

We marched through the woods in silence as Sigvarðr led us along a narrow deer path. Every so often, he would stop at a tree or rock carved with ancient runes and murmur something under his breath. Stick figures hung from branches, swaying slightly in the cold air. Small shrines made of moss-covered stones and charred firepits lined the path like echoes of a forgotten faith.

It felt like Sigvarðr had spent centuries weaving protection into this place, carving out a Norse safe zone in the middle of a death trap. As far as I was concerned, this whole place reeked of myth and doom.

Tension coiled tightly in every step. Half a day passed before we got a pee break—more like a prison walk than a real stop.

"Jensen, go with Esther," Cooper ordered, splitting us into pairs. "Don't go far. Just behind the closest trees."

I moved with Jensen behind a large oak. He turned and strode a few steps into the woods, giving me space.

"Not in a million years did I think I'd die in some Norse spin on *The Blair Witch Project*," he muttered, scanning the forest.

Relief hit as I squatted down. "My life was already shot to hell before this," I countered. "Now I just need to find my sister, or whatever's left of her, and kill the witch so I can bring my sister home and bury her next to my parents."

"Man . . . that's fucked up. Sorry."

"It's all good. Life's a—"

"Oh, shit! Look!" Jensen's voice cracked with excitement.

My body tensed, and I yanked my pants up. "What?"

"Look! It's a squirrel!"

A breath hissed through my teeth. "Jesus. You're fucking kidding me? I thought some man-eating monster was about to rip our faces off."

"Esther, come *quick*!"

I fastened my pants and strode over, rolling my eyes—until I saw it. A bright red squirrel perched on a low branch, its huge ears twitching at every sound. Its eyes gleamed strangely, reflecting the dim light. Without warning, it flipped backward, landed cleanly, and stared right at us.

I chuckled as the squirrel did it again. Then again—this time, with a twisting somersault.

Jensen crouched and stretched out his hand as if he had food. "He's coming closer. Let's catch him."

I smiled. The little thing moved with unnatural grace, spinning and leaping like a performer in some twisted woodland circus. We were drawn to it as if under a spell, a fleeting spark of joy in this godforsaken place.

It hopped closer. Almost within reach.

But then the bush beside us crackled, and a white blur lunged forward.

The white fox!

It sprang after the squirrel, jaws snapping shut just as the squirrel darted out of reach. The animals twisted and spun through the underbrush in a frenzied chase. A high-pitched screech cut through the air before both creatures disappeared into the trees.

"Shit," Jensen cursed. "Damn fox."

We turned to look back to the path—but something was wrong. The oak I had just peed behind was suddenly much *farther away*. The whole landscape had shifted as if the forest itself had nudged us along with the squirrel.

Jensen's worried gaze found mine.

"If you two are done *wasting our damn time*, feel free to join us again!" Cooper's voice rang out from the path.

Jensen hesitated. "Should we go after it? It kinda made me feel really good."

"Hell no. We need to be more careful." We marched back to the group.

"Of *a squirrel?*"

"Yeah. Of freaking *everything* out here." My gaze flicked to the trees, where I caught a glimpse of white fur slipping through the shadows.

When we stepped onto the path, Erickson and Sigvarðr were waiting.

"Dude, we just saw the craziest shit." Jensen grinned. "Some squirrel was doing Cirque du Soleil flips for us."

Sigvarðr's expression darkened. "Don't fall for its tricks again."

"Why?" Jensen shrugged. "It was just a squirrel."

"That was *Ratatoskr.*" Sigvarðr's voice was deep, like a warning carved in stone. "Hark, fools and wanderers. Keep your distance from the trickster beast that scurries upon Yggdrasil's sacred boughs. That wretched thing weaves mischief, whispering falsehoods and fanning the flames of discord. Even the gods do not understand its tricks."

"Mm . . . okay," Jensen mumbled.

My eyes drifted back to the trees. White fur flickered between the branches, then vanished. "Woh-lee-oh-nee," I said before I had time to think.

The meaning of the words suddenly hit me—I had just thanked the fox in my people's language. I didn't know how I'd remembered that, but I could only hope that the fox had been listening.

25

Esther

We reached the third hut just as night swallowed the forest. Although this was the shortest march yet, time seemed to have passed the fastest today.

The hut sat in a clearing, just like the others. It was a small wooden structure no bigger than a hunting cabin, surrounded by the same ancient runes carved into stone. Sigvarðr stopped at the edge of the clearing and studied the runes like he was reading a message on their weathered surfaces.

"It's late," he muttered. "I will return to my hut with the morning light."

He pulled a massive horn from his back and blew. The deep, haunting sound rippled through the trees, vibrating in my chest.

A warning.

It was getting dark. The beast would be on the hunt.

Inside the hut, Sigvarðr had started a fire whose flames threw flickering shadows against the wooden walls. The place smelled of old wood and smoke. Dust clung to every surface. A pile of rusting ammunition sat in the corner next to a few grenades. The walls were lined with black-and-white photographs—soldiers through the ages, staring back with hollow eyes. Some wore uniforms from the Civil War.

"How long . . . have we been doing this?" I asked, my shocked gaze turning to Sigvarðr. "Feeding humans to Yrsa to keep her quiet."

His gaze darkened. "For a long time."

We sat on whatever we could find—wooden crates, the floor—or leaned against the walls. Sigvarðr settled near the fire where, with his heavy drinking horn resting on his knee, he tore into dried meat with sharp teeth. The rest of us picked at cans of food salvaged from the supplies. Beans, old energy bars, and whatever we had left. No one spoke much. Exhaustion had set in, along with the creeping unease that had followed us since the last hut.

My gaze settled on Sigvarðr. He seemed . . . tired. Maybe it was the realization the pictures brought—the weight of how long he had been trapped here. Alone.

I knew that feeling.

I had been alone ever since my sister went missing. Two years of hell.

But to live like this for lifetimes . . .

"It must have been very . . . *hard* for you," I said, taking a seat next to him.

At first, he ignored me and just drank deeply. The liquid ran down his beard before he wiped it away with the back of his hand.

Finally, he spoke. "If you slay Yrsa and break my chains, my sword and shield are yours until my last breath. I am Sigvarðr Þorsteinsson of Eystribyggð, son of Þorsteinn the Iron-Headed. They call me Fjallgarðr, the Mountain Guardian, and by that name, I swear this vow is true."

I swallowed a bite of cold beans. "If we die, what will you do with Erin and Ava?"

He didn't look up, just took another bite before answering. "I shall lead them out of this forest if that is their wish."

The civilian in the wool sweater looked up. "That was a fucking *option?*" His voice snapped with anger.

"Not for you, it wasn't," Cooper cut in sharply, barely looking up from his food. "We need *nine* people to present to the witch. I won't risk this mission or a *natural disaster* killing my family because of you, *coward*."

The man's jaw clenched, but he didn't argue. Not with the death stare in Cooper's eyes.

I looked over at Erickson, who stared into the flames, deep in thought. The fire popped, sending embers drifting toward the chimney. Outside, the forest had gone silent. Even the wind had stilled.

Something shifted in my gut. It was the same creeping feeling I'd had when we first entered these woods, when we stepped past the runes.

"Um, guys," called out Dawson, who was standing guard by the window.

We all tensed.

"Why the hell is there some huge ass man standing past the fucking Viking protection stones?"

The cold weight of panic dropped into my stomach. We rushed over to the two windows that looked out over the grassy clearing. A figure loomed in the darkness just beyond the boundary stones, its dark shape barely visible. Eight feet tall, maybe more. Thick and broad, built like a mutated football player but *wrong*—too bulky, too dense, its body almost fused with the night itself.

Erickson stood next to me, his eyes locked on the thing.

"I thought the stones with symbols protected this area," Cooper said.

"They do," Sigvarðr countered.

"Then how the hell did *that* get past them?" Jensen shouted.

"Because," Erickson said, his eyes locking onto Sigvarðr's, "that stone thing isn't Norse."

Sigvarðr pushed past me and grabbed his sword and shield from the floor just as a low, grinding sound rumbled through the trees like stone scraping against stone.

"Run north!" Sigvarðr growled before wrenching the door open and vanishing into the night.

Then the night exploded.

The first giant tore through the wall as if it were paper, slamming into the hut with bone-rattling force. Wood splintered, and shards flew through the air.

Gunfire erupted. Someone screamed.

I spun and fired at the massive thing. The bullets barely left a mark against its thick, stone-like skin. The rounds ricocheted off like we were shooting at a goddamn boulder.

"Grab the grenades and blow them up outside!" Cooper yelled.

The hut turned to chaos. People scrambled for the exit as the thing lunged forward. Its hand closed around Collins.

His scream barely left his throat before two massive hands closed around his head.

CRACK.

His skull burst like a crushed melon.

Then the giant turned to me. Its black eyes narrowed before it let out an ear-splitting growl.

Before it could lunge, the unmistakable metallic *click* of a grenade pin cut through the chaos.

Erickson yanked me hard, hurling me over a wooden table before flipping it and shoving me behind it, using his body to cover mine. The explosion erupted. Stone shattered. Glass rained down, slicing through the air. A jagged piece shot through the table and buried itself in my leg like a bullet.

"Let's go!" Erickson barked, yanking me to my feet.

Instead of the door, he ran for the broken back window. With the butt of his M4, he smashed out the remaining glass and shoved me through. We landed hard, then bolted for the forest.

Behind us, Sigvarðr's roar split the night. For a moment, I could picture him—swinging his sword and axe like a beast unleashed. A bloodcurdling scream from one of the creatures almost made me believe he had taken one down.

Dawson's voice tore through the dark. "GRENADE!"

"RUN FOR THE WOODS!" Cooper bellowed just before a wave of explosions lit up the night.

The darkness of the forest swallowed us. Darkness upon darkness. Nothing but shadows and trees under a thick, cloud-covered sky.

We sprinted. Boots pounded against the ground. Gunfire cracked. Roars rattled the trees. The giants were slower than us, but every step they took sent vibrations up my legs.

Erickson led us like a wolf with night vision. Suddenly, he pulled me down behind a fallen tree. My chest heaved, and my lungs burned.

Then a growl.

A massive shadow loomed over us.

We waited. Not even breathing.

Until it moved on.

Erickson had done it again. Saved my life in these cursed woods.

But there was no time for thanks. There was only time to run.

My heartbeat pounded in my ears. My vision blurred from exhaustion. But the giants weren't stopping. They crashed through the trees behind us, slower but relentless.

So we ran. Then we hid. Then we ran again. And hid once more.

Always one step ahead.

But for how long?

I couldn't keep this up. My legs trembled. It didn't take long until my foot snagged on a root. I hit the ground hard.

"Get up," Erickson ordered.

I pushed up, but the first giant burst from the dark tree line just feet away.

Then another.

And another.

Towering figures stepping closer. Growling. There was no way we could run again. We were trapped.

Erickson jumped in front of me, his fists clenched. Of course, he stood no chance. This would be over soon.

But just when I thought this was it, whispers tore through the canopy of trees high above us. Soft at first, curling through the air like wind in the branches. Then they grew louder. Words I didn't understand threaded through the trees, wrapping around the night like a net. The giants froze. And for a moment, the world stood still.

Then the giants seemed to make out the source of the whispers, and their mouths stretched into wide, shattering screams. It was a sound like stone cracking, something untamed from the inside out. Their heads jerked back and their mouths gaped beyond rage.

The wind started howling, growing louder and louder until the trees shook violently. A mighty storm erupted with rain slamming down in sheets. Thunder rolled through the forest like the growl of an unseen beast.

A woman's voice rose above the storm. Low. Guttural. Ancient. Norse?

The giants shrieked and swung their arms at something unseen. An enemy they couldn't touch.

I grabbed Erickson's hand reflexively and squeezed it tight. Maybe because I didn't want to die alone. Maybe just to feel something real.

A massive branch cracked above us. My gaze shot up as it came crashing down.

Everything went still. There was only darkness.

26

Esther

I woke up sprawled on a wooden bed in a small hut. The air was damp and thick with the scent of old wood and something herbal. A slow pulse throbbed in my head.

I shot upright.

The wound on my leg—gone. Completely. Like it had never been there.

Light from a stormy sky seeped through a narrow window. It cast long, shifting shadows across the rough walls.

A shape stirred in the corner.

My hand shot to my side pocket, where my fingers curled around the knife. I yanked it free, heart pounding as I pointed it at the dark corner of the room.

Suddenly, the darkness itself seemed to shift.

A figure.

My pulse continued to hammer, loud and erratic, in my ears.

"Erickson!" I shouted.

The figure moved. It was hunched and shrouded in a long, flowing gown. The way it stood—its shoulders bowed, its head tilted at an unnatural angle beneath the fabric—almost made it look like the Virgin Mary from a prayer card. But then I saw its eyes. Ice-blue and staring. Its hand lifted, gripping the scarf wrapped around its mouth as if it were afraid to let me see what lay beneath.

"Erickson!" I called again.

The creature halted. Then, slowly, it stepped forward.

"Stop," I snapped, scrambling backward on the bed until my spine hit the wall. I turned to the old wooden door. I could make it. If I lunged now, if I got just one stab into this thing's throat—

"Esther."

The whisper barely reached me. It was more like a breath than a voice.

My grip tightened around the knife. "How do you know my name? Where is Erickson?"

The figure moved closer. Then, slowly, carefully, it lowered the scarf.

I wished it hadn't.

Its face was burned raw. The flesh had melted into dark, cracked leather. No clear features remained—only the grotesque suggestion of what was once human. A nose, barely more than two black holes. Lips—if they could even be called that—that were thin, dry, a ruin of scar tissue.

A sickening cold crawled up my spine as it reached toward me. Leathery fingers stretched through the dim air.

"Esther," it repeated.

No, not *it*.

She.

I froze.

That voice. It was a woman's voice. But not just any woman's.

And those eyes.

I couldn't breathe. The air vanished from my lungs as my fingers loosened around the knife.

The woman yanked the scarf back up and turned away. She bowed her head as if she were a servant waiting for punishment.

"J . . ." My voice broke. The knife slipped from my hand and hit the floor with a metallic clang.

"Jasmine?"

The woman flinched, then turned away from me. "She was right. It was too early—"

"Jasmine!"

The scream tore from my throat before I knew I was moving. I lunged forward, spun her around, and crushed her against me. My arms tightened around her frail body, squeezing so hard I must have knocked the wind out of her.

Sobbing, gasping, raw, pitiful tears. Joy, agony, terror, and some fragile, impossible flicker of hope overcame me.

"Maybe it's better if you don't look at me," Jasmine whispered, yanking the scarf over her face again.

I shook my head violently. "I don't care. You're alive!"

"No. Please," she begged, tightening her grip on the scarf covering her mouth and nose. But I caught her wrist, and my hand trembled as I slowly pulled it down, gently uncovering her face.

It hurt.

Like fire eating me from the inside out.

Like staring at something I could never unsee.

But . . . she was alive.

I swallowed hard, forcing my shaking hand to rest against her cheek. Her skin felt rough, leathery, unnatural. A brutal reminder of whatever hell she had been through.

And still, I smiled. Soft. Accepting.

"I look like a monster," Jasmine whispered, tears carving a path through the hardened ruin of her skin.

"No," I murmured. "You're my sister. I love you no matter what."

She shuddered, and then we clung to each other like we were the only two people left in the universe.

I buried the horror, the shock, the thousand things I wanted to scream. Right now, I had to be strong.

I had her back.

And I wasn't losing her again.

Then rage sparked inside my chest. It built fast, hot, like a match striking gasoline.

I grabbed Jasmine by the shoulders.

"Who did this to you? Was it Yrsa? The witch?"

Her gaze softened. She didn't answer.

That silence only fueled the fire. I snatched the knife from the floor, gripping it tight.

"Erickson," I said, voice sharp. "The man with the tattoos on his hands. We need to find him."

Jasmine still said nothing.

I rushed over to the window and pressed my back against the wall, then peeked outside. The view was straight into the woods.

"He'll help us kill her." The words left my lips in a murmur. My mind was already working, scanning the room for weapons.

A small wooden table sat against the wall. Food and mugs were scattered across its surface. Useless. But the plate—

I grabbed it and smashed it against the ground. Jagged shards spilled across the floor. I knelt and picked up the biggest one, testing the edge with my thumb. It would do.

"We might have to change plans and strike now. How long have I been out?" I turned, handing the shard to Jasmine.

She took the shard and held it between her fingers, then slowly set it back into my palm. She was calm and silent, with something unreadable in her eyes.

"What's wrong?" My voice faltered.

"Esther," she said gently. "Listen to me. Yrsa . . . she's not your enemy."

"Oh, God, no." I shoved away from her. "She's brainwashed you." My breath hitched. "She tortured you into submission, didn't she?"

"Esther—"

"Don't be scared of her," I said. "I know how to defeat her."

"Esther—"

"I can kill her. Then we can get the hell out of—"

"Esther!"

The way she said my name—sharp, commanding, full of the woman I used to know.

I froze.

For a second, I saw my sister in this woman's eyes again.

Proud. Unbreakable. She had never let anyone take that away from her. Not even at her worst.

And yet here she was now. This thing Yrsa had turned her into . . . some cult-like slave.

"I know it will take time to understand," she said softly.

"No." My head shook violently. "No! There is nothing to understand. Yrsa is a monster!"

Jasmine sighed. "You've been through a lot. It's only normal that you're afraid and confused. Yrsa said this would happen. And Yrsa is always right."

"Are you fucking joking? She kills people!"

"She saved you from the Gici Awas."

"You mean those rock giants?"

Jasmine nodded.

"What are they?"

"They're evil creatures. Old demons our people believed in. They crush anything in their path. Without Yrsa, you would be dead. She saved you at a great cost."

I shook my head. None of this made sense. Yrsa must have done terrible things to her. Tortured her. Broken her.

My head sank into my hands. Then, slowly, I looked up at my sister. I tried to keep it together, but the tears came, tracing warm paths down my cheeks as my hand reached for hers.

"Oh, Jasmine," I mumbled. Lost. Desperate. How could I fix this? Her real scars ran deeper than the burns on her skin. This wouldn't be fixed with an argument, not here. Not with a woman as stubborn as my sister.

I needed a plan.

The devastation of it all must have been written across my face, as Jasmine squeezed my hand.

"You need time. And more rest. Just like Yrsa said."

She guided me to the table. I noticed the food.

Bread. Cheese. Apples. Even soup.

I was starving. But I just stood there.

"The men who were with me . . ." My voice came out flat. I wouldn't sit. I wouldn't eat. Not until I got answers. "Are they—"

Jasmine shook her head.

The tight, crushing weight in my chest dropped. "Oh, thank God . . . Erickson." I gripped the backrest of the chair to steady myself. He was alive. At least for now.

My gaze found my sister's. Her blue eyes were sharp with distrust. She was watching me carefully, analyzing me.

I forced a breath, yanked the chair out, and sat.

"Yrsa is right," I said quickly. "I'm just tired. I need more rest."

Jasmine's expression softened.

I reached for the bread and cheese but hesitated.

A small giggle escaped her leathered lips. "It's good to see you haven't changed. Your trust issues are as strong as ever."

I stared at the bread in my hands.

"If she wanted you dead, do you really think she'd go through all the trouble of healing your leg and reuniting us just to poison your organically fair-trade sourced bread? I thought you were into that shit."

"I see your bad jokes are still going strong, huh?" I smiled. She was still in there. My sister. Somewhere.

I took a bite. Then another. Before I knew it, I was hogging down everything in reach, barely chewing before swallowing. The food tasted really good. Homemade and fresh.

Jasmine watched me, her lips curving into a soft smile. "I'll be back later tonight. Then you can meet Yrsa."

"Meet her?" The words tasted sour in my mouth.

She nodded with something close to pride. "She is the sun and the moon and everything that happens in between. I can't wait for you to see the truth."

I ignored her nonsense and grabbed her hand. "Where are you going? Please don't leave." I had spent two years thinking she was dead. I couldn't let her walk away now—not back to the monster who did this to her.

"I have to," she said gently, peeling my fingers away. "Yrsa gave me work to do."

She pulled me into a quick hug, her arms squeezing just long enough to leave a sting in my chest.

"I can't believe you did all this to find me," she whispered. "Crazy ho."

Then, just like that, she was gone, slipping through the door and shutting it behind her.

I sat there, chewing like an animal, gulping water from a mug, shoving down everything I could as fast as my body would let me.

We had made it out alive.

But something told me not for long.

My sister might have been brainwashed by Yrsa the "Amazing" —or whatever the hell she wanted to call her—but my money was on Sigvarðr. Yrsa wasn't banished to America when the Vikings first sailed here because she was Yrsa the Rainbow.

She was Yrsa the Cruel.

Too brutal even for Erik the Red, one of the bloodiest Vikings to ever live.

I needed to play along. Meet Yrsa. Find Erickson.

Seeing my sister hadn't changed my plan. If anything, the hatred burning inside me had grown hotter.

What she had done to my sister—to her body and soul—fueled the rage in my heart like a hurricane.

I would kill Yrsa.

Or die trying.

27

Ryder

The cave was little more than a deep hole in the ground, cramped and stifling. Cold, damp stone pressed in from all sides, and the air was heavy with the stench of rot, waste, and filth. The floor was slick with moisture, dirt, and urine that had pooled in the corners. A single opening at the top—barely wider than a shield and barred by rusted metal—let in a sliver of light. Water dripped from the ceiling, merging with the filth below.

"I wish she would just fucking kill us," groaned the man in the wool sweater as he walked over to the dark hole in the ground. "This is worse than death."

Jimmy.

That was his name. Introductions in a circle hadn't been a priority. Not when survival came first. Not when everything was dying in an endless nightmare.

It was crazy to think he had made it this far. That he was here, trapped with us.

When the man had finally come to himself, Cooper had asked his name, like Jimmy had somehow earned the right to have one.

A name meant you mattered.

A name meant you weren't just cargo to Cooper anymore.

"Dude, you just shit ten minutes ago," Dawson snapped at Jimmy.

"I get diarrhea when I'm nervous," Jimmy shot back, already unbuckling his belt.

The stench of shit and urine was about to get worse again, thanks to Jimmy. The disgusting football-sized hole in the corner was a reminder of how long we'd been stuck here.

Three days.

Food was tossed down the hole like we were animals, and we licked moisture from the stone walls just to stay alive.

The cold had settled deep into my bones, and the slick rock beneath me was wet and hard. My wrists ached from the iron shackles clamped around them. Everything about this screamed medieval dungeon.

Collins was dead, but somehow, the rest of Echo had made it out alive. And Jimmy. Thanks to Yrsa's storm, eight of us were left.

At some point, when the silence stretched too long and the damp rot of the place felt like it was pressing in from all sides, I tried to pray.

To Yggdrasil, the mighty tree. To my goddess. To the wind. The river. My grandmother. Anything that might still be listening. I asked if Esther was still alive. The thought that she might not be weighed heavily on me.

But there was no answer. It was as if the gods had turned their backs on this place. It felt both dead and alive at once, like nothing here was as it should be.

"So what the fuck now?" Carter spat, rubbing his raw, cracked wrists. Three days of fighting the shackles had left them torn and bleeding.

"We just gonna sit around here until she kills us?" Graves asked.

Cooper blinked up at the hole in the ceiling, his face unreadable. "We wait," he said.

"Wait for what?" Martinez grumbled.

A whisper cut through the still air. "Erickson—"

Our heads snapped up as a shadow passed over the hole. Moments later, Esther's face appeared.

She looked exhausted. But she was alive.

"Her," Cooper murmured as we scrambled to our feet, shackles clinking.

"You said you just wanted to see him, then we would leave," said a voice from above. A woman's voice. One I didn't recognize.

We'd seen nobody. Woken up in this cold, wet cave-prison, food tossed down. No explanations. No warnings.

"Are you hurt?" I asked.

Esther shook her head.

My shoulders loosened. The tension in my chest eased.

But there were only eight of us left now. And Yrsa the Cruel needed nine for the sacrifice.

"Collins is dead," I said carefully.

Esther nodded, seeming to understand exactly what I meant. I couldn't speak freely. Whoever was up there with her was listening. But Esther knew what I was saying. She knew she might be in danger too—that she could be the ninth.

"We have to go!" the woman's voice snapped. "If Yrsa—"

"Erickson is the only reason I'm still alive," Esther cut in. "Just give me a few seconds."

Cooper and I locked eyes.

The way Esther spoke to this woman—there was familiarity, something personal. It had to be her sister.

"I'll come back later," Esther said.

"No, you won't," her sister said. "We have to go now. If Yrsa gets mad . . ."

Esther met my gaze, then mouthed the words: *I will be back.*

"Esther!" I called out.

"We have to go now!" her sister insisted, pulling her from view. But Esther fought her way back into my sight.

"Use this," I said quickly, tapping my head. I mimicked the same gesture Esther had made back at the hut when she'd promised she didn't need a sword to kill Yrsa. *Just one cut to the right artery.* Hopefully, she would get the message. I was asking her to kill Yrsa if she got the chance.

She locked eyes with me, holding the moment just long enough for me to know she understood. A quick nod.

Then she was gone.

Silence swallowed the cave.

A rat scurried over my foot, then darted toward Jensen. He kicked at it lazily, sending it skittering back into the darkness.

"Let's hope she will—" he began, but Cooper cut in.

"No more talking," he ordered, his eyes locked on mine.

We had no idea who was up there. Who might be listening.

One by one, we sank back into our spots on the cold, wet cave floor.

Waiting for whatever the hell came next.

28

Esther

Jasmine's grip tightened around my wrist as she dragged me away from the pit. I twisted, resisting. Once we were several feet from the hole, the air shifted. The stench of feces and urine was still thick in my nose. My legs felt weak, but I forced myself to stand and glanced one last time at the pit carved into the ground. Iron bars stretched across its opening like a rusted dungeon gate.

We were in a clearing, wide and unnatural, as if the forest had been cut open and left to fester. A firepit sat at its center. Runes were etched into its stone edges, their deep carvings worn smooth with time.

Nine towering wooden poles jutted from the earth in a circle around the firepit. Their surfaces were scarred with blood and more runes. They reminded me of the pyres used to burn women accused of witchcraft, the kind you'd see in medieval paintings—tall and cruel.

With each step we put between us and the pit, my sister's grip around my wrist loosened. Finally, I twisted free.

"What is this place?"

She ignored me, leading me toward a narrow path at the edge of the clearing.

"Don't act like you didn't hear me," I growled.

She turned sharply, her expression tight, her eyes dark with warning. "We don't talk about it unless Yrsa brings it up."

Then she turned and walked down a small path in the woods. Norse runes were carved into trees and rocks.

"Yeah . . . I see. You don't talk about it unless Yrsa the Great brings it up," I muttered, sarcasm thick in my voice. "Or was it Yrsa the Psychopath? Serial Killer?"

Jasmine's pace quickened. I stayed on her heels.

"Kinda funny because if you ask me, those nine poles back there look like some crazy sacrifice shit."

"You don't understand," she snapped.

We pushed past the trees. There, the thick woods gave way to an open field by a river. For a moment, I almost forgot where I was.

The land stretched before me, pristine and untouched. It didn't belong in this nightmare. A tiny village lay beyond, small but carefully built—barns, grazing animals, fruit trees, gardens bursting with herbs. The air here smelled different, clean, carrying the crisp scent of sage and thyme.

It was . . . beautiful, even under the gray sky.

But it didn't matter.

I stepped in front of Jasmine, blocking her path. My hands found her shoulders, and my fingers dug in just enough to keep her still.

"Jasmine," I said, my voice low, steady. "This is insane. Yrsa is killing people. Women. Kids. Please tell me you understand that."

"It's not that simple," she countered, looking away.

"Dammit!" I shook her, forcing her to look at me. "The thing they did to you two years ago—the disappearances, the sacrifices. They do it every year. They take people. Just like they took you. Send them to Yrsa so she can kill them."

She flinched.

"This time, there was a girl on the truck."

Jasmine's expression faltered. A crack.

"A . . . girl?" she asked.

I nodded. "Ava. She's only fifteen. A child, Jasmine. A child."

Jasmine looked away.

My grip on her tightened. "Is that what you do now? Kill children?"

She didn't answer.

Words kept pouring out, everything crashing down at once. For two years, I had pictured her dead in a ditch. Every death I'd witnessed since stepping into this cursed forest weighed on me. Even my own hands weren't clean. The woman by the swim hole—her blood still felt warm on my skin. And now this.

My sister, a mindless slave to the monster responsible for it all.

"You're killing kids now, Jasmine?" When she stayed silent, I kept after her. "A fucking child murderer?"

A voice cut through the air from behind me. "I see you're recovering well."

The tone was thick and guttural, with rolled r's and clipped vowels. Rough yet rhythmic, just like Sigvarðr's.

I spun around and found a woman standing a few feet away. She was watching me with the cold amusement of a king watching his jester.

The woman looked to be in her forties. She was beautiful in a unique way. Her nose had been broken, and the healed bone was crooked, but the effect gave character to her face. Her pale blond hair was pulled into thick braids, and her icy-blue eyes were as cold as a frozen lake.

She wore a Norse dress of deep blue wool layered under a white fur cloak. Her arms were wrapped in metal plates, and thick leather lined her belt. At her side hung a sword secured in a worn scabbard. Its hilt peeked out like a silent warning. This woman had fought beside men like Erik the Red, and somehow, she was still standing.

I stumbled back and ran into Jasmine, who caught me before I fell.

"Yrsa the Cruel." The name barely made it out.

Slowly and deliberately, her lips curled into a smile. It wasn't warm or kind.

"Is that what Sigvarðr the Coward now calls me? Once, it was Yrsa the Fierce."

She spoke English far better than Sigvarðr—smoother, less broken. Her accent wasn't as thick.

I remained silent.

Yrsa tilted her head, studying me with unsettling calm. "No need for lies," she said. "I am certain the old fishwife filled your head with tales of slaughter and blood. Made me out to be some beast. A half-human thing with claws like a bear and teeth stained red with blood. The gods are my witness, even the wind grows tired of Sigvarðr's endless squawking."

Her grin widened, but I didn't share her amusement.

A creature like that would have made more sense to me. A monster looking like a monster. But this—this woman was something far worse.

I didn't speak, didn't move. My feet were rooted in place. My heart thudded against my ribs.

"Don't be scared, Esther," Jasmine said softly from behind me.

I exhaled sharply. "That's a little hard, considering there are people here being held like livestock for slaughter." My voice was steady, but there was no mistaking the tension behind it. My eyes never left Yrsa.

She held my gaze, unblinking. Then she nodded.

"I see it now. Healers run in your blood," she said. "A long line of shamans, bound to the old ways, their roots deep in the very earth beneath us."

She reached out, and her fingers pressed against the rough bark of a towering tree. Her eyes fluttered shut, her breath slow and measured. "This forest is unlike any other I've ever seen. Its spirits never left. Its trees still speak their minds." Her voice dropped lower, almost reverent. "It was different even then before I came and bent it to my will. It is restless, powerful."

The air shifted, and the branches overhead trembled. Leaves whispered, though I couldn't feel a wind. It was a faint rustling, like voices carried through the trees. Yrsa tilted her head, listening, her expression unreadable.

Then, slowly, her eyes opened. Sharp. Knowing.

She let out a slow breath and nodded. "Yes . . . I see clearly now." Without another word, she turned.

Just like that, the moment was gone. The forest seemed to exhale as if nothing had happened at all.

"Come. There is something I would have you see," Yrsa said.

Jasmine brushed past me and fell into step beside Yrsa as they started down the path toward the stone house.

I didn't move.

Every instinct told me to stay where I was, to turn and run. Where the hell was she leading me? A pit of human bones?

Yrsa stopped without looking back. "It is nothing of the sort."

A cold shiver ran down my spine.

"But if you do not wish to see the truth," she continued, "then keep standing in your blindness."

"The truth?" I asked.

A slow smile ghosted over Jasmine's burned lips. "You have to see this, Esther. It's beautiful."

There was something creepy about the way she said it. I hesitated a moment longer, then slowly followed.

We walked past the barn, where goats and horses wandered without a care, then the herb garden, heavy with the smell of sage and thyme. It was so peaceful. Too peaceful. Like the land had been tamed into something it was never meant to be. Everything looked untouched, as if it had been this way forever, almost frozen in time.

But I wasn't falling for it. Erickson was trapped in some dungeon, waiting to be butchered—just like all the others before him. Just like my sister was supposed to be.

My fingers slipped into my pocket and curled around the cool metal of my knife. If I moved quickly enough and caught her off guard, maybe I could end this. One deep cut, one severed artery, and it would be over.

Yrsa didn't turn, but her voice drifted back, calm and measured.

"Don't be foolish."

I stiffened.

"I am permitted to defend myself, even here, even against you," she said, walking with unhurried grace. "The forest may be displeased with me, but the balance allows it still." She glanced over her shoulder, her icy-blue gaze glinting. "I have spent much to keep you breathing. Do not spit upon my gods by wasting such sacrifice."

"What sacrifice?" I asked.

Jasmine threw me a sharp look and shook her head.

We walked in silence for another ten minutes or so. The wind stirred the trees around us. Somewhere in the distance, an owl hooted.

Then, suddenly, we stopped.

The woods opened up to the edge of a cliff, where the land plunged into a vast expanse beyond.

Jasmine's face glowed with something like joy as she turned toward me. Yrsa stood motionless, an all-knowing expression carved into her sharp features.

I hesitated before stepping forward. Not close enough for her to push me over. Just enough to see.

And then I did.

I sucked in a sharp breath, and my chest locked so tight I thought I might collapse.

"But . . ." The word barely made it past my lips.

I stared, my mind struggling to catch up with what I was seeing.

Jasmine smiled as if she had been waiting for this moment her whole life.

"That's . . ." My voice faltered. My head shook. "That's impossible," I whispered.

Deep in the valley, nestled among towering pines and the golden-red glow of autumn maples, lay an Abenaki village—untouched by time, hidden from the world.

Birchbark wigwams sat in a careful cluster on a rise beyond the river. Their domed frames were covered in tightly woven mats and sheets of bark. Smoke curled lazily from openings at the top. The village had been built just far enough from the water to stay safe from flooding but close enough for easy access to fishing, drinking water, and canoe travel.

By the water's edge, men stood knee-deep, spearfishing, their bodies motionless as they waited for the perfect strike. Others were weaving large fish traps from reeds, their hands moving in steady, practiced motions. Farther upstream, a group worked in silence, peeling bark from a freshly cut birch log and shaping it into a canoe.

Back in the village, women stretched deer hides over wooden frames, scraping them smooth with tools. Some worked near the fire, softening the leather with smoke, while others pounded something in wooden mortars. The steady rhythm blended with the rustling leaves overhead.

Laughter carried through the clearing as children played between the wigwams, their small feet kicking up dust as they did. A few boys tested their aim with small bows, loosing arrows at a target of bundled reeds. Their voices rose in playful competition. Young girls sat cross-legged in the shade, giggling as they wove baskets from sweetgrass.

I stared down at them all, my stomach twisting.

"Are they Abenaki?" I whispered.

Jasmine nodded. "Pequawket," she said, pride in her voice. "Our people, Esther."

"But . . . how?"

"Yrsa the Generous," she said. "She is protecting them. From the real monsters. People like the ones who killed our family."

I took a step back, my mind spinning. The government had locked down this entire part of the state, turned it into a no-go zone —because of Yrsa. Their agreement to send people to her had kept her quiet, but it had also kept the outside world away from them. The village below had been left in peace, untouched by modern hands. Untouched by cruelty, greed, and hate.

"Do they know about you?" I asked, my throat dry.

"They think I am a forest spirit," Yrsa said, her gaze locked on the village below. "We live beside one another, but we do not speak. I do not bother them, and they do not bother me. It is best this way. They live off the land, as their forebears did before them. Long before white people came to their land with greed and slaughter in their hearts."

My gaze snapped from the village to her. "You mean raiders.

Like yourself. Isn't that why the Vikings like you came, Yrsa? To kill and steal land?"

Maybe it was the shock. Maybe I'd had enough. But the words came out before I could stop them.

Yrsa's eyes narrowed, a flicker of something unnatural flashing beneath the ice. A yellow glow.

"Esther, shut up!" Jasmine hissed. She turned toward Yrsa in panic and dropped to her knees. "My goddess," she pleaded, grabbing Yrsa's hand and pressing desperate kisses to her knuckles. "Please forgive her. She's tired, confused. Blind. She doesn't know what she's talking about. Even when we were kids, she spoke before thinking. Please, my goddess, forgive her." She whimpered, her fingers clutching Yrsa's hand like her life depended on it. Or mine.

Silence hung heavy between us. Then Yrsa placed her hand on Jasmine's head, petting her as if she were a puppy.

"I do not strike at barking dogs," Yrsa said. "Take her to her hut. Night is coming, and much is to be done."

"Yes, my goddess," Jasmine mumbled, kissing her hand again. "Yes."

It made me sick. Watching all this. Not doing anything. But I needed to talk to Erickson. Needed a plan. Yrsa was on guard, always careful, always watching. An outright attack on my end would be suicide.

And then there was tonight. What the hell did she mean by "much is to be done"?

Yrsa stepped past me, her hand resting lightly on the hilt of her sword. Then she stopped. "You and I are not foes," she said. "It was men who burned your kin, as they sought to do to me. It is their way —war and blood, ever the same no matter what land. Theirs. Mine. Yours. But when we women take up their games, when we best them at it, they strike us down like frightened children."

She turned her head just enough for her gaze to cut through me like a blade.

"Think about your people before you call me your enemy, Esther." Her voice dropped lower, rough as smoldering embers. "Think of the charred bodies of your kin. Men did that. Men."

The world tilted, and the memory of my burning home slammed into me, too vivid, too sharp. The house swallowed by flames, dark smoke blinding me, the heat licking at my skin. But something was wrong. This wasn't a memory. The heat felt real. Actually burning me alive this time.

Then came the screeching. Not human. Not animal. A sound that didn't belong in this world.

My knees hit the dirt, and my hands clutched at my head as if I could force it all out. The pain from the fires burning me and the screams—it was too much, too real.

"Stop!" I yelled, but the fire kept consuming me, biting deep, crawling up my arms as if it were alive. Heat crushed the air from my lungs. My skin sizzled, and the stink of burned flesh choked me. Every breath pulled fire inside me. Every scream fed the flames. Pain exploded everywhere at once. There was too much to fight, too much to process.

Then I saw them.

My father. My mother.

Walking toward me, their bodies blackened from the fire, their faces gone—no eyes, no mouths, just empty, charred husks.

"Stoooooooop!" I screamed again, louder this time, desperate.

In an instant, it was all gone. The fire. The smoke. My parents.

I was on the forest floor, gasping for breath, my body shaking. The edge of the cliff was just inches away. Jasmine was wrapped around me, holding me so tight I could barely move. Had she stopped me from falling? Or had I tried to jump?

With an unsteady hand, I wiped the sweat from my forehead. My chest heaved, and my lungs choked on smoke that wasn't there anymore. My eyes burned, my throat was raw, and my head was pounding.

"You shouldn't have angered her," Jasmine whispered, tightening her hold on me. She started rocking, slow and steady, the way our father used to when we were kids.

I let her. I let myself move with her, back and forth. Anything to push away the horror still crawling under my skin.

I wanted to ask if this was what had happened to her. If this was how she'd been burned. If this was why her mind had shattered, why she clung to Yrsa as if she were something holy.

One thing was certain—Yrsa had just revealed her true colors. She wasn't a protector of my people. She wasn't a savior. She was a monster, no different from the men who killed our family.

Jasmine needed to see it. And I needed to get to Erickson and try to free him. Come up with a plan. But right now, I couldn't speak. I just sat there, breathing in the crisp forest air, rocking with my sister.

29

Esther

We sat in the small hut, the fire crackling low in the stone chimney. Jasmine handed me the tea she had brewed over the fire. The air was thick with the scent of cedar, sharp and earthy, curling in the steam that rose from the wooden cup in my hands. The heat brushed against my face, offering a small comfort.

I took a sip. The taste was bitter, and my face twisted before I could stop it. "Still tastes like boiled tree bark," I muttered, forcing a small smile.

Jasmine laughed softly. "Remember when Dad used to make us cedar tea when we were sick?"

I nodded. "Yeah. Remember when I tried to hide from it? I was burning up with fever, and he couldn't find me anywhere."

"You were curled up under the old laundry pile," she said, shaking her head. "He searched for an hour, cursing the whole time. I should have told him where you were."

"But you didn't," I said, smirking.

"I wasn't allowed to watch *She-Ra* that night," she said, her voice warm. "And you almost boiled your brain with that fever. If I could go back, I'd tell him now. You needed the cedar tea . . . and the Tylenol."

We both smiled at the memory. A rare, good one.

Then Jasmine's expression shifted. "I would do a lot of things differently now to protect you, Esther. I'm so sorry for everything I've done to you."

My head jerked back. "What?"

"I've been a terrible sister."

"Don't say that," I shot back. "You saved me from the fire. You're the only reason I'm still alive."

"Yeah," she whispered, staring into my tea. "But then I put you through a different kind of fire when I should have been there for you."

I shook my head. "It wasn't easy for you either. Losing Mom and Dad and Grandma like that. Then being shoved from one foster home to another, separated from me. Our names changed. Our father and our people erased from our memory."

We sat in silence for a while.

Jasmine broke it first, forcing a small smirk. "I still can't believe you impersonated a sniper just to find me," she said, nodding at my dirty, bloodstained uniform. "My little Esther. The same girl who cried and wet herself when Mufasa died in *The Lion King*."

"That was a traumatic moment, all right?" I rolled my eyes.

Jasmine laughed and shook her head.

I grabbed her hand, my fingers tightening around hers. "There's something I need to tell you," I said. "It's one of the reasons I did all of this, I think."

Jasmine's smile faded. Her gaze locked onto mine.

"A few years ago," I started, "I was already in the veterinary program, and my classmates and I were in Dover for a class trip. Our professor invited us to lunch. We . . ." I hesitated, swallowing hard. "We were walking downtown, looking for the pizza place. Then we saw a small crowd, people with their phones out, laughing and recording something."

I wanted to stop here so bad, but I forced myself to keep going. I pulled my hand back and fumbled with my fingers, my stomach twisting.

"When I got closer to the crowd . . ." The words caught in my throat. "I . . . I saw you. Sleeping on a bench. High."

Jasmine didn't say anything, just held my gaze as I sucked in a shaky breath and gripped the wooden tea cup as if it could hold me together.

"Your mouth was wide open. You'd peed yourself. People were laughing. Taking videos." My voice dropped to barely a whisper. "I wanted to scream. I wanted to make them stop. Cover you with my sweater. Get you out of there." I let out a trembling breath. "But I was so embarrassed. Even my professor made jokes."

A sob tore from me as Jasmine reached for my hand.

"I just kept walking. Left you there. Like a coward." My voice broke completely. "After you saved me from the fire, after every-thing . . . I just walked away."

"It's okay," Jasmine said softly, squeezing my hand. "I saw you there."

I froze. "You did?" I used the sleeve of my uniform to wipe away my tears.

She nodded. "I woke up for a few seconds and saw you walking away."

"What? Why didn't you say anything? Confront me?"

"Because, honestly, Esther, I was glad you did." She looked up at me, her expression soft. "You were doing so well in school. Top of your class. I kept telling myself that at least one of us had made it. It kept me going."

"No," I whispered. "Don't do that. Don't try to make it easy on me." I wiped my cheeks and chin, shaking my head. "I swore when you went missing that I would do anything to find you. Anything. I wouldn't stop. I abandoned you once, but I'd never do it again."

Jasmine smiled. It was the kind of smile that warmed my heart, if only for a moment. "Well, you sure as hell kept your promise. Goddamn, Esther. Lying to the government, impersonating a soldier, running from Garmr and the stone giants . . . you even shot a huldra."

I rolled my eyes and exhaled sharply. "If that's even what it was.

Erickson called it that. He saved me. He's the only reason I'm still here."

She nodded, her gaze flickering toward the fire. "The man with the rune tattoos on his hands and neck? Yrsa asked about him. She sensed something in him. A rare presence, she said. Strong." Her voice trailed off, her eyes distant. "But she can't keep him."

My blood ran cold.

"What do you mean, can't keep him?"

She hesitated. "We're already one short for tonight."

The mood shifted. The warmth of the brief family reunion was gone. Poof.

My stomach twisted into a knot. "What's happening tonight, Jasmine?"

Her smile faltered, and she looked away.

I watched her closely. "What's happening tonight, Jasmine?"

She exhaled sharply, shaking her head.

"I'm not a child anymore," I said. "I deserve to know after everything that's happened. You said we're already one short. One short for what?"

She didn't answer.

I grabbed her arm. "It's the sacrifice, isn't it?"

She swallowed hard. "Yes," she finally admitted, barely above a whisper. She pressed her lips together, and her eyes clouded with something I couldn't place. Regret, shame, fear? Maybe all of them.

"When I first arrived here . . ." she started, then shook her head. "No. When *we* arrived. There were nine of us on that truck."

I said nothing, waiting for her to continue.

"Yrsa knew I was from this land the moment she saw me. She sensed it. But you need nine to make it work. It's a sacred number in Norse beliefs. And because I was a halfling, she thought the forest wouldn't hold it against her. That she could offer me to her goddess, Hel, along with the others. A trade—for the power to bend the land to Yrsa's will." Her hands trembled as she placed them on the table.

My stomach twisted tighter. I knew what came next.

"She . . . burned me instead of cutting my throat in the hopes that the smoke of the juniper branches would cleanse the sacrifice.

But something happened," she whispered. "A storm. Or . . . something else. I don't know. I passed out from the pain. But I think the rain put me out."

I stared at her. I never knew I could feel this much hate for anybody. But right here, right now, I felt so much of it for Yrsa, I worried I might explode in rage. I opened my mouth, ready to spit every bit of that hatred into the air, nothing but raw fury lined up on my tongue. But Jasmine was faster.

"Esther, stop," she said quickly, grabbing my hand like she could physically hold me back from the words I wanted to shout. "Please, just listen."

I yanked my hand away. "Listen? To what, Jasmine? That Yrsa's a murderer? That she burned you alive, and now you worship her like a god? That she's about to kill more people, and you're just standing here, drinking tea like it's normal?" My voice shook as anger poured out of me in sharp, ragged breaths.

Jasmine's face twisted in frustration. "You don't understand. Yrsa knows she made a mistake. But it was too late. Ever since the incident, the forest has been different. Things have been out of balance. For our gods and hers. Hel's hound Garmr was released. Not even Yrsa knows why or how. The balance is too broken to make sense of it. It's been hunting us too. Then more and more Abenaki spirits started appearing as if the Norse gods and ours were at war over this land, and the forest was at war with them and us."

Her voice wavered. "Yrsa needs to make the sacrifice of nine tonight. To gain back control over this land. To close the gates of Hel's underworld and banish Garmr the hellhound and any other Norse spirits. Otherwise . . ." She trailed off, her eyes flicking to the flames. Then she swallowed hard. "Otherwise, a lot of people will die. Starting with the tribe in this forest."

My body felt numb. My mind struggled to keep up. But one thing was clear: It was a sacrifice of nine. And there were only eight of us left.

Unless—

My breath turned shallow.

"If Yrsa needs nine," I said slowly, my voice barely above a whisper, "are you . . . are you okay with her killing me?"

Jasmine's shoulders tensed. I pulled my hand away from hers.

"So you're just gonna stand there and watch your sister burn to death?" My voice broke on the last word.

She flinched, her eyes—wide and desperate—flicking to me. "She's not going to kill you, Esther."

Then it struck me like a sledgehammer to the skull.

I jerked back, my body going cold.

"No," was all I said.

Jasmine's lips parted, but no words came out. She didn't need to say it. I already knew. She wasn't offering me up.

She was offering herself.

"Yrsa was kind enough to wait until you woke up," Jasmine said quietly, "so I could see you one more time. So we could talk."

Her hand reached for mine, but I stood and stepped out of her reach.

"No. You can't. The forest—"

"It's not a sacrifice against my will, Esther." Her whole body was calm. She had already accepted it. "It's a willing gift I give to Yrsa to grant her the power to fix all this."

"A gift? This is insane!"

Jasmine stayed quiet.

"You're doing this to save me, aren't you?"

She hesitated. "No."

"Don't lie to me." I pointed at her foot—the way it tapped against the floor, just like it always did when she fibbed. "Don't lie, Jasmine."

She exhaled sharply and rose to her feet.

"Esther, please. Yrsa is not the monster you think she is. She's only—"

But then the world tilted.

The firelight blurred.

My limbs felt heavy.

I blinked hard. Too hard.

"What . . . did you put in my tea?" I slurred. My tongue felt thick and sluggish.

"It will make you sleep," Jasmine said, stepping closer, her face torn. "Until it's all done. Yrsa thought it would be better this way. Sometimes words can poison a person's mind, even those of a loved one."

"Don't do this." I stumbled, my fingers barely catching the edge of the table before my knees buckled. She caught me, easing me down with gentle hands. Like this wasn't betrayal.

"Once it's done," she said, brushing hair from my face like she used to when we were kids, "the forest will be back to normal, and you can go home. Go back to school. Marry. Have kids."

"No." The word barely made it out. My tongue was thick, my breath heavy.

She held me as if I were something fragile. "Think about me sometimes, will you?" she murmured, her voice breaking. "Not the woman on that bench on that warm summer day. But the happy child I was, checking on you while you hid in that laundry pile. Innocent. Lovable. Carefree."

No.

I fought to stay awake, but my eyelids were too heavy. My mind drifted, slipping away. The world spun around me.

I barely noticed the shard from the plate I'd broken earlier as I tucked it into my pocket.

Then—

Darkness.

30

Ryder

I rose slowly, careful not to make a sound, and stared at the hole in the ceiling.

Cooper and the others watched me.

"What is it?" Cooper whispered.

The sky was getting darker. Soon, evening would arrive. Then I heard it. A whisper.

"Do you hear that?" Jimmy said, panicking.

It was faint at first, like a breath carried by the wind. A woman's voice. The same voice that had whispered when the storm saved us from the rock giants.

It grew louder, curling around us, the words in old Norse.

"Cover your ears!" Cooper barked.

Echo and Jimmy clamped their hands over their ears. But I didn't.

Instead, I closed my eyes and shut out the whispers as best I could. There was no blocking this out with hands. No escaping it. The only way to fight Yrsa was with Yrsa's own medicine. The forest was angry with her. I needed to use it.

I took a deep breath and pushed past the way my skin prickled, the way the whispers crawled into my soul. They weren't just in the air anymore—they were inside me, pressing against my skull, weaving into my mind.

And still, I forced my mouth open. Forced the words out.

"Grandmother . . . please. Ask the goddess for her ear. Ask Yggdrasil to command its children to rise. To silence this seer's spell."

The whispering thickened. It coiled around me like a threat, choking off the air. One by one, the others slumped. Jimmy crumpled first, then Martinez, then Graves. The spell sank its claws into them, stealing them away into darkness.

I clenched my fists so hard that my nails bit into my palms.

"Freyja, my divine, I beg you. Ask Yggdrasil to order its children to fight! This land is not hers to claim with Hel and her dark tricks."

A sharp gust of wind ripped through the trees.

A response. Finally.

The branches above trembled softly at first, then violently, their leaves rattling in rage. It was a battle. The forest against the whispers. The trees against Yrsa's spell.

I fought against the pull of sleep, but my knees buckled.

Then, through the haze, I saw it.

A wooden ladder lowered into the pit. Followed by the creatures.

Dark shadows of old Vikings, tall and broad, their hollow eyes empty pits in rotting faces. Their flesh blackened and peeling.

Draugars. Vengeful undead warriors with inhuman strength and an endless hatred for the living.

With stiff, unnatural movements, they silently climbed down. One reached for me. The stench of death—wet earth and rotten flesh—hit me like a wave. I snarled and jerked back, my shoulder slamming into the damp stone.

But it didn't matter.

Cold, dead hands closed around my wrists. The iron shackles snapped open with a metallic clank. For a heartbeat, I thought I was free. But then the grip tightened, twisting my arms behind my back, yanking me upright.

I struggled, my boots scraping against the wet stone floor. One by one, the draugars hauled us up the ladder like it was something they'd done countless times before.

The wind howled louder, tearing through the trees as we emerged from the pit. Cold air slapped my face as the branches shook violently, struggling against her spell.

I sucked in a sharp breath.

"Freyja . . . Yggdrasil," I whispered. "Don't let her take what is yours. Fight."

The clearing stretched before us, bathed in the flickering glow of firelight. At its center, a massive firepit roared. Flames snapped at the darkening gray sky, stretching their long fingers toward the treetops. The air was thick with the scent of burning juniper, sharp and bitter, mixing with something heavier. Metallic.

Blood.

Nine wooden poles stood in a perfect circle around the fire. Each was carved with deep Norse runes. Some were fresh, with jagged and splintered cuts. Others had blackened with time, their meaning long swallowed by the elements.

Beyond the fire, the forest loomed. Dark. Watching.

Then I noticed the two women by the pit.

The first was wearing a blue wool dress. Her skin was badly burned—darkened and rough like leather. What little hair she had left clung to her scalp in brittle patches. She swayed slightly, her head tilted, as if listening to something only she could hear.

But the woman next to her stole the show.

She stood tall, wrapped in a snow-white wool dress, a white fox fur cloak draped over her shoulders. Her armor gleamed—metal plating across her chest, iron bracers over her arms, polished steel guarding her shoulders. A warrior. A queen of something old and dead.

Yrsa the Cruel.

She stood beside the flames, white-bladed sword hovering over the thick smoke, lips moving in sync with the whispers. The wind pulled at her words, carrying them into the night, spreading her spell.

The draugar dragged us to the poles, indifferent to the wind screaming through the trees. I fought against their grip, twisting and pulling, but it was useless. One by one, they forced us against the poles, then locked our shackles tight around the rough bark. Cold iron bit into my skin as my spine pressed against the splintered wood.

I glanced sideways, catching glimpses of the others—Martinez, Cooper, Carter, Jensen, Dawson, Graves, Jimmy. They were sprawled unconscious as the draugar retreated toward the clearing's edge. Their dark forms melted into the trees, leaving us behind.

Then Yrsa turned, and her eyes locked onto mine. The wind tore through her blond hair, whipping it across her face. However, she didn't stop whispering her spell. Her fury burned hotter with every breath.

I clenched my jaw, fingers curling into fists behind my back.

This wasn't over.

Not yet.

The forest was fighting back.

The wind howled through the trees like a wild beast. Flames in the firepit lashed side to side, struggling against the force. Branches shook, twisting against Yrsa as if they, too, had turned against her.

At first, she held her ground. But then the trees bent lower. Their branches stretched toward the poles, moving in ways they shouldn't.

For the first time, doubt flickered in Yrsa's eyes. She took a slow step back as the branches snapped, cracking like a whip. The fire shrank, choking under the weight of the wind.

The spell was breaking.

Suddenly, Yrsa jerked up her sword and whispered something new.

Then—silence. Her whispers cut off instantly.

The wind died and the trees stopped moving.

The fire steadied.

The stillness hit like a punch to the gut. Not a single branch creaked, not a single leaf rustled. It was as quiet as a graveyard.

Yrsa's eyes—sharp, calculating—narrowed at me. Slowly, she walked toward me, the sword still hanging loosely in her hand.

"It has been a long time since I last saw my people's marks etched into a man's flesh," she murmured, her gaze dropping to my hands. "These are the symbols of Erik the Red and my gods. Those who bear them are guided through war and stormy seas." She nodded toward the trees. "This is your doing, is it not?"

A faint groan cut through the silence. Cooper stirred, his head lolling before he blinked himself back into awareness.

The others followed, sluggish, like they were waking from a deep, drugged sleep.

I forced my voice to be steady. "Yrsa the Cruel, I assume?"

Her lips curled. Was she amused? It was impossible to tell.

Then Jimmy woke up—and lost it.

"Help!" he shrieked, yanking against the chains. "Please! Somebody help me!"

His cries filled the clearing.

"I don't want to die!" He yanked at the shackles binding his arms to the pole. "Please! Please don't kill me! Please, please . . . PLEASE!"

Yrsa strode over to him. In one smooth motion, her blade sliced through his throat like paper.

A spray of bright red blood hit the dirt. Jimmy's body jolted as his voice cut off with a wet gurgle. His mouth still worked as if he were trying to finish his plea, but the only sound that came out was a thick, bubbling noise. His eyes rolled back, and his body sagged against the pole, lifeless.

"Fucking cunt!" Jensen roared, his face red with fury. "I'll kill you!"

Yrsa barely glanced at him when she strode over.

"You bitch! You goddamn—"

Another swift swing. Another clean slice.

Blood poured from his throat as he choked, sagging forward, his body twitching. He made a strangled noise, then stilled.

"Shut the fuck up!" Cooper snapped. "All of you!"

Yrsa acknowledged him with a single glance before stepping back, careful to avoid the pooling blood. Her expression remained the same—calm, patient. She had done this before. Many, many times.

"This would have been easier had you all stayed in slumber," she said.

If anyone had expected a wild, chaotic spectacle—some chanting, some madness—this wasn't it.

This was a Norse sacrifice. And the Norse never made a fuss. The blood only needed to mix with the earth, the river, the roots.

That was it.

The forest shuddered as if forcefully feeding on the offering.

Then—movement.

From the darkness beyond the clearing, another draugar emerged. This one was carrying a body slung over its shoulder.

My stomach clenched. I jolted upright against the pole. "Esther!"

She didn't respond.

She was unconscious, her body limp as the draugar dumped her onto the dirt before grabbing a length of rope. Within seconds, it had tied her to the ninth pole, her arms yanked back.

"But—" the burned woman stammered, her eyes widening. "But you said Esther—"

Yrsa raised a hand, silencing her.

"She will not be harmed," Yrsa said. "Once it is done, she will be cut loose and return home. I will guide her safely from this forest."

As if on cue, the draugar dropped a leather bag beside Esther.

"Your offering will be honored," Yrsa promised the woman. "I see you. The gods see you. And we see your bravery."

The burned woman swallowed hard. Slowly, she nodded.

At this point, I had no doubt—this woman wasn't just another pawn. She was Esther's sister. And the ninth sacrifice.

Shit.

I exchanged a quick glance with Cooper. *Buy time*, his eyes said.

"You need nine, don't you?" I said, keeping my voice calm. "The sacred Norse number."

Yrsa turned to me, curiosity flickering in her icy-blue eyes.

"Why not kill two birds with one stone?" I pressed.

She stepped toward me, slow and deliberate.

"The Viking in the hut south of here . . ." I let the words sink in, watching closely for any reaction. A flicker of something dark passed over her face—hate.

"Sigvarðr, son of the Iron-Headed," I continued. "The man who betrayed you. He did betray you, didn't he?"

"He did indeed," she hissed, her grip on the sword tightening. "Sigvarðr and Erik the Red. Two cowards who feared my skirt more than death itself."

"Well, I guess we have that in common then," I said. "I was betrayed by Sigvarðr too." I nodded toward Cooper, who threw me a *what the fuck* look.

"They promised me freedom and land," I continued, my voice hard and bitter. "But I was lied to. They sent me here on false promises, knowing they were sending me to my death." I tilted my head back, eyes on the sky. "May my goddess hear me now. Freyja, if my fate is sealed tonight, let me sit among my kin in Sessrúmnir." I met Yrsa's gaze again. "But why not wait a little? Strike a deal that benefits us both instead?"

She tilted her head. I pressed on.

"I'll bring you Sigvarðr. His hut is south of here. I'll find my way back and bring him to you—so you can have your ninth, along with your revenge."

Yrsa's lips twitched, amused. "And in return, you ask that I let you go?"

I shook my head. "No. This old dog is ready for Folkvangr." I nodded toward Esther's sister. "You let her go instead."

Yrsa studied me, her glacial eyes sharp, measuring. Then she exhaled slowly.

"I sensed something great in you when I first put you in that cave," she said. "I have longed for my kind for centuries. It is a lonely thing to be cast out into eternity alone. The warmth of a man, the pleasure of drink and raid and fucking—" She paused, a smirk ghosting over her lips. "It is not easily forgotten."

Silence stretched between us.

Was it working? Would she cut me loose? Give me a chance to attack?

"But," she continued, her tone shifting. "The forest will not grant me another day, I am afraid. The rock giants have been unleashed, and they do not bow easily to will. What is done is done. And it must be done tonight." She tilted her head, a gesture of respect. "Take your place in Sessrúmnir tonight. Eat. Drink. Fuck. Your silver tongue and bravery have been proven here before the gods."

Then, without hesitation, she turned and approached Martinez. His eyes widened, and his body twisted against the restraints. "No—"

The sword cut through his throat in one clean motion.

"No!" Dawson roared, his voice raw.

Martinez gurgled, his shoulders jerking violently as blood gushed down his chest. His head lolled forward, his body sagging against the pole.

Frantically, I scanned the ground behind me. Nothing sharp. No weapon.

But—a rock. A large one.

If I hit my hand hard enough, I could break the bones and slip through the shackles.

"I hope the wolves tear your fucking head off!" Carter spat, drawing Yrsa's attention.

I used his outburst to cover the first hit.

Pain shot through me, hot and blinding. I bit down on my own scream. The metal cuffs dug into my wrist. Flesh tore. But it wasn't enough. Sucking in a sharp breath, I braced myself. Twisting my left hand into an awkward angle, I stretched my thumb as far as it would go, trying to make it smaller.

Another hit.

Pain exploded up my arm, and a sickening crunch split through my skin. Fire shot through my nerves. My breath hitched and my vision blurred, but I didn't stop.

I clenched my jaw, biting down hard, tasting blood.

Yrsa was already moving toward Carter.

Another clean slice.

His throat opened, and blood poured out in thick, pulsing waves. His body twitched. His legs kicked weakly before he fell still.

"Stop it!" Cooper demanded.

But Yrsa had already moved on—to Graves.

"Fuck you!" Graves sobbed, his head jerking wildly as his gaze fixed on the growing pool of Carter's blood beside him. Then he, too, was gone.

Dawson had given up fighting. He was praying frantically, his hands shaking, his voice cracking. "Jesus—please—I'm sorry—I'm sorry for stealing my father's retirement check, I'm sorry for the boy I killed in Syria—"

Yrsa silenced his prayers with one smooth motion.

Blood sprayed over the dirt, seeping into the ground. The forest drank it up like rain.

Then she turned to Cooper.

He thrashed against the cuffs, his eyes blazing. "You fucking bitch!"

I sucked in a breath and struck again as Yrsa strode toward Cooper. She stopped as they locked eyes.

"Would you like to speak to your gods before you go, leader?"

Cooper spat onto the ground. "We'll square off in hell, bitch." He grinned calmly. Ready. No regrets.

I was out of time. However, finally, the bone gave way with a sickening pop. My thumb bent the wrong way, dislocating completely. I gasped as nausea rolled through me. With a sharp inhale, I twisted my hand and fingers, forcing the shattered bone through the tight ring of metal. The torn skin burned, but I was able to wrench my hand free. I left behind a slick smear of blood against the steel.

I was free. The metal cuff still dangled from my other wrist, but I was off the pole.

Yrsa froze, her sword hovering inches from Cooper's throat. He froze too, his chest heaving, his eyes flicking between me and her, caught between rage and the sharp edge of hope.

At first, I thought Yrsa had sensed me breaking loose. My pulse pounded as I lunged for the long, sharpened branch from the firewood pile—almost like a spear—and gripped it tight.

Esther's sister gasped and stumbled back, mumbling something under her breath like she thought I'd come for her first.

But Yrsa wasn't looking at me. She was looking into the woods.

A deep, guttural roar tore through the clearing. The real reason she stopped.

"YYYYYYYRSAAAAAAAA!"

The name ripped through the air like a battle cry.

Yrsa's knuckles whitened as she gripped her sword.

"YYYYYYYYRSAAAAAAAA!"

Sigvarðr burst through the trees. The Viking stood like a mountain, his fur-lined cloak barely moving in the wind. His massive hands clutched his battle-worn shield and axe. Blue war paint was streaked across his face. His eyes flicked to me, brief and knowing, then locked onto Yrsa.

Suddenly, he hurled his axe toward her. It spun fast, a deadly blur. Any other person would've been split in half, skull to ribs. But Yrsa stepped aside with ease. The blade missed her by an inch and embedded itself into a tree near me with a deep, shuddering thud.

My weapon.

Sigvarðr didn't waste time. The moment his axe left his grip, he drew his sword. His stance was solid, ready for battle.

"You traded my head for the woman's, já?" His grin was sharp, wolfish. "Like a lame horse at the market."

"Hard to call it a trade when the buyer refuses to take the deal," I shot back, smirking.

Sigvarðr let the grin linger a second longer before hardening his face. His focus snapped back to Yrsa. In a thick voice weighted with centuries of rage, he said something to her in Old Norse.

She answered in kind, her voice like steel.

Then Sigvarðr muttered a prayer in Norse and let loose a raw, earth-shaking battle cry.

I didn't think. I just moved. Bolted over to the axe and yanked at it, but it barely budged. My shattered hand throbbed with every pull. I clenched my jaw and growled through my teeth. "Could've just fucking handed it to me."

Bracing my foot against the tree, I gave it another brutal wrench. One more drag, one more pull—it was about to tear free.

31

Esther

A nibble at first. Something small, quick.

Then a sharper bite.

I stirred. Consciousness crawled back in, sluggish and thick like I was surfacing from drowning. My head spun as the heat from a fire warmed my face.

Another bite.

My eyes shot open.

For a moment, I didn't move. Just took in the chaos around me. I was in the clearing with the pit. A fire roared high, wild embers snapping into the darkening sky. I was bound to one of the nine wooden poles surrounding the pit. The thick scent of burning wood and blood filled my nostrils. My pulse hammered as my head snapped left. Then right.

Bodies.

Slumped against the poles, lifeless. Their heads hung forward, their skin ashen in the firelight.

Except for one. Cooper.

"Kill her!" he roared, his voice hoarse from screaming. He was tied up just like me, but his rage filled the clearing. He spat those same two words over and over again.

Yrsa and Sigvarðr clashed in front of the fire, their swords striking in a blur of steel. It wasn't just a fight—it was a war.

Their blades moved faster than my eyes could track. Each clash rang out like thunder echoing through the forest. Sigvarðr had the advantage of a shield, which he wielded in defense and as a weapon, slamming it forward when Yrsa dodged a strike. She danced around it, fluid and unshaken, her white dress—untouched by dirt or blood—swirling around his blows.

I twisted my hands, fighting against the rope. Where were Jasmine and Erickson?

There.

Erickson stood near a tree, his body tense as he yanked an axe free from the bark. He turned with an expression ready to kill and bolted toward the fight.

Jasmine was by the fire.

Frozen.

Her hands were raised to her lips, and her eyes were locked on the battle. Fear. Confusion. She wasn't moving to help anyone.

"Jasmine!" I screamed.

My sister's head barely flicked toward me. She was focused on the fight. Yrsa and Sigvarðr were locked together again, their blades pressed tight. Then Sigvarðr used his strength to push her back with his shield.

Another nibble.

I stiffened, twisting my head as far back as I could.

Something was behind me. Biting me.

The white fox.

I realized her sharp teeth weren't biting me. The fox was tearing into the rope tying my wrists. She pulled at the fibers with quick, jerking bites.

"Good girl!" I encouraged her. But would it be fast enough?

I focused again on the fight. Erickson was closing in, his axe raised high, but his left hand—

Fuck.

His left hand was drenched in blood. His grip faltered, slick on the handle. His movements were sluggish.

He swung anyway, from behind, but Yrsa sidestepped the blow easily. Her body moved like a shadow, and Erickson's axe cut through nothing but air.

Sigvarðr lunged again, his sword flashing toward her exposed side. But Yrsa twisted, dodging in time, her face impassive even as the blade almost got her. Then Erickson swung again.

The first sign of her stumbling.

She was fast. Deadly. But even she couldn't block two attacks from different directions forever.

"Kill her!" Cooper bellowed again from the pole.

The fox bit down harder. The rope jerked, snapping another thread. Almost free.

A few more brutal exchanges between the three. Steel clashed, ringing sharp in the night. Blades flashed, glinting in the firelight. Sigvarðr, Yrsa, and Erickson were locked in a violent, deadly rhythm—strike, counter, dodge.

Then Erickson took a risk—a desperate, reckless lunge against her body, swinging the axe with everything he had. Yrsa twisted, dodging the axe's blow, but his body caught Yrsa's side, slamming her back a step in what could only be described as a suicide move.

Her response was instant and unforgiving.

And her blade caught him.

It punched through Erickson's stomach, steel gleaming, slick with his blood.

"No!" I screamed, thrashing desperately against the rope. My wrists burned as I twisted, fought, kicked. "Erickson!" The name tore from my throat, raw and ragged. My vision blurred—rage, grief, everything crashing at once.

Erickson staggered. A sharp, choked sound escaped his lips.

Sigvarðr seized the moment. As Yrsa yanked her sword from Erickson's gut, causing his blood to spill hot onto the dirt, Sigvarðr swung his blade in a vicious arc. But she was fast—too fast. She twisted at the last second. The blade missed its mark, and his sword plunged deep into the ground instead. Yrsa's eyes snapped toward his. A wicked grin curved her lips. However, Sigvarðr didn't give her the chance to counter. In an instant, he shifted tactics, swinging his shield with full force. The edge of it cracked against Yrsa's face with a sickening thud.

Finally, Yrsa staggered back. She spat blood onto the dirt as Erickson crumpled to his knees. His axe slipped from his fingers and hit the ground with a dull thud. Then he collapsed.

Sigvarðr pulled his sword free, ready to bring it down—but Yrsa's hand snapped up, fingers curling like claws. She whispered something in Norse, and Sigvarðr froze mid-strike. His body locked up like he'd been turned to stone.

A slow, wicked smile stretched across Yrsa's lips. Blood dripped from her mouth, but she wiped it away with the back of her hand, never breaking the low, steady whisper of her spell.

Sigvarðr's eyes widened. His chest heaved violently.

Yrsa's bloody smile deepened. Her voice was a low, rhythmic chant.

Sigvarðr's hands started to shake. His breath turned ragged, and his lips moved soundlessly. He mumbled, then full-on rambled in panic.

Then came the roar.

It ripped from his throat, raw and gut-wrenching. His shield and sword clattered to the ground as his hands flew to his head. They gripped his skull like he was trying to claw something out. His eyes were so wide, their whites gleamed in the darkness. He was like a man trapped in a nightmare from which he couldn't wake.

I knew this nightmare.

The burning house. The screams. The suffocating smoke. The illusion Yrsa had thrown at me back at the cliff when I'd angered her.

"Jasmine, do something!" I yelled, my voice shaking. "Fucking do something!"

But she just stood by the fire, frozen in fear, hands clenched to her chest.

Yrsa moved toward Sigvarðr. Her sword glinted in the firelight.

"No!" I screamed, thrashing against the rope. "Sigvarðr, fight it!"

But it was too late. Yrsa's blade rammed through him, slicing him open like a slaughtered pig. His insides spilled onto the dirt, steaming, pooling around her boots. His lips still moved, whispering, trapped in whatever nightmare Yrsa had cursed him with. Then his head lolled forward, and his mighty body slammed lifeless to the ground.

Yrsa exhaled through her nose, then flicked her sword to shake off the blood.

"I wish I could say it was a good fight, Sigvarðr. But I doubt this will be enough for Fólkvangr—unless the goddess now welcomes cowards."

Her gaze turned to me.

"You're a fucking monster," I spat, my breath coming fast. "My sister might not see it, but I do."

Yrsa started walking toward me, slow, deliberate. She stopped right in front of me.

"Yrsa . . . what are you doing?" Jasmine's voice wavered as she stumbled toward us, panic flooding her face.

Yrsa ignored her. She only had eyes for me.

"You're just like the others," I spat. "A raider. A killer. You never cared about the people in these woods. If you could, you'd kill them. But your hands are tied."

"They were tied indeed," Yrsa said, her voice edged with something amused, almost bitter. "I was promised this land. A kingdom of my own. But the lying pigs who brought me here feared a woman's power and banished me. A tale as old as the gods' very breath." Her gaze drifted to the fire, whose flames licked at the dark like restless spirits. "They bound me here with treachery and spells. Shackled me to a debt with Sigvarðr. Cast me into this wretched forest far from home, praying it would swallow me whole."

Her lips curled, flashing teeth in the firelight.

"But this land was never theirs to give," she continued. "It belonged to itself, to its spirits, to its gods. There was great power in every rock, tree, and blade of grass—a power waiting to be claimed. But the forest wanted neither me nor my goddess here. It fought me with wind and root, with storms that howled my name like a curse. Each morning, when the sun kissed its dirt, it tried to spit me out." She exhaled, shaking her head. "So I carved my own path. If the forest would not yield freely, then I would bend it. I turned to Hel, the mistress of the underworld, and I gave what was needed. Flesh. Bone. Blood."

The fire crackled, casting flickering shadows across her face. Her voice deepened, reverent now. "The price of such power is always blood. And no spirit of this land, nor tree, knew how to fight it."

The wind stirred, twisting through the clearing.

Yrsa's gaze flicked upward toward the towering trees that loomed like silent watchers. "But when I tried to sacrifice your sister, the forest rose against me once more." Her voice hardened. "Its spirits bared their teeth in the dark. It sent storms to break me. Giants to hunt me. It lashed against me with the beasts of my own gods."

Her eyes gleamed like ice in the firelight.

"But Hel does not grant favors to the weak," she continued. "I am still here. And after tonight, the forest will bow once more. Just as it has for hundreds of years. And"—she let out a slow, satisfied breath—"I was given one final gift. By you."

Jasmine's lips parted. Her breath was shaky. "Yrsa—"

Yrsa lifted a hand, silencing her.

"I have to thank you," she said. "Sigvarðr is dead. And I am free."

My stomach twisted.

"I can now walk wherever I wish, far away from this forest," she continued. "Conquer whatever I desire. Kill whoever I choose."

She lifted her sword to my throat. The tip pressed against my skin.

"There is no longer any need to please this land. Or its people. I can kill them and simply leave."

"No!" Jasmine lunged. She threw her arms around Yrsa in a desperate grab.

Yrsa barely spared her a glance before swinging the hilt of her sword onto Jasmine's head. My sister crumpled to the ground like a rag doll. Unconscious.

"Jasmine!" I thrashed against the rope, my wrists burning from the friction. I was almost free—so close.

Then Yrsa's gaze snapped past me.

She froze.

Her face twisted, not with rage or victory, but with something almost like awe.

"The white fox . . . from my dreams," she murmured as if she were seeing a ghost. "It led me to the rock giants. To save you from them. And now . . . Sigvarðr is dead. And I am free! My omen from the goddess!"

I yanked harder at the rope. The last fibers were beginning to give way.

Yrsa stepped closer, circling the pole, her eyes locked on the fox behind me, her lips parted as if in worship. However, as she moved, her expression shifted. The awe drained from her face. It was replaced by something colder. Sharper.

"You are not here for me," she whispered. She realized it was freeing me. The words had barely left her lips when the last bit of rope snapped.

Yrsa's eyes flicked back to me—too late.

I was already moving.

My hand shot to my pocket. My fingers closed around the shard from the hut.

I launched upward, driven by more than instinct—by the desperation of a girl who had watched her parents burn, the grief of a sister who had seen addiction rot away someone she loved, the rage of a woman who had searched through ditches and alleys for two years, clawing through filth and hopelessness. The strength of someone who had fought through a forest of horrors, who had killed, bled, and crawled through hell—to watch the only man who had ever treated her with worth and respect die in front of her.

Fire surged through my veins. Clutching the shard, I struck with the force of someone who'd fought too hard to get screwed over by life one more fucking time.

I wasn't just a survivor anymore. I was a storm.

A scream ripped from my throat as I rammed the shard deep into Yrsa's neck, right into her carotid artery.

Her body jolted. Her ice-blue eyes widened in shock. Her lips parted, but no words came out—only a wet, gurgling noise as blood spilled from her neck and stained her white dress.

Her sword arm trembled. Her grip was failing. For a second, I thought she would drop it. But Yrsa was a warrior. Even as she died, she fought.

With one last, desperate breath, she raised the sword high, ready to drag me to hell with her. Fair enough. My sister would live, and Yrsa was dead. I was ready.

But then a metallic blur flashed in front of me, and a blade swept through the air. Yrsa's head separated from her shoulders. For half a heartbeat, her body stood as if it hadn't caught up to what had just happened. Then, like a puppet whose strings had been cut, it collapsed.

Her head rolled and stopped near the fire. Her eyes were still wide, frozen in that last moment of disbelief.

And there stood Erickson.

He was barely on his feet, barely breathing, but he was standing. Sigvarðr's bloodied sword was clutched in his good hand. His other hand was pressed to his stomach. Dark red blood slowly spilled between his fingers.

"Erickson!" My breath hitched as tears flooded my eyes. I didn't think—I just ran.

I crashed into him, my arms locking tight around his battered body. The force sent us both to our knees. His sword hit the ground, forgotten, as his good arm wrapped around me, holding me just as fiercely.

I sobbed into his chest. For the first time in what felt like forever, I let go. No more fighting, no more survival, no more forcing myself to be unbreakable. I clung to him, shaking, gasping through the storm of everything crashing over me at once.

He just held me. Both of us were barely breathing, barely alive, but still here.

We both knew that from this day forward, we shared a bond—one that would remain unbreakable until death.

I pulled back, my hands shaking as I checked his wound. It was deep and ugly, but no artery had been hit. If it had, he'd already be dead.

"We have to stitch that up," I said.

He gave a small nod, his face tight with pain.

I scrambled over to Jasmine, who was still out cold. I pressed two fingers to her neck, searching—there. A pulse. Faint but steady. Just as I thought. Her head wound wasn't bad. Yrsa hadn't hit her to kill. It was as if she was too attached to her dog to put her down.

I let out a shaky breath and pulled Jasmine into my arms, holding her tight—just for a second. Long enough to feel her warmth, to know she was real, safe. Then I set her down gently and pushed to my feet, my pulse still hammering in my ears. I turned to the woods. My gaze locked on the shifting darkness between the trees.

"The witch is dead!" My voice cut through the stillness. "The evil that came to rule you is gone. She won't summon her Norse gods anymore. No more blood spilled to keep you bound. No more human lives fed to your roots like chains around your spirit." I swallowed hard, my chest tightening as desperation clawed at my throat. "You are free. Free to breathe, to grow, to exist without her shadow. Close the gates to hell. Shut them forever—hers and yours. Let this end. Please. I beg you. Let this end . . ."

The silence that followed was suffocating. The air itself felt like it was waiting, thick with something I couldn't see. Then the trees moved. A slow ripple, a whisper through the leaves. Not the wind—something deeper. It felt like . . . acknowledgment. Maybe even relief. Then trees went still again.

I bent down and grabbed the axe from the dirt. My fingers tightened around the rough handle. No time to waste. I turned and ran to Cooper, then raised the axe high. The sharp metal clanged against the shackle, sending a jolt up my arms. Another hit. Then another. The iron groaned, then snapped apart.

Move. We had to move. Erickson was losing too much blood. If we didn't get him to Yrsa's hut to stitch him up, he wouldn't last long.

We had made it.

At a terrible cost. We had lost too many good people. People who deserved better.

But we had done it.

Yrsa the Cruel had finally been sent to hell.

32

Esther

The morning sun cast long shadows across the clearing. The last of the night bled into streaks of deep purple. Smoke still hung thick in the air, clinging to my skin and filling my lungs.

It smelled like endings. And beginnings.

We stood around the burial pit Jasmine had shown us—an old, gaping wound in the ground, once used for the bodies Yrsa discarded like trash. Now it would be Sigvarðr's send-off.

No one was celebrating this victory. By killing Yrsa, the forest's order had been restored. No more giants. No more Garmr hunting us. But the weight of everything we'd lost pressed down like a goddamn boulder on my shoulders. Jasmine's fingers laced through mine, grounding me.

Erickson stood at the edge of the pit, holding a torch. The flames grabbed hungrily at the wood. Within the pit, the pyre had been carefully stacked around Sigvarðr's body. It was waiting to be set on fire.

Cooper had spent the night burying the others—Martinez, Carter, Jensen, Dawson, Graves, and Jimmy. They didn't get warriors' send-offs. Cooper thought one large grave was more suitable.

But Sigvarðr was a different story.

"Sigvarðr," Erickson said, his voice strong. "Son of Þorsteinn the Iron-Headed. Fjallgarðr, the Mountain Guardian. You fought like a warrior. You died like a warrior. And now you'll drink in Freyja's great hall."

The firelight from the torch carved deep lines into Erickson's face. Shadows settled under his eyes.

"May Fólkvangr's gates open for you," he continued. "So you can eat, drink, and have some fun. Your axe at your side, your shield whole again. Your war is done."

He lifted Sigvarðr's drinking horn—the one the Viking had kept on him, even in battle. Erickson took a slow sip, then poured the rest onto the ground. It sank into the dirt like an offering.

"Go party," he murmured before tossing the torch onto the pyre.

The fire caught instantly. Flames roared up, devouring wood, cloth, and flesh. Heat rolled off in waves, thick enough to sting my face. Embers drifted into the sky like restless spirits. Sigvarðr, the last of the old warriors, was finally going home.

None of us spoke.

We just watched.

Eventually, Cooper moved. He walked toward the leather bags and sorted through supplies for our hike south.

I turned to Jasmine, holding both her hands.

"You sure about this?" I asked.

She didn't hesitate. "Yeah. I belong here. I'm at peace here. There's nothing left for me out there." She nodded toward the world beyond the trees—the one with pavement, phones, billionaires, and sirens. "I will try to talk to our people." She smirked. "Besides, you'll visit, right? I bet you're into all this organic-living hippie shit."

I let out a rough laugh. "You're an idiot."

"Says the woman who never held a gun before but impersonated a Special Forces sniper," she countered, quieter now. "You sure you don't want to stay?"

I swallowed hard. "I wish I could. But there are things I need to do. I want to finish school. I always wanted to be a vet. Now . . ." I thought about the white fox. "Now more than ever."

Jasmine studied me, then nodded. She didn't argue. Didn't push. Just accepted it.

We hugged. Tight.

Then it was time.

I slung a leather supply pack over my shoulder and adjusted the weight as I turned to Erickson. As he lifted his own, he groaned, his face twisting with pain. I'd done what I could for his wound—stitched it, packed it with herbs Jasmine swore by—but it wasn't enough. He needed real medical attention.

"You gonna make it?" I asked.

"I'm fine," he muttered, his teeth clenched.

"Let me take your bag, at least."

He shot me a look. "Don't let all this witch-killing hero shit go to your head," he grunted, but there was a flicker of amusement under all that exhaustion. With another grunt, he dropped his bag at Cooper's feet.

Cooper, already packing up, muttered something under his breath.

I turned to watch Jasmine one last time. She stood on the path where we'd left her, raising a hand in a final wave. I lifted my hand as well, holding her gaze for just a few seconds longer. Memorizing her like this. Alive. Safe. Free. I would miss her so much. But this was good.

Then we walked south.

The forest felt different.

The air wasn't as thick. The trees didn't loom as heavy. For the first time since I set foot in this place, I could hear birds and see the sun. Squirrels rustling in the underbrush. The land was breathing again. Whatever hold Yrsa had on it—and the forest's furious answer to it—was gone.

It took two hours to reach the third hut. The place where Collins had died.

The blood was still there, dark stains sinking into the wood. The walls were cracked and splintered from the fight with the rock giants. The wind pushed through the gaps, whistling softly.

"You wanna wait here?" Erickson asked.

Relief hit me. I nodded, sinking onto the stairs. "Yeah."

I didn't want to go inside. Didn't want to see what was left of Collins.

Cooper was already moving, grim-faced, ready to do what had to be done. Erickson hesitated, then reached out. His hand landed on my shoulder.

He didn't say anything.

He didn't need to.

Then he turned to go, but before he could, I grabbed his wrist.

He stilled.

Our eyes met.

I needed to say something, but the words tangled in my throat, stuck somewhere between too much and not enough.

Erickson waited patiently as if ready to do whatever I asked. Whatever I needed.

But I said nothing.

Eventually, I released his wrist. He shot me a look—unreadable yet knowing—before turning and heading up the wooden stairs into the hut.

33

Ryder

The sun slashed through the trees, turning the mist into streaks of gold and violet. The woods felt . . . too still. Like the forest itself had gone quiet to watch us dig.

We had been at it for over an hour, shoveling dirt in silence, the only sounds the rhythmic scrape of metal against earth and the occasional grunt of exertion. The pit was deep enough now. Cooper handled most of it, but I helped out here and there, despite his objections.

I kept watch, Collins' M4 in my hands, scanning the tree line. Esther had his pistol. The forest seemed safe, but none of us trusted that peace yet.

It was eerie how fast things had returned to normal. No howls from the wolves last night. No rock giants shifting in the distance. No unseen eyes crawling over my skin. It was as if the forest had exhaled the moment Yrsa died.

Collins lay beside the hole, wrapped in an old sheet we'd found in the hut. His body was stiff and cold. Cooper wiped a muddy hand across his forehead as sweat dripped down his temple. He climbed out of the hole and, standing at the edge of the grave, took a long pull from his water.

This was the most logical time to do it.

I lifted the M4 and aimed it at him.

His eyes flicked to the M4. Then he laughed.

"Fucking goddammit, Erickson," he muttered.

"It's nothing personal," I said.

"I know." He dropped the shovel, shaking his head. "But what if I promise you I won't kill those two women waiting at the Viking's hut? Or your lying Native friend?"

I shrugged. "I wouldn't believe you, Cooper. You're not a bad guy, but you put the mission first. That's your purpose. And the mission doesn't allow for witnesses. You know that. If you don't do it the moment we get Erin and Ava out of here, someone else will."

He exhaled sharply, nodding—actually nodding—like he agreed. Like he had already made peace with it.

"You beat me to it, then." A smirk pulled at his lips. "Never liked you much. But they were right. You're the best at what you do."

I accepted the compliment with a small nod.

He looked up at the sky, squinting against the sunlight that broke through the canopy. "So what's your plan, then? What do you tell them when you make it back out? Even if you kill me and smuggle those women out, sooner or later, with the witch gone, someone's gonna notice the Natives in this forest. They'll come back."

I met his gaze. "That's why the witch isn't dead."

Confusion flickered in his eyes. "What?"

"After I lead the women out on the east side of the forest, Wager and I return to base. The mission was successful. Echo is dead. Wager and I are the only survivors, and we dropped the cargo at the coordinates. Completed the mission."

He stared at me, letting the words sink in.

"I'll offer myself as head of future cargo drops," I continued. "Lead the missions from here on out. I survived this one. That makes me valuable enough to be useful to them. Just like you were. And as long as they think the witch is still alive, they'll stay out of this forest."

Cooper remained silent, watching me carefully. "And future cargo missions?"

I shrugged. "I'll make a small change to the program in the selection process. Every year, I'll handpick the people sent here. No more women. No more kids. No more poor bastards just down on their luck. The only people we send through those trees from now on are rapists. Murderers. The absolute worst." My grip tightened on the rifle. "And God knows we'll never run out of those."

"And you'll kill them in these woods yourself? Like the pianist woman from that book *I Kill Killers*?"

I remained silent.

Cooper let out a low breath, a mix of disbelief and grudging respect. "You can't keep this up forever."

"I'll figure something else out down the line," I countered.

He tilted his head back again, letting the sun warm his face. His eyes closed.

"You think the people we killed are waiting for us in hell?" he asked. "Lined up, ready to collect the debts we owe?"

I shrugged. "How the hell would I know?"

Cooper cracked an eye open at me.

"I'm not going to hell," I said simply. "I'm going to Fólkvangr."

Then I pulled the trigger.

The gunshot shattered the silence, sending a flock of birds screaming into the sky.

Cooper's body lurched, then toppled into the grave.

I exhaled slowly, lowering the rifle. Walked over. Pushed Collins in after him.

A branch snapped behind me.

I turned.

Esther stood there, eyes glassy.

"Don't," I said. "Not for him."

She swallowed hard but stayed silent.

"Cooper would've put a bullet in all of us the second he got the chance. For the mission. We just beat him to it. We protected the kid. The Natives in this forest. And we protected your sister."

Quietly, she walked forward and grabbed the shovel. Then she started to bury Cooper and Collins.

"I don't know if I'll ever sleep again," she murmured.

I watched her for a moment, then dropped to my knees beside the grave, using my good hand to help push the dirt over the bodies.

"Just call me when you can't," I said. "I'll be up."

34

Ryder

I sat in my truck outside my ex-wife's house. My chest was tight, my stomach twisted. Nervous as hell.

My son.

I was about to see him again.

And I was twenty-five minutes late.

Too fucking scared he'd look at me and decide he never wanted to see me again. That he'd change his mind at the last second and slam the door in my face.

So I sat there. Stuck. Heart hammering, hands gripping the wheel. Too much time was slipping by, but I still couldn't move.

Esther's voice crackled through the car speakers. "Just do it, Ryder."

"What if he hates the gift?" My voice was tight, my throat dry. I looked down at the football in my lap. The shape was obvious through the wrapping paper. "Do kids even still play ball outside? Or is that just some old-man fantasy of fatherhood?"

What the hell did I know about Minecraft or TikTok?

"It'll be fine. Now turn the car off and knock on that door."

I wiped my sweaty palms on my jeans.

"Ryder . . . I swear to God. If you don't get your ass out of that goddamn car, I'll—"

"Alright." I grabbed the gift. "I'll talk to you later."

"You'll be fine."

I nodded like she could see me. Then I hung up and stepped out of the car.

Every nerve screamed at me to turn around. But I kept walking.

My legs felt heavier than they should have. Like they knew this was a different kind of battlefield. I was excited. I was scared. That damn mission had changed me. Watching Esther and her sister fight for each other had made me realize something I couldn't ignore anymore.

If my son didn't want me in his life, I'd respect that. But if he did—if he wanted my tired old ass around, wanted me to take him camping, teach him how to drive, toss a damn football in the yard—then there wasn't a chance in hell I'd deny him that.

I forced myself up the steps, one foot in front of the other.

With the help of the government, the courts had painted me as a goddamn hero. My sentence had been overturned. The official line was that I had acted in self-defense against a monster. The public had rallied behind me, the grieving father who'd killed his son's abuser. A man like that shouldn't rot in a cell. No, they'd reinstated me. High rank. Full honors. Like none of it had ever happened.

I'd be doing their dirty work now. Once a year. Every fall, I'd load the scum of the earth into a cargo truck and drive them into the woods. Alone. No more teams.

Amazing how a story could shift in the right hands.

Once a murderer. Now a hero.

At least in their eyes.

Didn't mean I'd ever forget Sigvarðr. Or Echo. The civilians who died. Yrsa, too.

And of course—Esther.

The craziest woman I'd ever met. And the bravest. We were close. Talked mostly at night, when neither of us could sleep.

First thing I did when we got back was demand that Wager be

discharged from the military—immediately. The real Wager had no problem with that. No one ever found out she wasn't the one who'd gone into those woods with me.

Esther was off doing her own thing now. Trying to get back into vet school.

And soon, I'd be leading her back into that forest—to find her sister.

We'd go in from the east. Same way we got Ava and Erin out.

Ava was with her grandmother now. Erin was finally sober and reunited with her family.

"If that ain't a happy ending," I muttered, shaking my head as I reached for the doorbell.

Before I could ring it, the door flew open.

And there he was.

My son.

Taller now—at least a head—but still him. He lunged forward, slamming into me.

The gift slipped from my hands as I wrapped my arms around him. For a moment, I stood there, frozen, gripping him as if he might disappear. As if I'd died in that damn forest and landed in a beautiful dream.

This was everything. This was all I ever wanted.

"Dad," my son choked out, his face buried against my shoulder.

I squeezed him tighter, breathing him in, his hair, his warmth—until he coughed, and I loosened my hold just a little.

"Dad . . . I missed you so much."

"Me too, Champ. Me too."

35

Esther

I'd been sitting in my car outside John Bear's house all day.

Ryder had tracked down his address—a few acres on the edge of the woods, not far from the Penobscot Nation up north in Maine. It was the kind of place where the trees stood taller than the buildings, where the land stretched quiet and undisturbed. A place that felt untouched, as if time moved more slowly there.

His truck pulled into the driveway as the sun dipped lower, causing warm streaks to bleed through the trees.

He looked confused when he spotted my car parked outside his home. However, when I stepped out and he saw it was me, his sun-darkened face brightened. A wide smile spread across his lips.

"I have been praying for you to find your way back to us," he said as he approached.

I nodded, returning the smile. "I was wondering if your offer still stands. To help me go back to school. If not, I totally under—"

"Of course. Come inside. I want you to meet my wife."

"I don't want to be an inconvenience."

"Oh, please, stop," he said, waving off the thought. "She has been praying for you too, ever since I told her about our meeting and how you saved the fox. I stopped by the clinic again, but they said you were no longer working there. I tried to find you after that. I felt like it was my fault you lost your job."

We started walking toward his house. It was an old farmhouse. Nearby stood a red barn, its paint faded from years under the sun. A handful of horses grazed lazily in the pasture. A single chestnut horse lifted its head and flicked its ears toward us before returning to its slow, steady chewing. The air smelled of fresh hay and damp earth—grounding in a way that felt different from the wild, untamed forests I had left behind.

"I released the fox back into the woods," John Bear said as we reached the porch. "I want to thank you again for saving her life."

I smiled as he opened the door and stepped aside to let me in.

The house was warm, lived-in, and filled with Abenaki touches —woven baskets stacked neatly in corners, wooden carvings of animals resting on shelves, and intricate beadwork draped across the walls. A fire burned low in a fireplace.

"Funny you say that," I said, glancing around. "Because I actually wanted to thank you. That night you came to me, it saved my life."

John Bear studied me for a moment as if weighing whether to ask for details. Then he nodded as if he already knew.

"Martha!" he called out as he shut the door behind us.

For just a moment—before the door fully closed—I swore I saw her.

The white fox.

Standing at the edge of the forest, her fur glowing in the fading light.

I walked up to the window and looked out, but she was gone.

"What is it?" John Bear asked.

"Nothing," I murmured as my lips curled into a soft smile.

Just a friend saying goodbye.

Epilogue
JASMINE

Carefully, I set the basket beside the flat river rock, then smoothed out the folds of the blue wool dress inside. The spot was just off the main path, where the villagers came to collect water.

I waited.

Hours passed. The sun crawled through the sky. I kept my back to the trees, my pulse steady but my senses sharp, watching the bend in the path.

Then I saw her.

She moved with quiet grace, her dark braids swaying over her shoulders as she walked. A Pequawket woman—mid-thirties, maybe older. She wore a fringed deerskin tunic dyed in soft earth tones. Beaded accents had been stitched carefully along the sleeves. A wrap-around skirt fell just below her knees. Intricate quillwork lined its edges. Hugging her calves were leggings made of supple leather tied neatly just above her soft-soled moccasins. She had the quiet confidence of someone who had always belonged to the land, who had never once questioned its place beneath her feet.

And this time, she wasn't alone.

A small girl clung to her side. She peeked at me with cautious, wide eyes. Her tiny hand gripped the woman's skirt.

I didn't move. Let them come to me.

We had been trading like this for weeks. First, small things— bundles of herbs left on the rock when no one was around. Then, one day, I'd seen her. She'd been standing just beyond the trees, watching me. We didn't speak, just nodded, acknowledging what we were doing. After that, the trades became more frequent. Sometimes, she smiled. Today, for the first time, we stood face-to-face.

She reached for the wool dress in the basket and lifted it carefully, running her fingers over the fabric. A soft, pleased noise escaped her lips, and a quiet smile lit up her face. Then she unfastened the bundle in her other hand and offered it to me.

A dress.

Deerskin, like hers, decorated with delicate white shell beads down the front. It was beautiful—simple, functional, but made with care. I took it gently and held it against myself. It smelled like woodsmoke and river water. The scent was so natural, it felt like it had always belonged to me.

I looked up and met her eyes.

She nodded.

So did I. With a genuine smile.

She pressed her palm lightly over her heart, then lifted it toward me—a gesture of goodwill. Maybe gratitude.

I mimicked it.

The woman chuckled softly, then lifted her hand in farewell, her fingers flicking outward. I returned the motion.

She turned and led the girl back down the path. Their figures blended into the trees.

I watched them go, the weight of the deerskin dress warm in my hands. My heart swelled. I couldn't wait to tell Esther about this. I was getting to know our people. Slowly but surely, I was making my way home.

That night, I sat near the fire. Its flames flickered strongly against the stone chimney.

Yrsa's house—no, my house—was nothing like a modern apartment. It was built in the old Norse way: sturdy timber walls, a steeply slanted thatched roof, and thick animal pelts draped over the wooden furniture. A warrior's home. But cozy too.

I had made it my own in small ways. Dried herbs hanging from the beams, bundles of sage and cedar, along with a few beaded necklaces, some of which had been traded by the villagers.

I sat at the table, grinding a thick herbal paste in a stone mortar. Honey and ash. An old Norse remedy for wounds. It had worked well enough when I'd nicked my finger a week ago while cutting potatoes.

My fingers moved by memory, but my thoughts drifted.

To my sister.

I knew she was coming to visit me soon. I could feel it, like a pulse in the land itself. I thought of her the way I always did— strong-willed, relentless. Kind. Selfless.

The firelight flickered over my reflection in the polished metal pot beside me. I barely recognized myself.

But I didn't care anymore.

The burn scars . . . they were just skin. The real scars—the ones buried deep inside me—were gone.

I had found peace and beauty even in the ruin of what Yrsa had done to me.

I was whole. Happy.

The wind shifted.

I looked up as it hit the house with sudden force, rattling the wooden shutters. The fire snapped violently in the hearth. Its flames stretched high, twisting unnaturally before settling again.

I froze.

Outside, the wind howled through the trees.

No—not the wind.

Voices.

Whispers. A woman's voice. Tangled in the night air like a message.

I rose slowly, my heart pounding. Carefully, I moved to the doorway. The cold pressed against my skin as I stepped outside.

The night was darker than it should have been.

The wind carried the woman's voice to me. Her words swirled just beyond understanding.

It was a language I didn't know, but the longer I listened, the more the syllables began to weave together. They took shape, twisting into something familiar.

Old Norse.

Yrsa had prayed in it many times. I had heard it. I had learned some.

I swallowed. "What was that?" I asked.

The air felt different—heavy. However, I wasn't afraid. If anything, I felt safe. Almost like the darkness was a friend, not an enemy.

Then I heard it.

"Daughter of Two Bloods."

The word drifted to me—clear as day—in old Norse, though it sounded like English in my mind.

I took a step forward. The trees shifted around me, the shadows stretching.

"Daughter of Two Bloods," the voice whispered again. "Your father's blood runs deep in your veins. But so does your mother's."

Something stirred inside me. Ancient. Alive.

I stepped into the forest's darkness.

Power rose within me. Hot. Hungry. Forbidden.

The voice returned, soft and certain.

"This land . . ."

I stopped and listened—but I was damn sure ready to fight too. Down to the last bone and breath.

Because I already knew what words would follow.

I felt it in my bones. My heart. My soul.

"This land," the voice said again—this time, demanding.

"Rule it."

. . .

244

Afterword

Thank you for reading You Can't Stay.

Though *You Can't Stay* is a work of fiction, its roots lie in real history —of colonization, erasure, and survival.

This story is about what was taken, and how the land and its spirit remain strongest in the hands of those who truly belong to it. The Vikings represent an early face of colonizing violence.

The Abenaki people—although nearly erased—are still here. And they carry strength, knowledge, and connection that no force could ever destroy.

This book isn't a literary masterpiece. It's a wild, Hollywood-style fun ride that asks you to suspend belief and enjoy the chaos. But it plants seeds—names and histories that might never reach certain readers otherwise. And that means something.

Thank you for caring. I'm so grateful.
S.T. Ashman

A Few Notes

Germanic/Norse Mythology and Traditions

Fólkvangr and Sessrúmnir: A Warrior's Afterlife Nearly Erased

In modern books and TV shows featuring Norse mythology, nearly everyone knows Valhalla as the grand hall where brave warriors go after dying in battle. But when we turn to the original Norse texts, a more complex picture emerges.

According to both the Poetic Edda and the Prose Edda, not all fallen warriors go to Odin's Valhalla. In fact, the texts clearly state that half of the slain are taken to Freyja's realm, called Fólkvangr. The name roughly translates to "Field of the People" or "Field of the Army."

In *Grímnismál* (Poetic Edda), stanza 14, we read:

"Fólkvangr is the ninth; there Freyja rules / the seating in the hall. Half the slain she chooses every day, / and half Odin has."

The *Prose Edda (Gylfaginning)*, written by Snorri Sturluson in the 13th century, echoes this:

"Freyja is the most famous of the goddesses. She has in heaven a dwelling which is called Folkvang, and when she rides to the battle, one half of the slain belong to her, and the other half to Odin. As is here said:
Folkvang it is called, And there rules Freyja. For the seats in the hall. Half of the slain. She chooses each day; The other half is Odin's. Her hall is Sesryn-mer, and it is large and beautiful."

These quotes come directly from the primary sources. There are slight variations in translations, but the meaning remains consistent across all versions.

Fólkvangr and Sessrúmnir are mentioned only a few times in the surviving texts, but that doesn't mean they're unimportant. Some scholars even suggest that Freyja might have had first pick of the slain, as she is named first and is said to "choose," while Odin simply "has" his half. The texts don't say this outright, but the wording opens the door to that interpretation.

So why is Valhalla a household name while Fólkvangr is largely forgotten?

Some argue it's not about Freyja's role being minor—it's about how the myths were preserved. Norse mythology was preserved through oral tradition for centuries before being recorded in writing. A great deal has been lost.

The stories were eventually written down by Christian scribes, who might have emphasized the gods who aligned with their worldview. Odin, the god of kings, warriors, and poets, fit comfortably. Freyja, a goddess of death, magic (seiðr), independence, and sexuality, did not.

But we can't say for certain—these are just theories as to why Fólkvangr became a myth within a myth. And none of this diminishes Odin's importance or his popularity among the Germanic and Norse tribes.

But we have to remember that a lot of the old stories have been lost.

Take Sinthgunt, for example—the sister of the sun goddess Sunna. She's mentioned only once, in the *Merseburg Incantations* from the 9th or 10th century. Scholars believe she might have been a moon or star goddess, and her presence alongside deities like Wodan (Odin) in such a brief poem suggests she once held real significance. That single mention hints at entire mythologies lost to time. Just like Sinthgunt, richer stories and details about Fólkvangr might have disappeared with the rest.

So while Freyja's realm is mentioned less often, it's not a side note. She has her own hall, her own land, and an equal share of the honored dead. That's significant.

Modern pop culture—from Wagner's operas to Hollywood films—has leaned heavily into the image of Valhalla. Its roaring feasts and endless battles make for great visuals. But so do a beautiful meadow and a grand hall ruled by a goddess who welcomes both men and women. And we have texts suggesting that Freyja received women into her hall.

In *Egils saga*, Þorgerðr says, "I will eat nothing until I join Freyja." This implies that noble women, too, could enter Fólkvangr.

It's a quiet reminder that Freyja's realm was once seen as a worthy afterlife—maybe just as important as Odin's, and perhaps more inclusive as well.

Here's a personal thought. Just a fun theory.

The warriors in Valhalla feast, yes—but they also prepare for Ragnarök, the Norse end-of-the-world showdown. A final battle between gods and monsters. They don't just drink and celebrate forever; they're training, destined to take up arms again when the world burns.

If Freyja not only receives half the slain but possibly gets first pick, isn't it possible that the most heroic warriors were given a different kind of reward? A place of peace, feasts, mead, women, and no more battles? In Freyja's Sessrúmnir—where they might reunite with brave men and women from their families?

Whatever the truth is, one fact remains:

Freyja gets half of the warriors who die in battle.

Shield-maidens

Both written and archaeological sources suggest that some women took up arms in Norse society. While this was not necessarily the norm, examples appear in saga literature and at burial sites.

In the sagas, figures like Hervör (from *Hervarar saga ok Heiðreks*) take on traditionally male warrior roles. Meanwhile, exploration sagas describe Leif Erikson's half-sister Freydís Eiríksdóttir as fierce and combative, even while pregnant.

Archaeologically, the Birka warrior grave (Bj 581) in Sweden is the most famous example. In 2017, DNA testing confirmed that the warrior buried with full weapons and battle gear—originally assumed to be male—was biologically female. Debate continues as to how common female warriors were, but this grave has become a touchstone in discussions about gender and combat roles in the Viking Age.

A detailed academic discussion supporting the interpretation of the Birka grave as that of a female warrior can be found here: https://www.cambridge.org/core/journals/antiquity/article/ viking-warrior-women-reassessing-birka-chamber-grave-bj581/ 7CC691F69FAE51DDE905D27E049FADCD

Yggdrasil and Ratatoskr

Yggdrasil is the mighty World Tree that holds the Nine Realms together. A mischievous squirrel named Ratatoskr runs up and down the trunk, carrying messages and insults between the great eagle at the top and the dragon (or serpent) Níðhöggr gnawing at the roots. In a sense, Ratatoskr stokes the ongoing rivalry between these two powerful creatures.

There are no known sources showing that Yggdrasil was directly worshipped. However, both Germanic and Norse tribes regarded trees—especially oaks and lindens—as deeply sacred. People gathered beneath them to hold rituals, offer sacrifices, and seek signs from the divine. Tacitus wrote about secret ceremonies in forest groves dedicated to a mysterious Mother Earth goddess. That specific rite is lost to time, but the sacred status of trees endured.

Adam of Bremen described a grove at Uppsala as so holy that

"each of the trees is believed to be divine." He detailed mass sacrifices in which blood was offered to appease the gods, and the bodies of animals and men were hung from the trees.

Similarly, in *Hervarar saga ok Heiðreks*, a horse is sacrificed, and its blood is smeared on a sacred tree.

We also see this reverence in the story of Donar's Oak—a massive oak that became a focal point of Germanic pagan rites before its symbolic destruction by Saint Boniface during the Christianization of the region.

The Number Nine

The number nine seems to symbolize completeness or a full cycle in Germanic and Norse cosmology. It's considered a sacred number and appears repeatedly throughout the myths:

• Odin hung on Yggdrasil for nine days and nights to gain the wisdom of the runes (*Hávamál*, stanzas 138–139).

• The cosmos is often described as nine realms connected by the World Tree, Yggdrasil.

• Certain rituals and sacrifices were arranged in cycles of nine or involved the number nine.

A notable historical example comes from Adam of Bremen, who, in his 11th-century chronicle *Gesta Hammaburgensis Ecclesiae Pontificum*, described a massive sacrificial festival held every nine years at the Temple of Uppsala. During this event, nine male victims of every species—including humans—were offered to the gods, and their bodies were hung in a sacred grove. He also wrote that "each of the trees is believed to be divine."

Human Sacrifice in Norse and Germanic Traditions

Human sacrifices were a documented part of rituals in Norse and Germanic societies. These sacrifices were often performed to honor the gods, ensure fertility, secure victory in battle, or avert disaster.

As noted earlier, according to Adam of Bremen, during the great pagan festival at the Temple of Uppsala (held every nine years), nine males of every species—including humans—were sacrificed, and their bodies were hung in a sacred grove.

Other sagas and sources mention ritual drownings, stabbings, and burials, often tied to major events such as the death of a leader, famine, or war. In the *Ynglinga Saga*, for example, King Domalde is sacrificed to restore prosperity after years of famine.

Archaeological confirmation is limited, but several graves and bog bodies found across Northern Europe suggest that ritual killings might have taken various forms.

Garmr, the Hellhound

Garmr is the fearsome watchdog that guards the entrance to Hel's domain, ensuring the dead stay where they belong. When the final battle of the gods (Ragnarök) arrives, Garmr is prophesied to break free and clash with the god Týr, leading to mutual destruction.

The Huldra

The huldra is a seductive forest spirit. She appears as a beautiful woman from the front but has a hollowed-out back like a tree (or sometimes an animal's tail, depending on the story). She can be both enchanting and extremely dangerous.

Draugar

Draugar are undead figures in Norse myths. They often leave their graves to attack the living, haunt locations, or guard buried treasure. Their stench and decay are frequently noted, and many are described as grotesquely bloated or physically powerful.

The Viking Voyage to Vinland—When the Norse Reached North America

Between roughly 985 and 1000 CE, Norse explorers sailed to North America. The best-known leader was Leif Erikson, who established a settlement called Vinland. Vikings reached the New World long before other European explorers. This is supported by archaeological evidence at L'Anse aux Meadows in Newfoundland, Canada—an authenticated Norse site dating to around 1000 CE. There, remains of Norse-style buildings, ironworking, and artifacts have been found.

Departure from Vinland

The Vinland Sagas—*The Saga of the Greenlanders* and *The Saga of Erik the Red*—make it clear the Norse didn't try to conquer North America. They faced hostile encounters with Indigenous people, constant threats, and tough conditions. *Greenlanders* outright says the land wasn't worth the danger. In *Erik the Red*, what starts as trade turns to violence. Both sagas end with the Norse deciding to pack up and go home.

Abenaki and Native Traditions

The Spirit Fox

In many Native American beliefs, foxes represent cleverness, adaptability, and, sometimes, a guiding presence.

The Sacred Forest

For the Abenaki and many other tribes, the land is alive with spirits. These spirits protect or punish based on how people treat the natural balance.

Balance Between Worlds

A core Abenaki view is that you can't truly "own" the land; you can only respect it and coexist with it.

The Rock Giants (*A-senee-ki-wakw*)

These stone giants come from Abenaki stories. They are said to roam mountainous areas, demonstrating immense strength and embodying the raw power of nature. Sometimes, they act as protectors, while other times, they are threats.

Medicine Men

Abenaki shamans or *m'teoulin* serve as healers, guides, and bridges between the physical and spiritual realms. They use herbal medicine, visions, and rituals to maintain or restore balance. Often, they help their communities navigate both worldly and supernatural challenges.

The Pequawket Tribe and Abenaki People

The Pequawket are a band of the larger Abenaki people who lived in western Maine and eastern New Hampshire, especially near the Saco River. Today, the Abenaki still live in Vermont, New Hampshire, Maine, and southern Canada.

What Happened to Them?

Like many tribes in the Eastern Woodlands, the Abenaki suffered huge population losses due to European diseases, warfare, and colonization. Some bands were forced north to Canada; others stayed but hid their identities for generations. Today, despite centuries of oppression, descendants of the Abenaki continue to keep their culture, language, and heritage alive.

psychological thrillers on the market.Don't Miss My Other Book!

What if the most dangerous serial killer is the one who hunts her own kind?

By day, Leah Nachtnebel is celebrated as one of the greatest pianists of our time. By night, she becomes a ruthless killer, using her brilliant mind to hunt predators who believe they've escaped justice.

But when her latest target unearths a connection to her dark past, Leah is thrust into the crosshairs of two relentless forces: an FBI agent determined to uncover her secrets and a sadistic serial killer who doesn't just see her as a traitor—he sees her as a trophy he must possess.

On a killer's playground, there's one rule: win and live, or lose and die.
Read here (FREE with Kindle Unlimited):
I Kill Killers READ HERE
Or you can find the paperback book on Amazon, Barnes & Noble, and at your local bookstore.

FREE Excerpt from I Kill Killers:

Prologue

When I was eight years old, I stabbed a boy.

He came from a troubled home, the kind where violence was the solution to any problem. His piercing eyes were a window to his sadistic soul, revealing a weariness far beyond his years. At thirteen years old, he tortured and killed cats and dogs. There were also rumors that he had molested a kindergartner in the school's bathroom.

I did my best to avoid him until one day, after school, I saw him lingering in front of the grocery store. At the time, he'd been suspended from school. He looked unkempt. His brown hair was sticky and long, and his face was smudged with dirt. Our eyes met for a split second before I stepped past him and into the store.

I was on my way home when I felt the unmistakable sensation of being followed. Glancing around, I saw his shadowy figure darting between cars, keeping pace with my strides. I felt no fear, only a nagging annoyance that he might make me late for my piano lesson.

I kept walking and entered a quiet street, where he managed to pull me behind a small patch of rosebushes. Concealed from the road, he threw me onto the leaf-littered ground and pulled out a knife, its blade glinting in the September sunlight. He told me he'd cut me open if I screamed. I nodded and asked him what he wanted.

"Kiss it," he said, grabbing his crotch.

I agreed but asked him to sit on the ground. "You're too tall," I said, which seemed to make sense to him.

He sat down in front of me. I knelt between his outstretched legs and waited for him to put the knife on the ground to unzip his pants. As soon as he did, I snatched up the blade and slashed his neck with a single smooth movement.

I'll never forget the look of horror on his face as he frantically pressed his hands against the deep crimson that gushed relentlessly from the wound in his neck. I'll also never forget the odd sense of emptiness I felt as I stood there watching him. No sadness or joy. Just a numb void that left me feeling detached from myself and the world.

When the first group of people gathered around the scene, gasping and screaming, I calmly walked straight to the police station and told them everything, bloody knife still in hand.

The boy survived, but my parents left me to rot in the Kim Arundel Psychiatric Hospital for the Severely Mentally Ill for the rest of the school year. I'd told the police that it was self-defense, and they'd believed me. But the composed and emotionless way I'd handled myself created a ripple effect in my small town, and CPS branded me a high-risk child in need of immediate intervention.

The therapeutic period that followed was mostly unremarkable. There were the standard programs designed to help normalize me: the grippy socks, the endless talk sessions. But what really left its indelible mark on my mind was the time I spent in the treatment center's library, a space shared by the children and adult units.

It was there, between the picture books and cleavage-filled romance novels, that I discovered a book about German National Socialism during World War II. Judge me how you want, but strangely, this book, as thick and heavy as three books combined, gave me hope.

My fascination with the book wasn't related to the horrific atrocities committed by the Nazis, nor was I fool enough to admire one of the greatest mass murderers in history. My obsession with Hitler stemmed from the peculiar fact that the same monster who was responsible for sending millions of people to concentration camps was also a vegetarian who had a deep affection for his dog, Blondi. At a time when a human's life meant close to nothing, Hitler passed some of the strictest animal protection laws ever written. He introduced penalties for animal cruelty and banned free hunting rights.

As I sat there on the library's torn and dusty couch, the worn book spread open on my lap, something stirred inside me. This, by itself, was shocking because I rarely felt any kind of emotion— hatred, joy, contentment, nothing. I understood the difference between right and wrong and derived no pleasure from witnessing animals or people suffer. Yet, on most days, I simply felt nothing—as if my inner world was a merciless desert devoid of even the slightest hint of life. Feeling that warm flicker inside me meant everything. Eventually I realized what it was: It was hope.

If a man as evil as Hitler could unearth the slightest bit of love within the depths of his icy, rotten heart—even if it was for animals —then perhaps, one day, I might be able to do the same.

Chapter
One

I'm here, Tim texted.

My phone's bright light illuminated the glass of water sitting beside it. It was 5:36 p.m. Tim was thirty-six minutes late. Men like him often were.

I was in a cheap Chinese restaurant, listening to the sounds of forks clinking against plates, the occasional peal of laughter, and the sizzling of grease against hot pans in the kitchen.

I picked up my phone.

About time, I texted. Waiting inside. Blonde girl with short hair, holding a red rose.

The familiar bouncing three dots indicated Tim was answering.

I'm late, and you got me a rose? That was my job. Want me to grab one real quick? Feel like a douche now. LOL

I took a sip of my ice water. Just kidding. No rose. But I'm the only one in a red dress. Get your sexy butt in here.

Exhaling deeply, more out of annoyance than anything else, I turned toward the window overlooking the parking lot. The sky was a canvas of fading orange and purple hues fighting against the encroaching gray of the night. Several streetlights illuminated the handful of scattered cars in the dim parking lot of the small shopping mall, which consisted of nine-to-five businesses such as an outdated fitness studio and a shabby tattoo parlor.

As I scanned the cars, my phone remained silent. A whole two minutes ticked by without a response.

He's debating leaving.

Many debated internally over whether to do 'it' just one more time, each motivated by their own reasons, in a constant back-and-forth.

I glanced at my phone, noticing the three dots bouncing again.

Shit, Tim texted. I'm so sorry, but work just called me in.

Oh no, I replied, hoping I could persuade him to change his mind. If he backed out now, it would complicate things significantly. My upcoming weeks were packed with concerts.

This late? I texted.

My boss says some older woman has a major leak in her ceiling, and our on-call guy won't pick up the phone. I'm so sorry. I feel terrible.

That's a shame. But don't feel bad. Work pays the bills. I get it. It's nice you're helping that elderly lady. You sound like a keeper.

There was another silence. Disappointed, I continued to stare out the window. I needed something to push him—quickly—or he might not bite. Something that preyed on his most primal instincts as a man.

Possessiveness. Jealousy.

My friend Mike is having a beer close by anyway, I texted. He begged me to meet up tonight. I'll just join him. No biggie.

Suddenly a pair of headlights turned on from the far end of the parking lot.

Bingo.

He'd been watching all along. I knew it.

He texted again: Hey, this might seem super weird…but do you want to tag along?

My green eyes narrowed at the headlights. Attaboy.

I just really want to get to know you, he continued. Could be a fun story at our wedding reception. LOL

Wedding reception? That was a little forward. He was attempting to exploit the loneliness of the type of woman I was pretending to be. A sweet and kind soul. One that longed for love and stability like a flower craves the sunlight.

Won't you get in trouble for that? I asked. Bringing me along to work?

Nah. It won't take me long to fix the leak. We could bring donuts and coffee and just talk in the car. Or grab dinner after. I know a fancy place and could make a reservation for nine thirty.

I waved at the young Asian waitress and reached inside my purse to grab twenty dollars. She hurried over. "Are you ready to order?"

"Sorry, but I have to go." I placed the twenty on the table. The soft fabric of my knee-length red dress slid over my thighs as I rose. I was wearing matching red ballerina shoes.

"Thank you," the waitress said, fingering the bill.

The door's bell tinkled as I stepped out into the parking lot and inhaled the cool autumn breeze. It smelled like a mixture of Chinese food and the fake floral scent of detergent from a nearby Laundromat. I waited a moment, then texted:

I'm outside. Just promise me you're not a serial killer. LOL

More dancing dots.

I promise.

The vehicle with the bright headlights at the far end of the parking lot started rolling toward me. Slowly. Under the dim light of a nearby streetlight, it revealed itself as a gray van that read East Coast Plumbing. We Do It Right! on its side. The van came to a stop in front of me. For a moment I stood there, waiting for Tim to get out. When he didn't, I walked around the front to the passenger's side. The door stuck a bit when I opened it.

As I got a closer look at Tim, I noticed the overwhelming difference between his dating-app pictures and reality. The photos were fake, of course. His once handsome cheekbones were now hidden beneath quite a few extra pounds. The striking blue eyes that could ignite a woman's wildest fantasies had lost their luster, appearing weary and dull. He was clean-shaven with an obscenely wide nose; only his brown hair and tall, imposing stature matched his photos. He wore a white protective coverall. Brand-new. Industrial, disposable.

He's a two out of ten, I thought and climbed up onto the seat.

"Wow," Tim said as I closed the door and strapped on my seat belt. It tightened against my chest, outlining my small breasts. Tim stared at them. Shameless. "You look even prettier than in the pictures," he continued.

I forced a playful giggle. "Stop it."

"No, really." Tim grinned, shifting the van into gear. "I'm a lucky man." His eyes lingered on me. "I don't think I've ever been with a woman as pretty as you." His gaze dropped to my legs before traveling back up to my breasts. "You could be a model."

He conveniently didn't address his own looks—or more the lack of them when compared to his pictures. Many of his kind were like this. Manipulative, dishonest, and yet with an air of entitlement, always prepared with an excuse to justify their self-serving actions.

Tim maneuvered his van out of the parking lot, smoothly merging with the flow of traffic as he joined the bustling street.

"Is the woman's house far?" I asked as the van snaked its way through the southern Boston suburb of Dorchester without stopping. I peeked over my shoulder into the back of the van—rusty toolboxes, pieces of white PVC piping, sponges, and buckets. Then my eyes settled on a very familiar five-gallon white-and-blue bucket of Fixx. The cleaning detergent used oxygen instead of chlorine. It was a fairly new cleaning product that erased all traces of hemoglobin, the oxygen-transporting protein in blood that was crucial in forensic tests.

Tim focused on the road. "No, not far at all. She lives close to the Blue Hills Reservation State Park."

The forest.

I stayed quiet. He laughed. "Don't worry. I promised not to be a serial killer, remember?"

Adjusting my dress, I forced out a chuckle. "Yeah, you did."

The houses gradually spread apart until the dark silhouettes of trees rose in the distance, marking the entrance to the large state park. I shifted in my seat. He glanced at me out of the side of his eye but didn't say anything.

Tim's headlights beamed into the darkness as he steered the van onto a dark road leading into the park. It was a smaller road, not the one that passed through the park's entrance and parking lot.

"She's pretty secluded out here," I commented, looking out my window at the endless black trunks of the trees now surrounding us. I sensed Tim smiling beside me, but he remained silent, driving deeper into the darkness of the woods until the road transitioned from concrete to gravel.

The stuffy air in the van grew even thicker, almost unbreathable. My heart started pounding against my chest as an icy adrenaline rush raced through my veins. This was the only time I felt excitement, and I often wondered why. Why did I feel this way before the storm hit? Why not later when his sweaty body violently pressed against mine?

I snapped out of my thoughts before Tim became suspicious of my silence.

"I…I think I want to turn back," I said in a weak, trembling voice. My fingers fumbled with the leather strap of my purse.

Tim remained silent, his dark profile starkly outlined against the window.

"Are we almost there?" I asked. "I think it's better if I go home. It's getting late."

Nothing but that stupid grin.

The van shook on the uneven gravel road as we ventured deeper and deeper into the woods. No one would ever come this way tonight. No one would be here to save me.

"I…I have to go home. Can we please turn around?" I pleaded, my voice rising in desperation.

His grin persisted, but he still offered no response.

Suddenly Tim stopped the van at a small bend in the road. End of the line. The headlights illuminated the never-ending rows of dense bushes and trees. To the left of the van, I could barely make out a narrow, overgrown path obstructed by branches, leaves, and rocks.

Turning toward his window, Tim gazed out into the night. Abruptly his hand jerked up to his hair, and he ran his fingers through it repeatedly, mumbling something to himself that sounded like "You're all the same."

"Tim?" My voice was a frightened whisper.

"Be quiet."

My throat started burning, suddenly dry, and I rubbed my hand against it.

There was nothing normal about any of this, and he not only knew it, but he loved it. He lived for these moments, craved my fear like a drug.

"Please," I said in a shaky voice. "I want to go—"

"I said shut up!" he snapped. His wide eyes locked with mine, and I noticed something flickering in his pitch-black pupils. Hate. Rage. Lust for pain.

Ah, the crude savage. Among the myriad of killers, I detested his kind the most, with their raw ferocity and absence of finesse.

Helpless whimpers escaped my lips.

"Stop that," Tim demanded, balling a fist.

I bit my lower lip and covered my mouth with my hand. The first tear rolled down my cheek, landing wetly on my dress. Whimpers emerged once more.

"I said shut up!" he yelled, slamming his fist onto the steering wheel. The loud honk of the horn echoed through the still night, making me jump in my seat.

"Please," I begged. "I won't tell anybody."

"Tell anybody what?" Tim yelled, pounding his fist on the horn again and again. "Tell anybody what, what, what, you cunt!"

I reached for the door handle, but just as my fingers wrapped around the metal, Tim grasped my arm and yanked me toward him.

"No!" I screamed. "Help! Help!"

In a matter of seconds, Tim was on top of me, his heavy body like a boulder crushing me into the soft seat. My stomach churned at his stale body odor and onion breath.

"No!" I screamed again as his large hand found my throat and wrapped around it. He used his free hand to lift up my dress and tear at my panties. The fabric cut into my skin until it finally snapped.

Scratching, biting, kicking, I fought every second, but it was no use.

"Please," I begged, my eyes beginning to water. "Please!"

But the hand around my throat tightened, cutting off all air. My eyes felt like they were bursting from my skull.

"You loose little whore," he huffed above me. "Want to abandon me to fuck that Mike, huh?" His dark eyes met mine, and I saw the evil flicker of a monster in them.

Trembling with excitement, he pushed my legs open with his knee and maneuvered his hips between them.

"A cunt is a cunt," he mumbled over and over again as if summoning a demon.

I thought about screaming once more. For help, to make him stop, but I knew it was futile. So I didn't scream. And he didn't stop.

I waited until he was fumbling with the coverall's zipper on his chest. Then I went still, dropping my arms abruptly like a puppet without strings.

That was when I started to laugh.

At first a weak chuckle escaped my lips, tentative and shy, but as soon as he loosened his grip around my neck, my giggles rose in volume and turned into a burst of uncontrollable, full-bellied laughter.

Tim's eyebrows furrowed in confusion as he removed his hand from my neck and pushed himself into a sitting position. Disbelief was written all over his face as he struggled to process the situation unfolding in front of him.

"What…what's so funny?"

I just kept laughing, gasping for air, my chest heaving up and down.

"What's so funny?" he yelled. The anger in his voice had returned, but this time it was the rage of a pissed-off man, not a manic psychopath.

With practiced ease, my hand reached into the pocket of my dress, finding the syringe. I slid it out and removed the needle cap with one hand, almost poking myself.

"You want to know…," I said, steadying my voice, "what's so funny?"

For a moment, the van lay in complete silence, as if time itself had stopped. Neither of our sweat-slicked bodies moved.

I narrowed my eyes at Tim. Emotionless. Cold.

"It's amusing that most of your kind share the same traits. Not one of you keeps going when I laugh. You need the screaming to feel powerful, don't you? But the truth is, there's nothing powerful about you."

I rammed the syringe into the side of Tim's neck and pushed

the contents into him. Tim jerked as if he'd been shot. Then he grabbed for my hand, yanked the needle out, and stared at it.

Quickly, from underneath him, I tugged at the door handle and kicked it open. Before he realized what was happening, I angled my legs and kicked him backward out of the van so he wouldn't collapse on top of me. With a heavy thud, Tim's large body crashed onto the ground, snapping a branch underneath it.

I scooted to the edge of the seat and carefully smoothed out the creases in my dress with my hands. "The propofol acts fast," I said. "We'll talk some more when you wake up again."

I stepped out of the van and onto Tim's chest. He coughed under my weight.

"Then you'll tell me where the bodies of Kimberly Horne and Janet Potts are."

Gasping for air, Tim somehow managed to squirm onto his side before he stopped moving. His vacant eyes stared into nothingness while his mouth was torn open, as if frozen in a scream.

I reached into my purse for my gloves and carefully slipped my hands into them. Bending down, I took off Tim's leather boots and slid them onto my feet. They were too large for me, and I was slightly unsteady in them, but I made my way to the back of his van just fine.

"Let's see what we're working with here," I said, adjusting the short blond wig on my head. It had shifted to the side a little during the fight. Short-haired wigs were my first choice when hunting. They perfectly covered my long hair, disguising one of my most identifiable features. The police rarely considered a good wig when searching for their persons of interest.

"You still with me, Tim?" I asked as I opened the doors of his van and climbed in.

No answer.

Want to know what happens next?

You can find the full book on Amazon, Barnes & Noble, or at your local bookstore.

I Kill Killers READ HERE

Thank you!

Dear Reader,

Thank you for reading *You Can't Stay*. If you enjoyed the book, please consider leaving a review on your preferred retailer's website (like Amazon, Goodreads, Barnes & Noble, etc.).

My Book

I have a small, mom-run author/publishing business, so every review, share, and kind word makes a huge difference and means the world to me.

Newsletter: https://www.ashmanbooks.com

Instagram: https://www.instagram.com/booksbyashman/

TikTok: https://www.tiktok.com/@ashmanbooks

Join Ashman's Dark Thriller Facebook Group to Meet the Author:

https://www.facebook.com/profile.php?id=100094353614873

Contact: hello@ashmanbooks.com

Thank you for your support.

S. T. Ashman

. . .

You Can't Stay

About the Author

S. T. Ashman is a German-American writer born and raised in Germany, now calling the beautiful U.S. Seacoast home. She once delved into the criminal justice system as a psychotherapist, a role that gifted her with a unique insight into the human psyche—both the beautiful and the deeply shadowed. In another life, she'd be a trench coat-wearing, mystery-solving female Columbo. Her mother's lineage traces back thousands of years to the Frisians, a fierce Germanic tribe from the north. A history lover to the core, she explores not only her own ancestry but also Indigenous cultures around the world. She weaves history and cultural awareness into action-packed fiction that keeps readers turning pages late into the night.